D0916051

Victorian Bookshop Mysteries by Kate Parker

THE VANISHING THIEF
THE COUNTERFEIT LADY
THE ROYAL ASSASSIN
THE CONSPIRING WOMAN

THE CONSPIRING WOMAN

KATE PARKER

JDP PRESS

The Conspiring Woman copyright © 2015 by Kate Parker

ISBN: 978-0-9964831-0-0 [print]
ISBN: 978-0-9964831-1-7 [e-book]

Published by JDP Press
Cover Design by Amber Shah,
Book Beautiful

Dedication

Lauren, Erin, John, and José,
you light up the world and my heart

CHAPTER ONE

"USE the downstairs door."

The neatly printed card reading "All tradesmen go to the door below stairs" shouldn't apply to me. I was expected, after all. The arrogant disdain from the tall, thin servant in a black suit was surprising as I stood with rain dripping off my umbrella and the cold creeping under my skirt.

I handed him my card. *Georgia Fenchurch. The Archivist Society.* "I have an appointment with Sir Edward Hale."

He stared at my card, making certain to stand protected from the weather just inside the entry. "You were supposed to be here by ten o'clock," he said, but he finally stepped back and let me in out of the rain.

I entered, swung around to furl my umbrella as I shook it, and then handed him my damp outerwear. He wasn't the only one who knew how to be difficult, but I was the only one with wet feet.

The hall clock struck the hour. "It's only ten o'clock now. The time of my appointment. Please take me to Sir Edward." It was a miracle I'd found the house at all. The winter fog outside had swallowed London.

Frowning, he plunked my umbrella in the stand and hung my cloak from an ornate mahogany hall tree. Then he led me up a flight of stairs with a marvelous carved railing and thick patterned carpet. The hallway and doors on this floor were dark paneled and blended together. Without a lamp glowing on a table, we'd never have found our destination.

After a knock, the man swung open the door. "Miss Fenchurch of the Archivist Society."

"You're late," said the pudgy man sitting behind his massive desk as he glanced at his pocket watch and then put it away.

I walked forward, refusing to speak until the man looked up and acknowledged my presence. Or, if he had manners, stood in the company of a lady. Newly rich industrialists in the Year of Our Lord 1897 seldom seemed to feel they had time in their busy schedule for something as unprofitable as manners.

Where I stopped was good for grabbing as much heat as possible from the fire and I hoped my feet would soon thaw. It was only the end of February, but I was hoping for spring to come soon. I considered walking over to study the mantelpiece of dark oak with scrolled carving, bringing me closer to the fire, but I decided this prospective client might not appreciate my boldness.

He finished perusing the documents on his desk and then stared at me. Removing his pince-nez glasses, he looked me over while I studied him. He wore a black suit with a burgundy colored waistcoat. A heavy gold watch chain hung down his wide stomach from his waistcoat pocket. His scalp showed through his fair hair. "You're the best they could send?"

Obviously, he was no more impressed than I was. "Either you want our help or you don't." The Archivist Society was small and select, with each member bringing different skills and contacts. I often acted as the face of the Archivist Society to our clients. We only took certain cases, usually ones that Scotland Yard had been unable to solve and frequently involving London's semi-elite. This time, however, we hadn't received sufficient detail before I came to see Sir Edward.

"Don't be snippy."

I decided a hard line would be best. "This is business. Don't waste my time."

The man nodded once, as if satisfied. "I want you to find my son."

"How old is he?"

"Edward junior, Teddy, is seven."

I hated missing children cases. We were generally successful in getting them back, but there was always the fear... "In whose company was he last seen?"

"He was with my wife. Still is so far as I know."

I barely suppressed a sigh of relief. "So Lady Hale is also missing?"

"Yes, but she can stay missing. I want Teddy back. He's my son and heir. I'm hiring you to return him to me."

Fortunately, most of our clients were not as reprehensible as this man. Otherwise, I think the Archivist Society would have given up long ago. "Is he also your wife's son?"

"What difference does that make?"

I snapped my mouth shut before I said something unwise. "I'm trying to obtain the facts in this case. Is your wife his mother or step-mother?"

"His mother."

I pulled my notebook and pencil from my bag and sat on the only other chair in the room. It was armless, but well upholstered and very comfortable. My legs were cold and tired after my trek up and down the street looking through the fog for the right address. "And her maiden name?"

"Now see here! I didn't give you permission to sit."

Terrible manners. He had continued to sit in the presence of a lady, and now he had the nerve to complain because I also sat. I made my tone dry. "Would you rather I continue to look down on you?"

His bulldog jowls reddened and his mouth clamped shut. I expected to be told to leave. With a snort, he said, "Very well. But I don't see why you need to know Alice's maiden name. We've been married nearly a decade."

What a tiresome man. Didn't he realize how lucky he was to have a wife and child? A family. The one thing I longed for. "Please, Sir Edward. We need all the facts we can gather."

"She was Miss Alice Newbury when I married her."

"When was the last time you saw your wife and son?"

"The day before yesterday at midday."

"And where was this?"

"In our front hall. I was on my way to visit my factories in Manchester. They saw me off."

"And you returned at what time?" Thick draperies at the window were pulled shut to keep out the cold. The only source of light besides the fire was a gas lamp aimed toward the surface of Sir Edward's desk. I could barely see to write my notes.

"Yesterday afternoon at tea-time."

"Your wife and son were missing then? What did the servants say?"

"That they left the house within a half-hour of my departure and hadn't returned."

"Did they use your carriage?"

"Why would I keep a carriage? Complete waste of money in town." He spoke as if he were proclaiming commandments from on high.

I resisted the urge to roll my eyes. "I'll need your detailed itinerary and an interview with each of your servants."

"What good will that do? I told you. They were here when I departed. When I returned the servants told me when they left. Now, go find my son."

"It does seem that you don't want the help of the Archivist Society. I suggest you contact the police and report them missing." I rose and started for the door.

"Don't tell me what I want or don't want. I wouldn't have called for you if I didn't want the help of the Archivist Society," boomed out behind me.

I stopped just short of the door. "We have a very good record for retrieving lost children, but it's because we run our investigations our way. If you have something to hide—"

"Hide?" He jerked upright, the whites clearly showing in his wide eyes. I watched him as he failed to look me in the face. "Why would I have something to hide? I want my son back."

Oh, he definitely had something to hide. I kept staring directly at his eyes. "Do you want our help or not?"

"Of course I do. Don't be ridiculous."

"Then we will carry on this investigation our way. Do not try to limit our inquiry in any way. Now, I'd like you to write out your itinerary in as much detail as possible while I question your staff."

His face turned so red I wondered if he'd have apoplexy, but he glanced back at my eyes. "How dare you?"

"You're asking for our help. If you want it, those are the terms."

"Very well. And your bill?" He picked up a picture frame

from his desk and studied it.

I couldn't see the picture. *Drat.* "Will be sent to you by Sir Broderick duVene." As a founder and the leader of our society, he arranged our assignments and handled the billing. Though we'd do our best for Teddy no matter what, I did hope he would make Sir Edward pay. "Now, have you contacted the police?"

"Whatever for?"

"It's customary when someone, particularly a child, goes missing."

"No."

"But—"

"No. Those are *my* terms." His thin-lipped stare told me he wouldn't shift from that point. That wasn't suspicious by itself. Many wealthy people had a fear of their neighbors seeing the police come to their door.

"Very well. Do you have a recent photograph of your wife and son?"

He showed me the photo on his desk. It was of a young boy, with fair hair and a cheery face.

"And your wife?"

"I believe there's one in the parlor."

I resisted a look heavenward. "May I take it with me?"

"Not this one." He snatched it to his chest and held on with a grip that death wouldn't release.

"The one from the parlor." No photograph of his wife in his study. He didn't want her found. Sir Edward obviously hated his wife. I wondered how she felt about him.

"If you must."

"If you'll instruct your footman to—"

"Butler."

Sir Edward must keep a large staff. "If your butler will

allow me access to the staff, one at a time, to answer my questions, I'll leave you to write up your itinerary. I won't need to bother you again today."

He continued to sit behind his large, polished mahogany desk, surrounded by ledgers, papers, pen and ink, and stared at me. I stared back. If this was how he carried on with his business, I'd hate to be a manager at his factories.

I wanted to refuse his case. He couldn't pay us enough to put up with him, and we seldom made more than would pay our expenses. Sometimes not even that much. But there was a woman and child missing in nasty winter weather. That was more important than my dislike of this odious man.

Finally, he reached over and grabbed the bell pull. The same servant arrived almost immediately. "Take Miss Fenchurch to speak to each of the servants, starting with yourself, and then return here to pick up a letter I will have for her. Oh, and let her take one of the photographs in the parlor."

Finished with me, Sir Edward turned to a line of figures in a ledger with an attitude of dismissal.

I turned to the servant. "Shall we?"

I quickly found a photo of a young boy with a woman who closely resembled him, except her hair was quite dark where his was fair. "Lady Hale and her son?"

The man nodded. He scowled at me, the unspoken word "thief" lingering on his lips as I put the framed photo in my bag.

He led the way downstairs to the butler's pantry and offered me a stiff, wooden chair. I pulled out my notebook and pencil while I waited for him to decide what attitude to take.

Apparently, he decided on a superior tone. He sat,

straight-backed, and stared down his nose at me. "What do you wish to know?"

Silly man. For all his airs, he was still a servant for an industrialist. A knighted industrialist, but still, new money. I'd never hired a servant, but I knew there was no status in his position outside this house. "Your name and how long you've worked for Sir Edward, for starters."

"Bartholomew Johnson. I've been with Sir Edward for three years now."

"And your position?"

"Butler."

This must be a large household, but I couldn't picture Sir Edward keeping a large number of servants and entertaining frequently. "How is he as an employer?"

"I have no complaints."

"Did you see Lady Hale and her son leave the house shortly after Sir Edward departed two days ago?" I decided to be as specific as possible with Johnson.

"Yes. I opened the door for them."

"Did Lady Hale say anything to you?"

"Say, miss?"

I stared at him, letting my impatience show.

"She said, 'Good day, Mr. Johnson.'"

No help there. "What staff does Sir Edward employ?"

"There's the cook, two maids, and the scullery maid."

"No housekeeper? No valet? No lady's maid? No nursery maid or governess for Teddy? And yet he employs a butler?" My voice showed my skepticism.

"Of course. Sir Edward directed me to handle anything in the household that Lady Hale didn't manage on her own. I act as valet as needed. And there was a governess." For the first time, Johnson seemed uncertain of how to proceed. "She was fired. By Lady Hale." He ground to a halt.

"When did she leave?"

"A week or so into January. A few days after she returned from the Christmas holiday to resume teaching the young master."

"Why was she fired?"

"You'd have to ask Lady Hale."

Interesting. "She's not here to ask, is she?"

"No."

"Again. Why was she fired?"

He looked away. "I don't know."

He was lying. I asked to speak to the cook.

Johnson took me into the kitchen and left. I told the cook why I was there. She told me in the four months she'd been employed by the Hales, she had never left the kitchen area except on her day off. She planned to leave "this madhouse" as soon as she found another position.

The scullery maid tried to be helpful, but her meager wits didn't allow her to notice things beyond food and dirty dishes.

As I spoke to her, I noticed a young redhead peek around the kitchen door. "Come in," I called out to the girl.

"I was told we're all to talk to you about Teddy going missing. Except he can't be, can he, if he's with his mum."

"Where can we talk?" I asked as I approached her.

She whispered, "Come on up the back stairs."

I glanced at the cook, who didn't seem to be paying us any attention, and the kitchen maid, who didn't seem to understand much. I nodded and followed her.

Four flights of stairs later, we were under the eaves. I gasped and collapsed against a wall, while the redhead didn't seem to be winded. "We're used to it," she told me.

She opened the door to her room. The cold hit me immediately. There were two beds with thin blankets, a hard wooden chair and a dresser. The room was dry, but I could see my breath in the light coming through the small window.

"I'm Georgia Fenchurch," came out amidst my heavy breathing.

"I'm Molly, and this is Rose."

Rose reached the landing and bobbed a curtsy. She was dark haired and maybe a year younger than Molly. Neither girl appeared to have reached the age of eighteen. "Hard work," I said, panting. "All these stairs all day long."

"It's not as bad as where I was before. And they pay every quarter without a murmur of complaint. At least they did while the missus was here. I don't know about him," Molly said, glancing at Rose for confirmation.

Rose nodded.

"He's miserly?"

"Cheap, I'd say."

Molly apparently had the same impression I did. Men as rich as Sir Edward often kept two menservants. The family would ordinarily have a housekeeper, a valet, and a lady's maid, though not a butler. Was Sir Edward in financial trouble? Then why a butler? "Did either of you see your mistress and the boy leave the day before yesterday?"

"Yes. And it's strange. They didn't carry any bags like they were leaving. Although I wouldn't have been surprised if she did go off." Molly lowered her voice even though there was only the three of us in this frigid space.

"Why?"

Molly and Rose shared a look, then Molly, who seemed to be their spokesman, said, "They argued something awful. He treats her like one of the servants, and lately she's been fighting him at every turn. I think that's why she was so quick to fire Teddy's governess and send her away without a reference. Sir Edward hired the woman and he wasn't here when Lady Hale threw her out."

No reference? That would ruin the woman's chances of future employment. What terrible crime had the woman committed? "What happened?"

"Sir Edward hired Susannah Forbes to get Teddy ready to go to boarding school. Lady Hale was against sending the boy away from home. When the mistress caught Miss Forbes in her room, she threw her out of the house immediately without a reference. When the master got back, they had a terrible row about it."

Rose nodded her agreement to Molly's words.

"When the master got back?" I repeated.

"He was gone overnight to visit his factories."

"He does that a lot?"

"Two or three times a week."

The Archivist Society would have to check on these trips of Sir Edward.

Before I could ask more, "Rose. Molly," came up the stairs in a baritone.

"Mr. Johnson," Molly whispered. "He keeps us hopping all day long and half the night."

Rose immediately ran down.

Molly continued, "Ask about Miss Forbes and the missing jewelry." Then she too hurried down and I followed more slowly. I'd have to talk to those girls again.

I met the butler on the ground floor. "Here is the paper you requested from Sir Edward," he said without meeting my gaze.

"Tell me, Mr. Johnson. Did Lady Hale complain of any

jewelry missing in the past month or two?"

"I couldn't say."

"Couldn't or won't? May I remind you that Sir Edward asked you to assist me in my inquiries into Teddy's disappearance?" I stared hard at the man.

"That has nothing to do with the child's disappearance."

"It might. Now, Mr. Johnson—"

He gritted his teeth. "She did complain of a bracelet and necklace missing about a month or six weeks ago."

"Jewelry given to her by Sir Edward?"

"Yes."

"What did this jewelry look like?"

"It's there. In the photograph you took. It's quite distinctive."

I pulled the photo out of my bag and studied the jewelry. The bracelet was made of diamond shaped links made of a shiny black substance with a tiny stone in the middle of each link. A pendant that matched the links hung from a gold chain. "It is distinctive. Were the police called in when they disappeared?"

"Certainly not." He sounded scandalized. "Sir Edward said she was just careless."

"Did he have the staff hunt for the missing pieces?"

"No. He said if she were careless she could do without."

Good grief. Expensive jewelry was stolen and the master of the house said it was just carelessness? That didn't match with my impression of a tight-fisted, or financially troubled, Sir Edward Hale.

Or maybe Sir Edward wasn't worried because he knew that soon his wife wouldn't have need for any jewelry at all.

THE FOG was so thick during my return trip to the

bookshop that twice I nearly turned at the wrong intersection. I'd learned this sort of bad weather either brought customers in by the cartload or cut us off from shoppers.

I entered the shop to find it empty except for my assistant, grandmotherly Frances Atterby. We were on our third day of cold fog with a misting rain, and business had been abysmal. If this weather continued, people would soon need to venture out to get more books and weeklies to read, and we would get needed trade.

On this day, however, we'd have plenty of time to work on the ledgers and dust the shelves. And read.

I repinned a few errant locks of my auburn hair and then telephoned Sir Broderick duVene, my mentor in the antiquarian book business and head of the Archivist Society. My report on the assignment was brief.

The telephone was still fairly new—I was one of the few shop owners on the street with one. But a year and a half ago the Duke of Blackford had ordered it installed to help out on a previous Archivist Society case, and I had to admit it came in handy. I also had to admit Blackford was farsighted when it came to business.

"Adam Fogarty is here," Sir Broderick said. "Let me put him on."

Then I heard former Metropolitan Police Sergeant Fogarty's grumble over the line. "What do you have, Georgia?"

I told him all I'd learned.

"Her maiden name was Alice Newbury?" His tone was sharp.

"Yes." What had he heard about this business? Sir Edward had said no police involvement.

"Was her father Lord Elliott Newbury?"

"I don't know. Why?"

"A missing person's report came into a West End station for a Miss Alice Newbury. Her late father was the financier." Fogarty spent his retirement keeping up with all the cases coming into the police and meeting the new constables. His help was invaluable to the Archivist Society.

"Could it be a coincidence?" If it wasn't, I was very much afraid for Lady Hale. "Who made the report?"

"Her sister. Countess Reinler. Formerly Prudence Newbury."

The papers had all reported the recent death of the incredibly wealthy Lord Newbury, last of a family of creditors to the very rich, including the sovereign. Since he had no sons, he'd left his daughters a fortune apiece. Now one of his heirs was missing, and she might be the wife Sir Edward Hale didn't want returned. Did he hope to get her money instead?

And why hadn't Prudence reported her missing under her married name? First her husband refuses to report her missing and then her sister confuses the search by using Lady Hale's maiden name. Didn't they want her found?

CHAPTER TWO

"ADAM, do you have an address for the countess?"

I heard the pages of a notebook ruffling over the telephone line, and then Fogarty gave me the address.

When I hung up, I told Frances what I'd learned and said I'd be back before we closed for the day. She nodded and went back to reading a new gothic novel.

I left to take an omnibus to Mayfair and the address Adam Fogarty gave me. As I rode along, other vehicles came out of the fog at us and disappeared again. I wouldn't have known we had reached the street I wanted if the conductor hadn't called it out.

As I turned onto the side street, the fog thinned enough that I caught my first glimpse of the wondrously large houses lined up along the pavement. It appeared as if a gauzy veil of cloud separated me from these houses built for the rich. Each had a portico held up by fine carved columns protecting the front stoop from the weather. Between these doorsteps, fancy wrought iron railings protected pedestrians from falling down the stairs to the tradesmen's entrances if the fog thickened again.

I found the house quickly enough and rang the bell. A footman in impeccable livery answered and I gave him my Archivist Society card, saying, "I'd like to speak to Countess Reinler about her sister."

He left me on the doorstep, but at least I was protected

from the drizzle by the portico. A minute later, he returned and gestured me to enter. Without a word, he took my cloak and umbrella before leading me down a hall.

Opening the door, he waved me into the room with a slight bow. Then he shut the door after me, leaving me alone in a lovely yellow morning room made gloomy by the weak daylight. I was standing by the fire, warming my chilled hands, when I heard the door open. I glanced up to see a dark-haired, dark-eyed woman of about my age walk in. She was every bit as beautiful as the photographs of Lady Hale.

"You have word of my sister?"

"Perhaps. Is your sister also known as Lady Hale?"

She lowered her head. "He's killed her, hasn't he?"

"Who is 'he'?" Did she suspect Sir Edward had already murdered her sister? I had hoped this woman would shed light on her sister's disappearance, not throw out allegations.

"Her husband. Sir Edward. He's killed her, hasn't he?"

"I don't believe so. While he was visiting his factories, Lady Hale and her son left the house and haven't been seen since."

Her hand went to her wide mouth. "Dear Lord."

"She hasn't communicated with you in the past two days, has she?"

"No." The woman began to pace the thick carpet, her dull black dress nearly skimming the carpet and reminding me I was in a house of mourning. "And you say Teddy is missing as well?"

"Yes."

"Then perhaps that odious man isn't involved. He'd never hurt Teddy. Please, sit down."

I sat in a delicate chair upholstered in striped yellow and gray material and pulled out my notebook and pencil. "Had you planned to see your sister?"

"Yes. We were to meet here in the afternoon two days ago. I waited all afternoon, but she never showed up. Then I reported her missing to the police." She sat down and twisted her hands.

"Why go to the police? Why not check at her house to learn if she'd changed her plans?"

"I sent a note. There was no reply. She'd have sent a note if she'd gone elsewhere or couldn't come here."

I'd have to check that with the butler. "Have you seen your sister at any time since the death of your father, Lady Reinler?"

She rose from the chair and began pacing again. "Of course. The last time I saw her was less than a week ago. The creature she married had gone to Manchester and she was free to bring Teddy here and visit as long as she liked. That's why we planned to meet two days ago."

"He objected to her coming here?"

"He objected to Teddy coming here. He didn't mind Teddy seeing his grandfather, but he hated any influence Alice or I had on the boy. Said we'd turn him into a weakling. When my father died and Sir Edward learned Teddy hadn't been left anything in the will, he blamed us and forbade Alice to bring Teddy here again."

"What was your sister's response?"

"What do you think? Alice has a mind of her own. Our father raised us to think for ourselves. It became obvious while we were still young that we'd have no living brothers, and our father wanted us to be able to manage our inheritance. Even with the Married Women's Property Act to help protect us, he made absolutely certain to arrange things so no husband would ever have control over our finances."

She kept in constant motion across the thick flower-patterned carpet.

"So there were just the two children? You and your sister?"

"There was one brother who lived beyond infancy, but he died at the same time as our mother. My father never remarried."

"Your brother was the youngest?" It seemed a reasonable guess.

"No. I am. My brother, Martin, was three years older than me, and Alice three years older than him. Despite the difference in our ages, Alice and I were very close."

Curiosity made me ask, "What killed your mother and brother?"

"Typhoid. We all had it. They succumbed."

"Excuse me, milady, but I'm not familiar with your family name. Your husband is the Earl of—?"

She paused in her pacing and gave me a smile. "He's not an earl, he's a count. Count Heinrich Reinler. He's Austrian, and he left just a short time ago to go back to his homeland. Otherwise, I'm sure he'd be as busy as I am searching for my sister and her son."

"Do you have any children?"

"Yes. Our son is two years older than Teddy. He's traveling to Austria with his father." She strode over and picked up a photograph from a table.

When she handed it to me, I said, "A handsome family." With an older husband, the young Countess Prudence, and a boy. "Are you his first wife? I ask because of the age difference."

"No. His first wife died many years ago. His older son by his first wife will be the next count. I don't have to worry about Dieter having to live far from England all his life." Hers was a proud smile.

"If something has happened to your sister, what happens to her share of the inheritance?"

"Don't think I failed to consider that when she didn't show up. That man—"

Before Countess Reinler had a chance to complain about Sir Edward, I said, "Did your sister leave a will?"

"Yes. Everything goes to Teddy, held in trust until his thirtieth birthday. The trust is to be managed by my father's solicitor and his business manager and me. The will was written shortly after Teddy was born at my father's insistence. Edward agreed." She smiled as if she'd won a prize.

"Sir Edward didn't have much choice?"

"No." She sounded smug about his defeat.

"And if they are both deceased?"

She looked shocked at my words, but I wondered if it was all an act. "Then all the money comes to me. That devil gets nothing, no matter what."

I couldn't help but think *why settle for half a fortune, when you can have it all?*

She walked around a table to stand in front of me. "I know what you're thinking, but I don't want the money. I certainly don't need it. I want Alice and Teddy back. When they didn't arrive and there was no word, I reported her missing. I'm worried. This isn't like her."

I gave the countess a hard look. "Are you certain their disappearance isn't linked to the fortune your sister just inherited?"

"I'm the only one who will inherit if they both die. And no amount of money could replace them in my life. If that weren't true, why would I have reported her missing in her maiden name?"

At my puzzled expression, she said, "If I'd used her married name, they wouldn't have taken a report from me. If by some miracle they had taken the report, the first person they would have asked would be her husband, and he'd deny everything. Edward didn't report her missing, did he?"

When I didn't reply, she stared at me suspiciously. "And if he wouldn't report her missing to the police, he certainly wouldn't be spending good money hiring the Archivist Society to look for her. I heard of your group when you rescued the Russian princess last autumn. The entire diplomatic community heard about you."

We'd been mentioned in the newspapers, something we hadn't wanted. Still, I doubted I'd do any harm to their relationship to tell her how the Archivist Society became involved. "He's hired us to look for Teddy, not your sister."

"Isn't that just like him?" She resumed her silent pacing across the thick carpet.

"Did your sister have any enemies?"

"Apart from her husband? I don't think so."

"When did your sister and her husband stop getting along?" Knowing that might speed our inquiries.

"Theirs was a whirlwind courtship. Father and I thought it would never work, but Alice was adamant. Unfortunately, we were right. It was a difficult marriage almost from the beginning. I think Alice would have left him long ago, but she found herself with child. Edward was thrilled with his son, and so the two of them kept up pretenses for Teddy's sake."

"And then?" From what I'd heard at the house, there must be an "and then."

"Edward is a bully. They were visiting us one day about

two years ago when Teddy did something—oh, I don't remember what. Something minor and childish. Edward verbally tore the child apart. My father took him to task. Words were exchanged.

"In the end, Edward threatened not to let my father see Teddy or Alice again because of his interference. My father threatened to call in Edward's loans on his factories if he tried such a stunt. You should have seen Edward's expression. My father had truly beaten him." Glee lit the countess's face.

"Had you known about the loans?"

"I had. Apparently Alice hadn't. I take a closer interest in finance and helped Father on occasion."

"What were things like after that argument?" I couldn't imagine it was pleasant to be in debt to the father of a despised wife.

"Edward and my father were very correct toward each other. Very cold. Edward didn't want Alice to come over here or bring Teddy to visit without him. Alice said they began to have terrible rows. It wasn't long after that Edward began to spend more time at his Manchester factories."

Was he hiding from his wife, or was there a reason he needed to travel there more often? I made a note to send Jacob, Sir Broderick's ward and errand boy for the Archivist Society as needed, to find the answer. "When did the governess arrive?"

"Miss Forbes? Early in the autumn. Edward wanted Teddy to begin more rigorous academics. My sister was fine with that until she found a letter from a boarding school saying Teddy had a place for the Easter term. She wanted him to go to a day school in London."

"This caused some disagreements between your sister

and her husband?"

"Flaming rows would be a better description."

"Did you or the servants witness these rows?" Servants overheard almost everything in a household, even with the doors shut. I waited to hear what Lady Reinler would say.

"Alice told me about them. They kept their arguments private, although she said they were loud enough the servants should have heard. She said even the neighbors should have heard them yelling."

"What did your sister tell you about discharging Miss Forbes?" That had also sounded unpleasant.

She paused for a moment and considered. "Alice was watching for her opportunity to get rid of her. My sister planned to make sure Teddy wasn't ready for the school Edward had chosen, and then have him sent to a day school in London until he caught up. She was also missing some jewelry at Christmas, and she suspected Miss Forbes of being the thief. When Alice discovered Miss Forbes in her bedroom while Edward was away, she saw her opportunity. Miss Forbes was gone from the house before Edward returned."

"Tell me about the jewelry that went missing."

She gave me a description that matched the pieces in the photograph and then said, "The odd thing is, everything that was taken was given to her by Edward. None of it came from our parents. Edward accused her of pawning his jewelry out of spite."

"Were the thefts reported to the police?"

"No. Edward wouldn't hear of having the police in the house. He blamed the loss on Alice and said if that's what she thought of his gifts, he wouldn't give her more."

Despite a dislike of having police on his doorstep, that didn't sound in character for a thrifty man like Sir Edward.

"What did Lady Hale think of the thefts?"

"She found it puzzling. The jewelry she received from our parents was more valuable than anything her loathsome husband gave her. Why steal the cheap stuff and leave the expensive?"

Why, indeed? "Who would your sister run to if she were afraid and couldn't reach you for some reason?"

"I don't know. I'll give you a list of her friends, but I can't believe she'd be with any of them and not send word." She pulled paper and pen from a desk in the corner and began to write. "It's a very short list now. Before she married Edward, she had a wide circle of friends. Over the years, he's alienated most of them by insulting their husbands. The man is a brute. A philistine. But the people I would see first are Sir Henry Carstaire and his wife, Lydia. They live around the corner from Alice and Edward."

THE FOG thinned as I traveled to the Carstaires' grand residence while trying to keep both my umbrella and my hairdo from flying apart in the cleansing wind.

The footman who answered the door took my *Georgia Fenchurch. The Archivist Society* card. In a dry voice he said, "Lady Carstaire is not at home."

"This is a business call, not a social one. A friend of Lady Carstaire is missing along with the woman's son, and I was hoping to speak with your mistress about the last time she saw her. Also, if she has any information that could lead us to the lady's present location."

"Yes, ma'am." The footman stood in the doorway, not moving enough for me to force my way inside.

Footsteps behind him made us both glance in that direction. The pretty blonde who moved to stand by his shoulder said, "I'm Lady Carstaire. Who is missing?"

"Lady Hale. May I come in and learn if you have any information that might help us find her and her son?"

"I'm sure I can't help you." Her voice was surprisingly high, but well-modulated and very cold.

As she turned away, the butler began to shut the door in my face.

The miserable weather and the dangers on the London streets for a woman and a young boy made me bolder than I normally would be. The boy was younger than Jacob had been when we'd first met on an early Archivist Society case, and Jacob had been streetwise. If Teddy was alone, he was certainly in peril. Even if he was accompanied by Lady Hale, the pair might be in trouble. "Wait!"

I shoved against the door with my hand, and the footman stopped and stared at me in surprise. "There's a little boy in jeopardy." Desperation made me beg, "Are you sure you don't want to help?"

The woman sighed, said, "Very well," and beckoned me with one hand. The footman stepped far aside as if I carried a contagion as she led the way toward the back of the house. I followed Lady Carstaire along the ground floor to her morning room.

She was a thin woman with a graceful carriage and delicate-looking hands. At this time of day, I expected her to be wearing a morning dress, but she was in a gown more suited for making afternoon calls. The material was a rich fabric of deep green. I hoped that meant I would be offered the hospitality of an upper-class house, but I suspected Lady Carstaire was on her way out and didn't want to bother with an unimportant person.

There was no fire in the fireplace and the room was

bitterly cold. Lady Carstaire remained standing on her thick carpet. No hospitality was evident here. I guessed this would be a short interview and was glad I kept my cloak, hat and gloves on.

"Alice and Teddy are both missing? I don't see how I can help you." She sounded genuinely surprised.

"This is the third day they've been missing. When did you last see them?"

"It's been over a week. Edward must be beside himself with worry."

"Indeed." I refrained from making any other comment about Sir Edward's hunt for his son. "Being neighbors, did you visit with the Hales often?"

"Often enough, I suppose. Alice and I were presented at court during the same season. Both of our husbands have been knighted due to their—service to the crown." I noted her hesitation before the word service. If she were a snob, she'd hate to admit her husband did anything within a million miles of earning his living.

"Do you have similar interests?"

"Yes." She didn't elaborate.

"Do you have children, Lady Carstaire?"

"Yes. Sir Henry and I were married first, so our children are older than Teddy. Some of us didn't think Alice would ever marry, she put it off so long." There was snobbish disparagement in her tone. Disparagement I knew I would face in the coming years as a spinster.

"So you kept in touch during those years you were married and Lady Hale remained unmarried?"

"Of course. My husband is not so feudal as to keep me from choosing my friends. As it happens, he was glad for me to remain in contact with Alice. He felt she improved my mind." For one second, she made a face as if she'd tasted something bitter.

How odd that a husband wanted his wife's mind improved. I saw the first crack in the edifice that was the Carstaire marriage and wondered if Lady Hale has caused any other damage. "Was Lady Hale also a friend of your husband's?"

Her eyes narrowed. "Alice had the mind of a man and the face of an angel. Men find that attractive." She strode toward the door in an unsubtle hint for me to leave. "She was far too dramatic for my tastes. And very depressed since her father died. That was just a month or two ago. I'm afraid I have no idea where Alice or Teddy might be, but if only Alice were missing, I'd suspect she'd taken her own life in a theatrical show of mourning." Her tone made clear what she thought of Lady Hale.

"Was she very close to her father?"

She made a face. "Abnormally so."

"Can you think of any female friends she might have taken refuge with?"

"Taken refuge with? What a strange idea. I didn't really pay attention to Alice's friends. She's not with her sister?"

"No."

"Well, if she were going to take refuge, as you say, I think it would be with Lady Imogen Fielding."

Now it was my turn to be surprised. "Isn't she—?"

"Yes. The scandalous sculptress." Glee shone in Lady Carstaire's eyes when she hissed out the name Lady Imogen had been christened with in the daily rags.

Countess Reinler's list of Lady Hale's friends hadn't included Lady Imogen Fielding. I wondered how a devoted sister hadn't known about a friend that a neighbor knew of.

All London knew Lady Imogen Fielding lived on Cheyne Walk because of the scandal three years before. She was the daughter of the Marquess of Hunterbrick, had a reputation as a talented sculptor, and had had a tempestuous affair with Lord Wilcox, the husband of a friend.

The whole thing ended up in court over the attempted drowning of Lady Wilcox in the Thames off Cheyne Walk. In the end, Lord Wilcox lost both women, who were no longer speaking to him or each other.

I headed for Cheyne Walk just past the Battersea Bridge in the thick fog that clumped along the river. I couldn't wait to meet the scandalous sculptress.

Just as the door opened to my ring, I heard a forceful voice with rounded aristocratic vowels call out, "Is it Alice?"

"No," I called back around the butler, "I'm looking for her, too." Then I handed him my card.

He called over his shoulder. "Milady, it's a person from the Archivist Society."

"Really?" replied the aristocratic voice. "How original. Show this person in."

My first view of Lady Imogen as I was escorted into the morning room was of a tall woman with light brown hair sitting on the floor in a multicolored tent-like garment. She and a young boy were playing with some wooden livestock spread over the carpet. A boy I'd seen in the photograph I'd taken from Sir Edward's.

"Lady Imogen," I said, curtsying, "and you must be Teddy Hale." My shoulders relaxed in relief. I'd found the missing boy. Then I stiffened as I realized someone was missing. "Where's your mother?"

CHAPTER THREE

THE boy studied me out of dark eyes, his serious face pressing his lips together in a thin line.

I turned to Lady Imogen. "How long has Teddy been staying with you?"

"For the past two nights, since Alice arrived. She said someone was following them. Was that you?"

I looked at her in amazement. "No. Who was following them? Why did they come here without any luggage if they were staying?"

"Alice came here precisely because she knew I wouldn't ask those sorts of questions. And that I wouldn't call Edward." She galloped a toy horse across the carpet after Teddy's horse.

I decided now was not the time to tell her who hired us. "Is she here now?"

"No." She studied me closely. "She went out at breakfast time. The fog was thinning, and she saw that the person who earlier might have been following her was now staring at the house. She left to confront him and told us not to wait breakfast." Now she had a cow chasing Teddy's pig. A tiny smile flicked across the boy's face.

"Did you see this person?"

"No. I don't know if it was a man or woman. I prefer not to know my friends' business. It makes for—safer friendships."

After her experience with the daily papers, I could see why she'd value "safe." "You said to confront *him*."

"Yes, I did. I don't know if I was repeating her words or if I assumed it was Edward and said him."

So I couldn't count on Lady Hale's follower being a man. "And you've not seen her since early this morning?"

"No." She sat up, giving me her full attention for the first time. "I expected her back long before now. I hope she's all right."

"If she doesn't return soon, what will you do with Teddy?"

He looked up at me when I said his name, but he didn't open his mouth.

"He'll stay here until I hear from Alice."

"What if Sir Edward—"

Her pale eyes shone with determination. "If Sir Edward shows up at my door, I can guarantee he won't find Teddy or Alice here. I can promise you they can search for a hundred years, but they won't find anyone we don't want them to find."

"We? They?"

Her chin went up. "Alice and I."

She was lying. There were more people involved in this than just the two of them. Someone as well educated as Lady Imogen wouldn't misspeak in such a way. I needed to do some research and then talk to Sir Broderick. "You should be safe enough for the time being. I'll let you know if I get in touch with Lady Hale. Please let me know if she returns. I hope she's all right."

Her eyes narrowed. "You won't report back to Edward? He obviously hired you."

I didn't deny it. "I want to speak to Lady Hale before I

talk to Sir Edward."

She nodded, apparently satisfied.

I wasn't. Who else was involved in Lady Hale's disappearance? And what had I blundered into?

INSPECTOR GRANTHAM rose from behind his desk when I entered his office in Scotland Yard, his hair tousled and his tie askew. I made a brief curtsy and immediately asked, "Have I come at a bad time?"

Grantham glanced at the constable standing in his doorway and sighed almost inaudibly. "No. How are you, Miss Fenchurch?"

"Fine. I hope your grandmother, Lady Westover, is improving." She'd been immensely helpful on some of our cases, and I always appreciated her old-fashioned opinions and her common sense.

Her grandson had tried more than once to keep her from aiding the Archivist Society. Lady Westover hadn't paid him any attention.

"She seems to be rallying. Lady Monthalf is taking very good care of her."

"I'm glad. And you seem to be busy." I cut off the small talk with, "I need a favor."

"If I can grant it." Grantham sounded wary, but he'd worked with the Archivist Society often enough to know he had every reason to trust us.

"I'd like to see your records on women missing from London in the past three years. Women of at least moderate means. Those whose bodies haven't been recovered or who haven't turned up alive later."

"If we ignore the East End, there aren't that many. Surprising for a city this size, but people still keep an eye on their neighbors. However, I'm afraid you'll have to sift through all the reports of missing women to find those that meet your criteria. What are you up to, Georgia?"

"I'll let you know if it turns out to be anything."

With a nod, Grantham said, "Constable, will you take Miss Fenchurch down to the records room and direct her to what she needs? And for heaven's sake, avoid Superintendent Marcum."

"Yes, sir." I picked up a look of fear in the constable's eyes.

"What's going on, Inspector?"

"We have a new superintendent, fresh from South London, with a reputation for following *all* the rules."

I nodded my understanding. I was certain he wouldn't appreciate help from the Archivist Society.

The records room was lit by both windows and electric lights, making the search easier on my eyes. A good thing, because the room was filled with cabinet after cabinet of reports, all I had to sit on was a hard wooden stool, and some of the reports featured really awful penmanship.

The constable showed me the drawers of files on missing persons and the notes on the reports that indicated if the missing had returned home, been found elsewhere, or their body had been discovered.

I kept going until the records office closed. I'd only looked through the past ten months, but I'd found five possibilities. Now to find out if any of these women were wealthy, like Lady Hale, and had just walked away from their homes and vanished.

The "we" that Lady Imogen used rung in my ears and made the hairs on the back of my neck stand up as I packed up my notebook and left.

BY THE time I closed up the shop for the day, I'd told Frances all about my unpleasant encounter with Sir Edward Hale and the questions raised by Countess Reinler and Lady Imogen Fielding. As we walked together through the persistent fog, Frances said, "Imagine being lost and alone in this."

It was all too easy to imagine, and I shivered. Streetlamps left a shimmery smear of light in the night air marking the edges of streets. I glanced at Frances, bundled against the cold, and said, "Can you find your way the rest of the way home?"

"Yes, thank you, Georgia." We split up then and I headed for Sir Broderick's. Fortunately, even hansom drivers were proceeding cautiously, or I'm sure I would have been run down trying to cross New Oxford Street.

Humphries, Sir Broderick's manservant, opened the door for me. "Dinner has already begun, Miss Georgia."

"Oh, dear." I handed him my outerwear and hurried toward the dining room. Shortly after my former shop assistant, Emma Keyes, left on her honeymoon, the other member of my household, Lady Phyllida Monthalf, moved out to nurse Lady Westover through a bout of pneumonia. What we thought would be a short visit had turned into a prolonged stay as the elderly woman fought for her life.

I discovered I couldn't manage the shop and the flat by myself. Worse, I couldn't cook, and Sir Broderick had the best cook in London in the person of Dominique. The West Indian adapted foods from her homeland to English cuisine with magical success. When Sir Broderick saw I was floundering, he invited me to stay in his huge, well-staffed townhouse.

I accepted in less than a second.

I'd known Sir Broderick since childhood, when he was my father's silent partner in the bookshop. He'd risked his own life, and nearly died, while helping me attempt to rescue my parents from a madman. Instead of the rescue we'd planned, I'd found myself an orphan at seventeen with only the bookshop standing between me and starvation.

I'd begged Sir Broderick for guidance. Despite being bedridden and in pain, he'd tutored me on dealing with publishers and antiquarian book collectors. I, in turn, gave him a focus beyond his sickroom. A reason to continue.

We'd been fast friends ever since.

When I entered the dining room, I found Sir Broderick in his usual place, his wheeled chair parked between the table and the roaring fire. Mrs. Hardwick, his housekeeper and companion, was sitting at the far end of the table from the blaze.

"There you are, Georgia. I was beginning to worry," Sir Broderick said as they both turned to look at me.

I sat midway between them. "Travel is slow going tonight."

Humphries set my fish course in front of me. They were halfway through this dish, and I'd missed the soup entirely. I dug in, trying to catch up, and discovered I was famished.

I realized as I ate that I'd missed luncheon. Once we finished the fish course, I'd slaked my hunger enough to say, "I found Teddy today, but not his mother."

"Excellent," Sir Broderick said. "At least we can reunite him with his father."

"Not yet. There's something else going on, I think involving other missing women and a whole network of people helping them disappear."

"Would this woman disappear without her child?"

"No. She saw someone outside where she was hiding and went out to confront him or her. That was before breakfast, and by mid-afternoon, she still hadn't returned."

"Then we must return the boy to his father."

Sir Broderick always believed in doing the right thing. The proper thing. Having met Sir Edward, I wasn't sure the proper and legal thing was the right thing. "Not until we know what happened to Lady Hale. The person she's staying with said if we try to take Teddy, he'll disappear and we'll never find him."

Sir Broderick threw his serviette on the table. "Then the boy is in danger. We must act."

"He's not in danger. I think there might be a network of women hiding other women, unhappily married women who can't obtain a divorce. Women who have money or property of their own to fund their disappearance and a new life elsewhere."

He looked at me as if I'd lost my mind. "Do you really think so? Lady Hale just snapped her fingers and an entire network—"

"I don't think Lady Hale is the first. I went through Scotland Yard's files on missing persons, and in the past ten months, I found five other possibilities. I want to check them out."

"It doesn't matter. The law is quite clear on this. The boy must be returned to his father."

I couldn't believe he'd come out so strongly for the letter of the law. "Please, Sir Broderick. Not until we learn—"

"It doesn't matter what we believe. The only parent that we can find is his father. The boy must be returned to him."

"Not yet. Let's at least find his mother first. She could have been snatched. Held for ransom. She's quite wealthy." I sounded like I was begging. Perhaps I was.

"I think you should investigate this further," Mrs. Hardwick said.

"Beatrice?" Sir Broderick had a puzzled look on his face.

I whirled around in my chair to stare at her. I'd never known her to voice an opinion about any of our cases.

"I had a friend who was married to a brute of a man. Well respected, but a brute. He beat her. He refused to agree to any sort of a separation or divorce. He said she could either live as his wife or she could die. There was no third choice. She ran away and hid in a small village in northern England. She had relatives there. But he found her and brought her back."

She picked up her fork. Set it down. Picked up her serviette and blotted her mouth. Set it down. "After three weeks, she returned home. In a pine box. I saw her body. It was horrible. And the police did nothing. Broderick, there's a need for a group to hide women like that."

After a long pause, Sir Broderick asked, "Did you hear anything about Sir Edward being violent?"

"No. But maybe I didn't ask the right questions. Starting with, had either of them mentioned divorce? And then there are the other five women. I want to ask some questions. Find out if any of them knew Lady Hale's friends. If any of them had their own property and what happened to it."

"They may have nothing in common with Lady Hale and their disappearances may not be related," Sir Broderick said. Then he paused and considered. "On the other hand, someone may have had a clever idea." I was surprised at the admiration in his tone.

"I agree." The Married Women's Property Act gave a woman control over her own property and businesses, allowing her to trade or make wills without her husband's permission. Independence for a woman of means. Too bad the divorce laws hadn't caught up.

A woman couldn't get a divorce without suffering humiliation, loss of a fortune, and probable separation from her children. With a hint of adultery on his wife's part, a man could easily obtain a divorce at minimal cost and the gain of all marital property, including the children. "This is something I need to check out. I'd like the Archivist Society to help me learn about these five women."

We stopped talking while the next course was brought in. Chicken stew, flavored with some of the spices from Dominique's homeland. The silence continued except for the sound of chewing.

As long as Sir Broderick was being agreeable, I said, "There's something else. I'd like Adam Fogarty to talk to his friends on the beat along Cheyne Walk. That's where Lady Hale was last seen, in the fog by the river early this morning."

Sir Broderick nodded. "It's a good idea. But since I don't have anyone to deliver messages in place of Jacob and he's currently out, can it wait until morning?"

I didn't want to wait. "I can deliver the message after dinner."

"Do you think it's safe?" Mrs. Hardwick asked.

"That depends on where I'd find Fogarty at this time of day." I gave Sir Broderick a hard look.

Sir Broderick gazed back, and apparently deciding he had no choice, looked heavenward. "There's a pub not far from Scotland Yard. The Key and Whistle. You might find him there. Or find someone who knows where he is."

"I'll go as soon as we finish dinner."

"Do you think that's wise? It's a pub," Mrs. Hardwick

said.

"I don't have to worry about my reputation anymore. Haven't you heard? I'm a spinster." The self-pity I'd been fighting leaked out in my voice.

"The duke will return. And you'll care when he does," she replied serenely.

It was my turn to toss down my serviette. "He's probably in America right now, wooing some heiress."

"I doubt it. He doesn't need the money. That's why so many of our peers look to America for brides. They're broke, but not your Duke of Blackford. He's free to choose anyone. Oh!" Mrs. Hardwick looked surprised at something that crossed her mind. "You had a letter in the second post today. I've left it on the table in the hall."

I finished my dish and leaped up. Hurrying into the hallway, I didn't bother to shut the door to the dining room. They knew I was hoping for another message from the Duke of Blackford.

He was a duke. I was a middle-class bookshop owner. I'd already had two letters more than I should have expected. I was surprised I'd heard from him at all during his trip to America. His messages sat in my room upstairs, read and reread so many times the words were memorized and the folds were wearing out and making holes in the paper.

And I kept hoping for another. I had hopes and dreams I was afraid to examine for fear they would turn to dust. He was autocratic, demanding, distracted by his duties and involved in a world of politics and nobility I knew nothing about. But still, when he focused on me, I felt everything and anything was possible.

With a sigh, I saw the letter was my daily message from Emma. I read it as I carried it back into the dining room.

"What does Emma say?" Sir Broderick asked as Humphries took away the chicken plates and brought in the pudding.

"They're leaving by boat to travel down the Dalmatian coast to Greece. The weather is sunny and mild. Oh, how I envy her." I disliked the sulfur-smelling soup that sometimes passed for air in London in the winter. "You'll have to read her description of Sumner exploring some ruins and the harbor where they're sailing from. His writing ability is rubbing off on her."

"How many books do you think he'll have planned by the time they get back to England?" Sir Broderick asked.

I shook my head. I was still trying to get used to the fact that brawny, scarred, former soldier John Sumner was the famous gothic novelist Mrs. Hepplewhite. And the fact that Emma Keyes, the shop assistant I'd raised since she was thirteen, was now Mrs. Sumner.

And the knowledge that at thirty, I was now officially a spinster in everyone's eyes. Including my own. I could hate it all I wanted; that was my life now.

I rose from the table. "I wish you wouldn't call him *my* Duke of Blackford. I'd better get going if I want to find Fogarty and ask Grace Yates to help me learn about the women who've disappeared."

"Will Grace be able to get time off from her job as Lord Barnwood's secretary and librarian?" Mrs. Hardwick asked.

"Old Barnwood is only too happy to let her have time off to work on an Archivist Society investigation. He knows we'll owe him when it comes to the next antiquarian book he fancies," Sir Broderick replied.

"Please ask Humphries to wait for me before locking up for the night," I said as I left the room.

The Key and Whistle turned out to be close to an omnibus stop. Its weathered sign hung above the pavement in faded colors. I entered and found every face in the crowded room staring at me as silence descended like snow. They were all male faces, and while they all wore civilian dress, I was willing to wager anything that they were all current or former constables.

I wondered if a woman had ever set foot over this threshold before. Certainly, no woman had scrubbed these scarred wooden floors in ages. They were filthy. Then I wondered why any woman would want to enter here. With the cigar smoke and the beer smell mixing with the odor of wet wool and bodies crowded together, this wasn't anywhere I wanted to linger.

A path opened in the crowd as Fogarty limped toward me. "Miss Fenchurch. What has happened?"

"I have an assignment for you, and you might want to pass it along to your friends. There's a woman missing, Lady Hale, who was last seen along Cheyne Walk in the fog early this morning. If any bodies have been pulled from the Thames today, find out if they are of a dark-haired woman in her thirties who has not been reported missing."

His lined face was solemn. "You think she jumped."

"No. I think she was pushed. She went out to meet someone, but the person who lives in the house where she was staying didn't see the person in the fog."

"And if a body is found meeting your description?"

"Pass the word on to me as soon as you hear anything. I think it's possible someone in her family is behind her death."

"But is it likely?"

I thought of Sir Edward not wanting his wife found, and Lady Prudence, her sister's heir if her son were to die, not mentioning the name of the person Lady Hale was staying with. Was this deliberate? "Unfortunately, too likely."

WE WERE busy in the bookshop for the first few hours the next day as the fog lifted, the rain held off, and the wind lessened. As close as we came to perfect weather in the winter. Customers came in to stock up before the wind, sleet and fog returned and kept everyone indoors.

Fogarty walked in, limping badly as he hurried to the counter.

"You found her?"

He nodded.

When he didn't speak, I knew it was bad news. I glanced around to make sure no one was within hearing distance. "Is she dead?"

He gave a single nod.

"Drowned in the Thames? Is there any sign she was pushed in rather than fell or jumped?" I didn't want her death to have been a senseless accident, leaving a young boy motherless. Injury and illness made too many children orphans. I'd like the possibility of getting justice for Teddy and Lady Hale.

"She didn't drown, although we found her in the river near Cheyne Walk. She was thrown in after she was stabbed through the heart. And Georgia, she was stabbed from the front with a longish blade. Someone looked her in the eye while he killed her."

CHAPTER FOUR

I looked at Fogarty for a moment with my mouth hanging open. Snapping it shut, I said, "There's no mistake? She was stabbed through the heart? And from the front?" I couldn't imagine anyone being able to take a life so viciously.

"It's a case of murder, all right. Inspector Grantham was assigned to lead the investigation."

"Oh." I let out a breath. He was accustomed to Archivist Society interference. "That's good then. Has her family been notified?"

"Grantham is doing that now."

Relief poured off me. Notifying people that their loved ones were dead was a sorrowful and thankless task. Grantham could fall back on his official status when delivering such news. I couldn't. "Then I'll wait until this afternoon before I visit them. I hope this weather holds up."

Fogarty grinned. "Don't we all?" With a wave, he limped out of the shop and disappeared down the pavement under the weak sunshine.

I used a lull in customers to telephone Sir Broderick and give him the news. I also told him where I planned to go before returning to his house. One woman had already been stabbed. I didn't want to become a second victim.

"I'll call together a meeting of the Archivist Society for tonight," Sir Broderick boomed over the line. "This case seems to be changing from minute to minute."

He was right. Our simple disappearance had turned into murder and a battle over a young boy's welfare.

Once Frances returned from lunch, I left for Sir Edward's. The welcome sunlight made it possible for me to see the features of passersby. I looked everyone over carefully once I climbed down from the omnibus, searching for anyone who might be connected to this case. There were plenty of people out on the streets, but they were all strangers.

Before I spoke to Sir Edward, I decided to check with a few more neighbors on Countess Reinler's list. One had come down with influenza before Christmas and hadn't received callers since. Another was traveling, and a third had no interest in anything that happened outside her home. The last one on the list, Lady Moffatt, was plump, middle-aged, and eager to speak to me.

"Lady Hale is dead and Teddy is missing? How sad for Sir Edward. Although I imagine his only concern is Teddy. He adores the boy."

She certainly had Sir Edward's measure. "When was the last time you saw either of them?"

"Perhaps four days ago. Lady Hale and Teddy were going out as I was coming in and we spoke. Nothing that would help you. Just that the weather was frightful."

Lady Moffatt seemed to be the most observant of the neighbors and was willing to share her observations with me. A real find in this neighborhood after my reception at the other houses. "If you were to guess, where do you think they'd have been headed?"

"Her sister's, I would suspect."

"No. Her sister was frantic with worry."

"Oh. Then I don't know. Unless..."

"Unless what?"

She eyed me closely. "I could be wrong, but I wonder if the two of them didn't run away."

"Why do you say that?"

"It's no secret Sir Edward and Lady Hale couldn't stand each other, and she had just come into an enormous inheritance from her father. It's just a possibility."

"You don't think she might have done away with herself?"

"Oh, my goodness, no. Now if Sir Edward had taken the boy, on top of her father's death, then perhaps. But as you say, Teddy is missing. She wouldn't have done anything to herself and left him alone. Whatever the manner of her death, it wasn't suicide."

With Lady Moffatt's words in mind, I continued to Sir Edward's. Oddly, I saw no funeral wreath, no straw on the pavement, no mourners, no sign that this was a house where death had visited. I knocked on Sir Edward's door. Tall, thin Bartholomew Johnson opened it almost immediately. "Sir Edward is not receiving guests."

"I bring news of Lady Hale and Teddy." I could see the butler's jacket didn't sport a black crepe mourning band.

"Lady Hale is dead. The police have already been here."

Stupid, stubborn butler. I stood on the step and looked up at him with my chin jutting aggressively. "Mr. Johnson, Sir Edward will not be pleased if he learns you have kept him from his business."

"If you'll wait here, please." He shut the door in my face, leaving me in the cold wind.

My temper kept me warm as I counted to sixty. If the self-important butler wasn't back by then, I would leave and return the next day.

Mr. Johnson opened the door on fifty-nine. "If you'll come this way, miss."

Sir Edward was again upstairs in his ill-lit study. Again, he didn't rise or offer me a seat in this cold room. I couldn't imagine how he could stand to work in there. "Have you found my son?"

Lady Hale deserved better than this from her husband. I stared hard at him as I said, "My condolences on the death of your wife."

"That is not your concern." The bitterness in his voice was etched in his face.

"Surely you have a funeral to plan."

"I'm not claiming her body. Let her sister bury her with her father."

A gasp slipped past my lips. That was unheard of. Funerals were England's premier social event and a way to display wealth and status. A man who employed a butler must have some interest in displaying his standing. Not to mention he must have some residual feelings for the woman. "You're not going to bury your wife?"

Sir Edward stared back and said in a dry tone, "You sound scandalized. You shouldn't. Now, have you found my son?"

"I saw Teddy yesterday after what we now suspect was the time of Lady Hale's death. He is fine and safe in the care of a friend of Lady Hale's."

He slumped with relief and closed his eyes for a moment. Then he glared at me. "Why haven't you brought him home?"

"When I saw him, I didn't know Lady Hale was dead."

"And now?"

I knew this wouldn't make me popular. "Now, you're a suspect in her death. A leading suspect. There's no point in bringing him home only to have him see you taken off to Newgate Prison."

Fury burned in his eyes. "How dare you? I didn't murder my wife. Now, bring my son home to me immediately."

"How will I know that you're in London and not in Manchester?"

He spit out the words as he said, "I don't leave for Manchester until Sunday afternoon. Return Teddy to me before then. That shouldn't prove too difficult for a woman of your talents." Then he began to read the papers on his desk, dismissing me.

"I need to speak to your maids."

"What good will that do? They won't know where my son is."

"Perhaps. Tell me, why do you employ a butler with such a small staff?"

His head jerked up and he stared at me without blinking. "That's impertinent."

I held his gaze. "Yes, it is. Why do you employ a butler?"

"To keep Alice happy. No need for that anymore."

I turned and marched out, finding Mr. Johnson in the hallway. Had he overheard our last conversation? "I need to speak to Molly and Rose again."

"I'll have to ask—"

"Now, Mr. Johnson."

"No. Not without the master's permission." He gave the closed door a calculating gaze and then escorted me to the front hall.

When I reached the hall, I stopped and asked, "Did Lady Hale receive a message from her sister on the day she disappeared?"

"No."

I couldn't believe the countess would lie about something so easy to check. "Are you certain no message came to this house for Lady Hale that day?"

"A message arrived from her sister, but Lady Hale had already left." Johnson looked pleased with himself. "So she didn't receive it."

Stupid man. Luckily, at that moment Molly came out of the door to the left of the hall. "Molly, I need to speak to you and Rose about your mistress's murder. Do either of you know anything about the disappearance of the jewelry or anything else that might help in the search for her killer?"

She looked from me to Mr. Johnson.

I tried to urge her into confiding in me. "She's dead. You can't betray her now, but you might be able to help us catch her killer."

I'd have continued, but Mr. Johnson broke in to say, "Get back to work, Molly. Sir Edward doesn't pay you to stand around gossiping."

"Yes, sir." She gave a bobbed curtsy and dropped her duster, polish bottle, and cloths.

Feeling guilty about making her nervous and possibly in trouble with her boss, I knelt down to help her pick everything up. Mr. Johnson remained standing, harrumphing his displeasure.

"Monday afternoon. One o'clock. End of the street," Molly whispered.

"Yes."

We both stood, with Molly in possession of her cleaning supplies, and nodded to each other. She curtsied to the butler again and went down the hall.

"I'm leaving," I said as I walked to the door. Since he hadn't taken my cloak, he had nothing to do but open the door, which he did with undignified speed. I wouldn't learn anything else here this day and there was no point in arguing with such a mule-headed man. I felt certain he'd have no trouble keeping his position in Sir Edward's household, with or without Lady Hale's desire for a butler.

I hurried to my next stop, to get Countess Reinler's reaction. I was shown into the parlor where the countess was waiting by the welcoming fire. She hurried up to me and took my hands in hers for an instant before drawing back. I could smell lavender on the handkerchief she pulled out from her sleeve. "The police have been here. There's no mistake? Alice has truly been murdered?"

"I'm afraid so. You must be grieving terribly. I'm very sorry."

She dabbed her eyes. "And Teddy?"

"I saw him in the home of Lady Imogen Fielding yesterday after your sister was killed. He was safe and unharmed. Your sister had been staying there but went out in the morning to meet someone." I unwound my scarf. The electric lights made the room feel hot with their summer brightness.

"This someone was her killer?"

"It seems likely."

She began to pace the carpet. "I had no idea she knew Lady Imogen Fielding. The woman is scandalous. And Teddy is staying with her? No, he must come here to me. He and my Dieter are good friends."

"By law, he should be returned to his father, who is his only living parent."

Even before the words were out of my mouth, Prudence turned on me. "No. Her husband must be her killer. She was afraid of him. I have letters from her saying that whenever he was home she feared for her life."

"When did she write these letters?"

The countess stalked a few steps away from me and looked down. "Years ago," she mumbled and slid her handkerchief in her sleeve.

"Anything written that long ago won't serve as evidence against Sir Edward or stop him from claiming his son."

She dropped gracefully into a chair. "I know. I know. But I'm still convinced the swine killed her."

I stared at her. It might not be the right time to say this to someone who just learned their dearest relative had died, but I had to say it. "You told me earlier that if anything happens to Teddy, you inherit your sister's money and property."

She glared at me as my meaning became clear. "I would never hurt my sister or Teddy. I love them. Good heavens. I hadn't finished mourning my father before my sister was murdered. I'm heartbroken, and you talk about Alice's money. No." She put up a hand. "I have enough of my own."

"Nevertheless, for your own protection, it would be better if Teddy were not in your care. In case he is also a target."

"Teddy? A target of a murderer? But he's only a child." A tear slid unchecked down her cheek. "That's monstrous. But Edward has the law on his side, and he would never kill his son. I may not like it, but I concede that Edward will have poor Teddy returned to him."

With that unpleasant topic covered, I dropped what I thought of as a bombshell. "Sir Edward refuses to claim your sister's body or provide her with a funeral."

I could see her stiffen her back and visibly draw strength from within. "Then I shall take care of it."

She sounded as if she was not surprised by his inaction and was glad to perform this service in place of Alice's husband. I found her attitude almost as shocking as his. "Are you sure? This is his right and his duty."

She rose and began pacing again. "He doesn't care about his rights and he has no sense of duty. That's what comes of being raised with the working classes. I shall see to my sister's funeral and she'll be buried in our family plot."

Working classes? Prudence Reinler sounded as if she carried the prejudices of the upper classes. Odd, since I'd learned her father was a descendant of self-made men like her sister's husband. "Is this what your sister would want?"

"Yes. I think so. Alice and Edward were married in name only. They tolerated each other under the best of circumstances. When they were disagreeing, it was much worse. Edward locked himself up in his study and Alice fled here." The countess pulled out her handkerchief again and wiped her eyes.

"In those situations, where would Teddy be?"

"Either he'd come with Alice or he'd stay home with his nanny, Mrs. Green."

"Mrs. Green?"

"She was his nanny until this past summer, when Sir Edward pensioned her off. She'd been with Teddy from the first and he loved her, but lately she'd been slowing down. Shortness of breath. Alice knew it was inevitable, but she was sorry to see Mrs. Green go. And then the bold, brilliant and beautiful Miss Forbes showed up."

What a strange way to describe a governess. "Is that how you felt about her?"

"Alice told me that's how she'd once described herself. Of course, she claimed to be quoting her previous employer, but

Alice and I both felt that's how Miss Forbes thought of herself. We took to calling her that between ourselves. And then we'd laugh." The scorn in her voice told me how she really felt.

The governess would need a healthy ego to survive an unwilling employer. Or perhaps the outsized ego came first, making it hard for an employer to appreciate her. "Do you have any idea where Miss Forbes might have gone after your sister threw her out?"

Her eyes and mouth rounded. "You think she killed my sister?"

I wasn't going to start speculating with Countess Reinler. I wasn't certain she hadn't killed her sister for the money. Or control over Teddy and the money. Her constant pacing made her appear nervous and guilty, not grieving. "There's no point in guessing who the murderer is. But Miss Forbes was in the house until shortly before Lady Hale died. She might have seen or heard something useful."

"Oh." She sounded disappointed. "I have no idea. Sir Edward should have an address for her."

"And you don't know how your sister met Lady Imogen Fielding?"

"No idea at all. I'm afraid I'm not being very helpful."

"Well, you could help by giving me the name and address of Lady Hale's business manager." I gave her an encouraging smile. I needed the information.

"Of course. It's the same man my father used and that I use." She walked over to a roll-top desk and pulled out pen and ink.

I moved to stand by a drapery-covered window. Amazingly, her draperies kept out the cold air the way I could only wish mine or Sir Broderick's would. "May I also have the name of her solicitor?"

Prudence nodded and kept writing. In a minute I held all the information I could hope for here.

"Can you think of anything else that might help us find your sister's killer?"

Her stare held the chill of the outside air. "You don't need to look any further than Sir Edward Hale."

BY THE time I sent Frances home and closed up the shop, I discovered Sir Broderick and Mrs. Hardwick had planned an early dinner and I was late. Good. I didn't need to feel guilty over ruining Dominique's delectable dishes.

I sat down at the table and said hello to Jacob, Sir Broderick's ward, as Humphries brought in my soup. "Jacob was telling us he's discovered a passion for the technicalities of the legal system," Sir Broderick said.

"So he can find a way to wiggle out of trouble when someone catches him using his lock picking skills? A skill you encouraged," I said, trying to hide my smile. I'd been glad more than once that Sir Broderick had Jacob tutored by a retired housebreaker. The Archivist Society did more than look through dusty records to solve crimes.

"I've decided to apprentice to a solicitor," Jacob said.

"Are you sure?" I looked across the table at the young man Sir Broderick and I had rescued from the East End during one of our first cases. He'd been an undernourished orphan, already on his way to a life of crime. Recently, Jacob had undergone training as an accountant and as a locksmith. So far, his only aptitude was for lock picking.

"I'll soon reach my majority. I need to find a career."

That was true, but it didn't answer the question on my mind. "Have you found a solicitor who would be a good teacher and be willing to work around your schedule with our cases?"

"His name's Mr. Wylie. I spent part of the day with him yesterday and had dinner with him last night. He's aware of the work we do in the Archivist Society."

"Aware of doesn't mean he'll allow you to drop everything and run around London for days at a time." I shot a glance at Sir Broderick and then looked back at Jacob. "Or will you be leaving the Archivist Society? No. Please don't tell me that. You're too valuable." I gripped my fork, making my knuckles whiten.

"No." Jacob gave me a grin. "Mr. Wylie believes we can set up an apprenticeship that will allow me time for working on our investigations."

"I've warned Jacob and Mrs. Hardwick we have a new case and will hold a meeting of the Archivist Society after dinner tonight," Sir Broderick said. "The rest of the group should arrive at half past eight." The housekeeper served tea and some of Dominique's fabulous scones at the start of the meetings, but then she would vanish.

"We'll need to start work on this investigation immediately. A mother and her seven-year-old son had been missing for two days." I looked at Sir Broderick. "Now the mother has been found murdered. This is after the father made clear when hiring us that he only wanted the son returned."

And if what I suspected was true, Lady Hale wasn't the only woman in danger...

CHAPTER FIVE

I'D worked with the Archivist Society on innumerable cases since its founding more than a dozen years before. In that time, I'd lost my ability to be shocked by humanity's cruelty, but it never failed to sadden me. People murdered their family members all too often.

"Have the police been called in?" Sir Broderick asked.

"No. Sir Edward refuses to speak to the police. I'm not sure I trust our client," I added with a dry tone.

"Wouldn't be the first time," Jacob said and turned his attention back to his food.

"How distressing," Mrs. Hardwick said, setting down her serviette.

"I'm sorry. I shouldn't have said anything." I was so used to discussing unpalatable subjects with other members of the Archivist Society that I hadn't curbed my tongue around a nonmember, and worse, at mealtime.

"No. You should feel free to discuss Archivist Society business at this table. I just worry about a child losing his mother at such a young age. And without a father that you feel you can trust. How frightened he must be." Mrs. Hardwick put on a hesitant smile and picked up her serviette and then her fork.

"When last seen, he was being well cared for in the household of a marquess's daughter. At least we don't have to worry about his safety from the elements," I told her.

Sir Broderick immediately picked up on my thoughts that the child might be in danger from people he trusted. He gave me a sharp look and we switched to more polite topics for the rest of the meal. Then we moved into the parlor to wait for other members of the Archivist Society to join us.

Adam Fogarty, formerly of the Metropolitan Police, was punctual as always. I greeted him with, "Have you heard about a new superintendent named Marcum?"

"Several of the boys have mentioned him. He's a stickler for the rules. Wants everyone's uniform clean and pressed. And no interference by civilians."

"The Archivist Society won't be getting any assistance from him, I gather," Sir Broderick said.

"That could be a good thing. He's tenacious. When he's after a culprit, that's a good thing. When he's got the wrong suspect, that's not so good. And they say he doesn't believe he's ever wrong." Fogarty gravely shook his head.

Frances Atterby, the plump, gray-haired widow who'd helped in the bookshop since before Emma left, was the last to arrive. She headed straight to Dominique's scones as she gave everyone a breezy greeting.

"As soon as Mrs. Atterby is ready, we'll begin," Sir Broderick said.

"Go ahead," Frances told him. "I've already heard most of it from Georgia between waiting on customers." Then she turned back to the tea table.

"Georgia, do you want to tell us about the investigation?"

I told them all I'd learned.

I finished with my theory that Lady Hale wasn't at Lady Imogen Fielding's because of a previous friendship, but because Lady Imogen was part of a larger group that helped wealthy women disappear from abusive or odious husbands.

Grace Yates, secretary and librarian for the antiquarian book collector Lord Barnwood, had already offered to help check on the women whose names I'd pulled from Scotland Yard files, as soon as she could get some free time from her employer.

When she spoke up I asked, "But don't you need to be at work tomorrow?"

"Lord Barnwood is having some colleagues to lunch. I'll have most of the day to myself. I'll take part of the list."

I appreciated Grace's willingness, since these names would take us all over London. "And I'll work on part of the list in the morning. Frances, you'll have the bookshop by yourself for a while."

She nodded. "If the weather turns bad again, that won't be a problem."

"We also need someone to follow Sir Edward's itinerary for his trip to his factories. That means travel to Manchester in this awful weather." Sir Broderick hadn't been able to stand the cold since his accident, spending his time in front of the fire in whatever room he was in.

"I'll do it," Jacob said.

"What about your solicitor training?" I asked.

"What solicitor training?" Adam Fogarty asked.

Jacob told the others what he had planned.

"And he'll allow you to just pick up and chase after information when we have an investigation?" Adam didn't sound like he believed Jacob's good fortune. I wasn't too sure, either.

"Yes. Mr. Wylie is a great admirer of our work. He says I've seen the situations where our laws and statutes have failed. Now he says it's time for me to learn where they've succeeded and how to make sure they provide the hoped-for result." Jacob sounded quite determined. I hoped Mr. Wylie would prove a good master.

"So you're willing to go to Manchester for our investigation?" I asked.

When Jacob nodded, I passed him the paper Sir Edward had written out for me. Jacob glanced over the list and then looked up. "He has three factories within five miles of each other in Manchester. Why does he live in London?"

"We'll have to find out," Sir Broderick said. "Can you leave in the morning, Jacob?"

"Yes."

"I have a photograph of Lady Hale and Teddy. The boy is seven, so this has to be a relatively new picture." I passed it around and heard several comments of "very handsome, both of them."

"The butler admitted that the jewelry Lady Hale is wearing in this photograph was stolen or mislaid a month or so before the lady and her son went missing."

The photo went around again, this time with the jewelry closely examined.

When it came back to me, I glanced at it once more. Lady Hale was, indeed, lovely.

Now she was dead, and a little boy would someday want to know why.

AFTER THE meeting, Grace agreed to find out what she could about three of our missing women and took their details with her. I kept the other two. Once I opened the bookshop in the morning and saw that Frances was settled, I went out to investigate my theory.

No one was home at the first residence, but I learned from a chatty neighbor that the lady who'd lived there had gone shopping several months back. She'd been run over by a hansom cab and had lain in a hospital bed for several days, unable to speak and unidentified, until someone in the family had checked hospitals at a distance from her home.

Apparently, no one had bothered to tell the police the woman had been found. And the woman owned no property.

I went to the neighborhood of the other missing woman. It was north of Hyde Park, new, respectable and monied. Unlike the first area, women here were not likely to answer their own doors.

I decided on an old subterfuge. I rang the doorbell, and when a maid answered, asked if Mrs. Gregory was at home.

"Oh, she's been gone six months or more," the girl said, her eyes widening.

"She's moved? I've done business with her in the past and hoped to again. Can you give me her new address?"

"No, ma'am. She sold the business and then just disappeared. The family's been that upset, I can tell you."

"Who's at the door?" A girl of about sixteen appeared behind the maid.

"This lady wanted to do business with your mother, Miss Anna. I told her the business has been sold."

"Yes. Forsyth and Summerhaye bought the firm. You'll have to speak to them. Now, shut the door before the cold and the fog come in." She walked off, clearly uninterested in anyone who'd done business with her mother.

I turned away, planning to speak to Forsyth and Summerhaye. But first I needed to check on my bookshop.

I needn't have worried. Frances had everything under control out front, and I only had to deal with a delivery of weekly illustrated magazines. After that, I took over the shop while Frances went home to eat luncheon with her son and his family at the hotel they owned.

She had barely returned when among the customers coming into the shop to stock up on reading material was a man wearing the garb of a successful professional. His outfit, in black and white and gray, was well tailored and included a black silk top hat.

However, his clothes seemed at odds with his coloring. His eyes were the brightest blue I've ever seen, and his hair and mustache were a rich light brown like an animal pelt. He was a pleasing height and had a trim build, but I was drawn to those blue eyes. His personality seemed to shine in his eyes, and right now, they were smiling.

"Are you Miss Fenchurch?" he asked with a small bow.

"Yes. How may I help you?"

"I'm Mr. Wylie. I'm the solicitor training Jacob. You have a lovely shop, Miss Fenchurch."

"Thank you. Are you here about Jacob?" I hoped I hid my worry. Jacob was so interested in studying the law, I didn't want anything to go wrong.

"Indirectly. Jacob said he was going to Manchester on an investigation. I wondered if you needed any help at this end while he's gone."

"No. We're fine. Thank you." This man was in his late thirties and, from what I'd heard, was a busy solicitor. Why would he suddenly offer to help the Archivist Society?

My skepticism showed in my voice. Wylie raised his eyebrows and said, "Well, yes. I also wanted to meet you. You are important in Jacob's life, and if I'm to successfully teach him the law, I need to know the people and the influences in his family."

"We're coworkers, not family," I said as Frances went to greet a regular customer who'd walked in, jingling the bell over the door.

"You underestimate your influence. From what Jacob has told me, the Archivist Society is more family than corporation."

At the words 'Archivist Society,' I shushed him. Stepping close to him, I whispered, "I prefer to keep my two occupations separate. Do you want to speak to me in my office?"

"If you don't mind, Miss Fenchurch."

He followed me back to my small, untidy office where I cleared off two chairs as I said, "Please pardon the state of my housekeeping."

"This room looks a lot like my office. Jacob will feel at home there." We sat down and looked at each other as if not certain how to proceed.

I decided to set the record straight. "Jacob doesn't spend any time in here. He runs books between the shop and Sir Broderick when I'm away on Archivist Society business, but he has no need to come into my office."

He nodded solemnly, then brightened as he said, "Sir Broderick is an interesting man."

"Yes, he is." If he wanted me to be indiscreet about my friends, he was out of luck.

Mr. Wylie turned his top hat in his hands for a moment before he looked at me with those bright blue eyes and said, "Miss Fenchurch. I'm not trying to spy on you or discredit Jacob in any way. I'm merely trying to understand his unique background. He told me he joined Sir Broderick's household as a child after he was involved in a murder investigation."

"Yes."

"Was that the first investigation by the Archivist Society?"

"No." I could have left it there, but for some reason, I didn't. Maybe I thought Mr. Wylie really was trying to understand Jacob's unusual life. "After my parents were killed, I tried to find their murderer without much luck, but with the assistance of my friends. When one of these friends came to me for help because Scotland Yard couldn't find her brother's killer, I involved Sir Broderick. He resisted my entreaties at first, but eventually I wore him down. The quest for that killer became the first Archivist Society case. We met Jacob about six months later."

Mr. Wylie's eyes widened. "And before that, Jacob was an orphan in the East End, doing odd jobs for prostitutes and blacksmiths after his mother died. He was very lucky."

"He was courageous. A prostitute who'd been looking after him was kidnapped by a murderer. He couldn't interest the police in the woman's disappearance, so he came to us. He helped us free her and bring a killer to justice. The newspapers called the man we apprehended 'the murdering earl.'"

I could never forget the case where I first met both Jacob and Lady Phyllida, who was the sister of the murdering earl as well as his prisoner and household slave. Jacob convinced us to enter the earl's fortress-like house, and Phyllida saved my life when her brother attacked me.

"I remember reading about it at the time. And Jacob was part of that investigation? How old was he?"

"He was eight or nine. I was only ten years older and hardly able to take him in. Sir Broderick had household staff who could look after the child, especially since he himself was still bedridden from the injuries he received trying to save my parents. It seemed like the best solution. We couldn't just leave Jacob where he was."

"So you became his family."

That was true in its own way. "Sir Broderick eventually made Jacob his ward and saw to his education."

"You've known Sir Broderick a long time. What sort of man is he?"

"He was my father's partner in this bookshop. He's loyal, brave, brilliant. And he's had the determination to carve out a career for himself with the Archivist Society despite being in a wheeled chair."

"I've been told he was injured in the same accident that claimed both your parents."

"It wasn't an accident," I snapped at him. I immediately regretted my outburst and took a deep breath, crunching my ribs against my corset. The pain eased my temper.

I saw his hurt look and felt a need to explain. "A madman believed my father was involved in the theft of a valuable book. He kidnapped my parents and myself and took us to an abandoned cottage just outside the suburbs north of London. I escaped and went straight to Sir Broderick who returned with me."

The rest was still hard to say. "We sent the cabbie off to the nearest police station for help while we tried to enter the cottage. The madman set the building on fire with my parents tied up inside. During the efforts to rescue my parents from the burning building, a beam collapsed on Sir Broderick. By the time I dragged him outside, the rest of the cottage collapsed, killing my parents."

Pain showed in those expressive eyes of his. "Good heavens. How old were you?"

"Seventeen."

"That is an impressive rescue by one so young. To drag a grown man from under a beam and away from a fire..."

It didn't feel impressive to me. "I wanted to save them all. I still wish I had."

"And the madman?"

"Still free to hunt for his stolen Gutenberg Bible and kill people who don't tell him what he wants to hear." I wondered if my voice betrayed the bitter taste those words left in my mouth.

He shook his head, amazement written on his face. "And you began to run a business all on your own at seventeen? Incredible."

"I received a lot of help from Sir Broderick. He was in great pain and near death, but I'd come to him each night and he would answer my questions as long as his strength allowed. By the time he was able to sit up on his own, I'd learned the day-to-day basics of running a bookshop and dealing with antiquarian volumes."

"I'm sorry for what you went through." I could see his sympathy in those blue eyes.

I didn't want his pity. "We had to suffer through that loss or we would never have formed the Archivist Society. It drives us on to help people get justice for their loved ones. We use more obscure sources of information than Scotland Yard in digging for the truth in those cases we take on."

"You get justice for others, but you can't get it for yourself." More of that pity. I was beginning to dislike Mr. Wylie.

"Perhaps I may yet succeed. In the past year, I've learned the identity of the killer of my parents. He is protected by the Austro-Hungarian government, as well as rich and powerful friends in this country. Still, I hope to get justice."

"And this is the family Jacob has grown up in." Wylie sounded amazed.

"Yes. Don't hold it against him. He's bright and hard working and a quick learner."

"And devoted to gaining justice for the powerless. That's a valuable commodity in a solicitor." Wylie stood and gave me a smile. "Thank you for your time, Miss Fenchurch. I've very glad to have met you. And I've heard tales of the successful work done by the Archivist Society. I would never hold Jacob's involvement in it against him under any circumstances. I think he's been quite lucky to have you in his life."

I rose and returned his smile. "We're all very fond of Jacob. He's an asset to the Archivist Society."

"And he's very loyal to you. But now I need to get back to work and I suspect you do, too."

"I'm glad to have met you, Mr. Wylie." I ushered him out of the shop.

He turned as he reached the door and pulled on his gloves. "Thank you, Miss Fenchurch. I hope to see you again soon." Giving me a final smile, he strode out into the wind and, clamping his hat on his head with one hand, disappeared down the pavement.

We were busy with customers during the afternoon. Being able to find their way about again without the terrible fog, people were venturing out, hurrying down the street and occasionally stopping in my shop. Illustrated weeklies and two-shilling editions of novels flew off the shelves. More serious tomes remained untouched. Apparently, no one had the will to engage in rigorous thought in this weather.

I made sure Fenchurch's Books was ready to serve their needs, no matter what they wanted to read.

A customer was just leaving with her purchase of gardening books when Grace walked in with a light step.

They nodded to each other and then Grace hurried up to the counter. "I think I've found something," she whispered.

She pulled off her coat and gloves, swirling cold air around us. "Two of them were washouts. One died and the other was visiting family and the note she left was lost. But the third is a possibility. The woman was quite well off, and she and her husband reportedly had a frosty relationship."

She leaned forward over the counter. "A few months before she disappeared, her daughter married after the girl's father forbade the wedding. When she married, the father banned the daughter from the house. The woman owned a lot of property around London that she'd inherited. She started selling the property before her daughter's wedding. She vanished about four months ago and hasn't been seen since."

"She matches a woman I learned about today. This woman owned a business that was sold to Forsyth and Summerhaye before she disappeared." I looked up as the bell over the door jingled.

Grace reached across the counter and grabbed my arm. "Oh, but Georgia..." she said before she dropped my arm and turned away. She nodded to the customer and went over to the scientific books.

I showed the older woman the newest novels, all the while wondering what Grace had learned. Each book I suggested reminded the customer of a story she'd read, and she ended up recommending more books to me than I had the opportunity to show her.

All the time I could see Grace pacing the aisles of nonfiction books, her gaze straight ahead of her.

Charles Dickens strolled up to us and rubbed against the woman's legs.

"Shoo, Dickens," I said and tried to grab the cat.

He hissed at me and swung a paw with his claws out.

"Oh, pretty kitty," the woman said and creakingly bent over. I held my breath, expecting Dickens to strike. Instead I heard his rumbling purr as she scratched him behind his ears. His eyes closed in bliss.

Was that all it took to win him over? I was the one who put out his food and water. Apparently, with a cat, that stood for nothing.

Or perhaps Dickens was like the Duke of Blackford. A clever hunter, a proud aristocrat, and a gentle soul with the meek. And one who might lash out without ever realizing that it would hurt me.

Ordinarily, I was interested in discussing books with my customers and didn't mind if they fussed over Dickens. But today, I couldn't wait to send the old lady on her way. At that moment, I was impatient to hear what had excited Grace.

Once the old lady chose a book and left the shop, Grace returned to the counter and grabbed my hand. "That's it, Georgia. I was speaking to one of the neighbors whose house was owned by Mrs. Matthews, the woman I was investigating. A few weeks before Mrs. Matthews disappeared, the house was sold. The firm that bought it was Forsyth and Summerhaye."

CHAPTER SIX

"WHO are Forsyth and Summerhaye?" I asked Grace. "They must be the key to this puzzle of disappearing women of means."

"Do you think they've all been stabbed and tossed into the Thames?" Grace asked.

"No. Why buy up their property and then kill them? There's something else behind this. Lady Hale could have been some sort of mistake. Could you follow up with the one left on my list?" I gave Grace the particulars on Mrs. Gregory as she pulled on her coat and gloves.

"I'll be glad to. May take a day or two, but I'll find out what I can."

Not long after that, I closed up the shop for the night. When I returned to Sir Broderick's, I found they had waited dinner for me. Jacob had managed to make his trip to Manchester a one-day journey and he sat across the table from me in his usual spot. I was able to fill them in on my day's discoveries during the soup and fish courses, and then turned to Jacob as the fowl course arrived. "What happened in Manchester?"

"Sir Edward has three factories there. They are his entire business."

"Then why live in London?" Sir Broderick asked.

Jacob shook his head. "I don't know. I spoke to all three managers, and while they know about Sir Edward from a business perspective, they have no idea what else he does while he's in town or who his friends are or why he lives in London. I did learn with the new fast trains, the journey isn't long. By leaving early this morning, I took care of my business and returned just a short time ago."

"What did they say about working for him? Is he a good businessman?" Knowing what others thought of Sir Edward might make understanding him easier.

"He's bull-headed and abrasive, but not nearly as bad as he was in years past. They said he's made some good decisions lately, and he seems to have calmed down as a result. One manager was on the point of leaving about a year and a half ago, but things have improved so much since then that he plans to stay indefinitely."

"Where does he live when he's visiting his factories?" I thought that could be the key to Sir Edward's life away from London.

"A small, shabby hotel that caters to commercial travelers."

"Is he that hard up?" I asked. Surely he'd want someplace more luxurious.

"No. From what the managers said and from what I learned around town, Sir Edward is well off."

"Then why—?" Mrs. Hardwick looked around the table. "Oh, dear. Excuse me. I'm interfering, but I'm afraid I've become involved in this case. I can't help worrying about that little boy who's lost his mother."

"Feel free to get involved. All of us first became part of the Archivist Society by worrying about a single case," I told her with an encouraging smile. "And that's my question too. Sir Edward doesn't have a lavish lifestyle, but a shabby hotel sounds too spartan even for him."

"It does have the benefit of anonymity," Jacob told us. "I went there and spoke to the proprietress. A sour-faced, cold woman. She told me nothing. Then I hung around and spoke to a man who was headed inside. He would have nothing to do with me. Said everyone there keeps to themselves, and that's the way they like it."

Sir Broderick set down his fork. "The next time Sir Edward goes to Manchester, you'll have to follow him, Jacob. In the meantime, you need to work extra hard for Mr. Wylie. He's being very generous in allowing you to help us, but he's your employer now."

"I'll be there all day tomorrow reading the law. It's going to be a long five years reading law books that are dry as dust."

Something in Jacob's tone worried me. "Do you think you've made a mistake?"

"No. Once I've read and understood all those tiring books and can put my learning into practice, I expect to find it fascinating." Jacob turned and gave all his attention to Humphries, who was bringing around the main course of ham, potatoes, and cooked fruits.

Once the butler had left the room, Sir Broderick said, "Georgia, we'll need you to find out when Sir Edward plans to go to Manchester again."

"He told me Sunday afternoon." My pleasure at knowing the answer to at least one question in this mystery deflated as I had to admit, "He wants Teddy returned to him before then."

"He should be. Georgia, I know how you feel about this, but Lady Hale is dead. Teddy only has one parent left, and that is Sir Edward."

I stared at him, knowing we weren't going to agree.

"What if he killed his wife?"

His voice was level. "Do you have evidence that he killed his wife?"

I felt myself shrink. "Nothing solid."

"Then you have to set your feelings aside and take Teddy back to his father. If it later turns out Sir Edward killed Lady Hale, the courts will decide what to do with the boy."

"He has financial guardians named in Lady Hale's will. Her father's solicitor, his business manager and Teddy's aunt," I told him.

"In that case, they may be assigned the guardianship role. Or Lady Hale's sister alone might be." Sir Broderick shrugged. "But the immediate situation demands that Teddy be returned to his father. Then we'll turn our attention to learning who killed the boy's mother."

"May it wait until morning?" I asked. My tone was more than a bit peevish.

"Of course. Take Adam Fogarty and Grace Yates with you. They may make the task less onerous." Sir Broderick's tone was even, but I saw compassion in his eyes.

I knew I wouldn't see kindness in Lady Imogen's eyes when I asked her to hand over Teddy.

LADY IMOGEN stood in her parlor, dressed conservatively and elegantly, with her height and aristocratic bearing adding to her intimidation. "On whose authority do you plan to remove Teddy Hale from my house?"

I looked up at her haughty expression, wishing I didn't have to do this. "On his father's authority as his sole living parent. Believe me, if Lady Hale had lived, we wouldn't be having this conversation. Please don't make this any more difficult, milady."

"I don't intend to make this difficult, Miss Fenchurch. You and your friends are free to search the house. Teddy Hale is not here."

"Where is he?" *Blast.* This was going to be awkward.

"He's not here. Beyond that, I have no desire to tell you. And don't think you can trick it or bribe it out of my servants. They are far too intelligent and paid far too well to fall for threats or enticements."

"Sir Edward can petition the courts to force you to tell him Teddy's location. With my testimony, it would become a case of kidnapping. A scandalous case."

Her smile was cold. "I'm no stranger to scandalous cases. But never forget who my father is. His power in the courts and in the government is not to be misjudged."

The Marquess of Hunterbrick was one of the most powerful men in the country. More powerful than Salisbury. Nearly more powerful than the Queen. Her threat was clear. One word from her father would have my testimony and Sir Edward's suit dismissed as lies and we would find ourselves the defendants in a libel suit.

"But please. Search the house. Assure yourselves the boy is not here." She gave a sweeping gesture with one arm.

Such an offer would make her look innocent and would convince everyone the boy had been taken elsewhere. What easier way to keep the boy safely here? "Thank you. We'll take you up on that generous offer."

I turned to Fogarty and Grace, who both looked shocked that I'd taken Lady Imogen's dare. "Sergeant Fogarty, if you'll search the downstairs and outbuildings, and Grace, if you'll take the public rooms, Lady Imogen and I will search the private rooms."

I faced Lady Imogen with a smile. "If you'll lead the

way?"

I was impressed with her equanimity in the face of my taking up her challenge. She led the way silently, her carriage straight, her gait graceful, as we went from room to room on the top two floors of her house. A smile kept playing at the corners of her lips.

The house was large enough and old enough to have any number of hidey-holes. She showed them to me and let me explore them with apparent indifference while I got dusty and sneezed frequently. I lingered, staring at the furnishings in each room. They were breathtaking, containing furniture and drapery I would expect to find in Blackford House. Her family not only had power; they had money.

When I'd seen the boy wasn't in any of the rooms or hidey-holes, I said, "Thank you for allowing us to assure ourselves that Teddy wasn't playing hide-and-seek in your home."

Lady Imogen blocked my way, an amused smile hovering on her lips. "I didn't think you'd take my word for it, but I was surprised you'd take up my offer and actually search my home. I'm the daughter of a marquess. That carries a lot of weight with most people."

I thought of Blackford and smiled in spite of my efforts to look professional. "I've worked with a duke on several investigations. I'm afraid I've lost the proper deference for titles."

"I've heard Blackford has been helping the Archivist Society. I can see why I'm not intimidating." The corners of her mouth quivered with the effort not to curl up.

I dragged my thoughts away from the duke's firm expression and warm embrace and back to the current search. "I wasn't disputing your word as much as I've learned not to take anyone at face value. This way, I can state you are not hiding the boy from his father. I suspect you know where he is, but that's not something I can prove."

"No. You can't confirm whether or not I know where Teddy is." She smiled and stepped back, letting me precede her downstairs.

I returned her smile. "But I believe you are too good a person not to be certain of his welfare before allowing him to leave here."

"Thank you for that. There are many who think me cruel and uncaring."

There was no reply I could make.

I met Fogarty and Grace in the front hall. They both shook their heads.

"What are you going to tell Sir Edward?" Lady Imogen asked.

"That we've assured ourselves Teddy is no longer here, and a search must begin." I didn't look forward to delivering that message. I had no idea how to find Teddy.

"What are you really going to tell Sir Edward?" Grace asked once we'd left Lady Imogen's house.

A rotting gaseous smell off the Thames that morning took my breath away for a moment. Turning my back on the river, I was able to breathe again. "Nothing yet. I'm going to visit Lady Hale's man of business and see what he can tell us. Thank you for coming with me this morning. I couldn't have done that on my own."

Fogarty coughed deeply before he said, "I learned one thing. When I was in the back yard, I was alone with a young maid. I said 'I know the child's not here now. How long ago did he leave?'"

We went up a side street away from the river before he

continued. "She told me the household learned that Lady Hale was dead soon after she was fished out of the river. The news was all over the neighborhood. Within an hour, a coach came and picked up Teddy. She said she didn't recognize the coach. Don't know if I believe her about the coach, but the rest of it's true. I'd stake a coin on that."

"So they knew Sir Edward had every right to take the child home, and they're stopping him. Why? Are they doing this for Lady Hale, to help Countess Reinler, or for some other person?"

I was deep in thought when Grace asked, "Who else might have a claim to raise Teddy?"

"No one we know of yet. Do you have a full work day at Lord Barnwood's?"

"Not so full that I can't find a little time to do research on my own." Grace smiled. "What do you need?"

"You already have Mrs. Gregory's business to look into. Will you have time to do more?"

"I'll give it a try and I'll let you know what I learn."

"Look into the families of both Sir Edward and Lady Hale. Find out if there are any other relatives who might want to claim Teddy, especially now that he's a wealthy heir. I'll go to the offices of Forsyth and Summerhaye after I talk to Lady Hale's man of affairs and see if I can learn anything there. We'll talk later."

Grace stopped and looked at me. "Did the knife thrust that killed Lady Hale take much strength?"

I glanced at Fogarty, who shook his head.

"Because," she told us, "I had to look in Lady Imogen's studio for Teddy. She must have great strength in her arms. She carves life-sized and larger statues out of stone."

"Of what?" Fogarty asked.

"Adult males and females. Nude. They're quite impressive."

"That would take a lot of strength as well as talent." I wished I'd seen them.

Grace nodded, and then she and Fogarty went off in one direction in the blustery sunshine and I went in the other toward the City of London.

The square mile of the City of London, the birthplace of the sprawling metropolis that served as the capital of Victoria's empire, held most of the business offices and banks in our city. The office of George Howard, man of business affairs for Lord Newbury and his daughters, was located on the second floor of a staid Georgian-styled office building.

As soon as I saw the elevator, I knew the building was much younger than its apparent age. The elevator boy took me up along with a middle-aged couple who were headed to another floor.

With a jerk, the cage-like contraption stopped at the second floor. As the gates opened, I rushed out of the shaky booth. Behind me, I heard it close its iron jaws once I'd stepped onto the firm wooden floor of the hallway.

Mr. Howard's offices were located in the front of the building. I knocked on the polished wooden door with its brass nameplate and then walked in. A young man looked up from the only desk in the room, one finger poised over a typewriter key. He immediately stood and, as he took off his sleeve protectors, said, "May I help you, Madam?"

I gave him my Archivist Society card and said, "May I have a little of Mr. Howard's time? It concerns the death of Lady Hale."

"Just a moment. Let me see if he's available." The young man slipped on his jacket and knocked before opening the darkly stained door.

He walked in and shut the door behind him, and I was free to examine the office in leisure. The room was lit with garishly bright electric light that nearly made me squint. Glass-fronted bookcases full of dark-bound volumes encircled the room. A second door opened off to one side, perhaps leading to a store room. On the young man's desk was a half-filled pottery mug and scattered papers. I forced myself not to read the papers after I made certain they had nothing to do with Lady Hale.

The young man opened the door and held it wide in an invitation for me to enter. I did so to find Mr. Howard standing behind his desk. He looked me in the eye as he gave me a correct bow. I curtsied in return and then he bade me have a seat with an expression of mild interest at my calling on him. Howard was either good at his job or had learned the external marks of a competent man.

I sat and found the chair in front of his desk was solid, rounded and uncushioned. Ample for carrying out business but too firm for anyone to linger, even with the multiple layers of clothing I wore under my skirt. I heard a small scrape and realized the young man had sat in the room with us out of my line of sight. Howard was having another pair of ears taking notes. He was good at his job, or at least cautious.

"I've heard that Lady Hale had sold much of her property in the weeks before her death. Is this true?" I guessed a direct approach would work best with this man.

"May I ask what your interest is in Lady Hale's affairs?" George Howard was a good-looking man in his late thirties, well dressed, but not at noticeable expense. His brown eyes studied me as closely as I scrutinized him.

"The Archivist Society has been asked by her husband to

discover the facts concerning the whereabouts of her son, and we are further investigating her murder."

"And you think her business affairs have some bearing on her death?"

"I think it likely."

"Why?" He asked with a tone of mild curiosity in his northern English accent.

"We know Lady Hale was specifically targeted. Hers was not a random killing. She was a wealthy woman. Therefore..." I let the rest of the thought hang in the air. Air that was tinted with a sweet pipe tobacco smoldering in an ash tray on a side table and with the odor of musty papers piled in a stack on his desk.

When he said nothing, I added, "It seems reasonable to ascertain whether some business affair could have led to her murder."

I could see on his face when he came to a decision. "What you've learned is correct. Lady Hale sold several of her properties."

"And the proceeds?"

"Her entire estate is now held in trust for her son."

"Who were the purchasers?"

"Forsyth and Summerhaye."

The same company that bought up the properties of another woman who'd gone missing. "For all of the sold properties?"

Howard visibly swallowed. "Yes."

"May I have a list of the properties that were sold?"

"Why on earth would you want that?" He sounded as if I'd surprised him with my request.

"Forsyth and Summerhaye has come to our attention in another matter. I would be less than thorough if I didn't follow up this lead."

Howard scowled as he studied me. "Since they are no longer in Lady Hale's possession, I suppose I won't be breaking a client confidence. My clerk, Mr. Smith, will provide you with a list."

"What did Lady Hale plan to do with the money? It must have been a large sum."

If I thought Howard would be so indiscreet as to answer with any information at all, I had sadly mistaken the man. A thin smile crossed his lips before he said, "That would be divulging client information. I'm sure you understand I can't do that. Is there anything else, Miss Fenchurch?"

He didn't have to glance at my card to remember my name. Ah, yes. He was very good at his job.

After receiving the list from the clerk, I headed to the address of Forsyth and Summerhaye a few blocks away. When I arrived, I saw it was as different from Howard's office as was possible. This building was truly ancient, probably thrown up in haste in the years after the Great Fire. I walked up a flight of dusty steps to find two doors. In the dim light I made out that one bore a tarnished plate saying Forsyth and Summerhaye, and the other Powell's Agency.

A disheveled man with beady eyes blundered past me on the landing. I opened Forsyth and Summerhaye's door and practically leaped inside to get out of the way before the unkempt man clomped down the stairs.

Only when I turned around did I look at the premises of Forsyth and Summerhaye. It was one large room in need of a coat of paint. A gigantic cobweb in the corner moved in the breeze that entered around the closed windows. There were two desks, both covered with papers that had yellowed with age. An unsmiling man of middle years with thinning hair and a grease mark on his waistcoat sat behind one of the desks. "May I help you?"

He didn't sound like he wanted to.

I gave him my Archivist Society card. "We are investigating the murder of Lady Hale. Forsyth and Summerhaye has done business with her recently. Could you shed light on the type of business transactions conducted between her and your company and if you noticed anything unusual about any of these transactions? Or if you noticed anyone following Lady Hale?"

"No."

"Excuse me?"

"No. I won't shed light, as you put it, on any business conducted by this firm." He had a deep voice for such a slender man of middling height.

I tried to put on my friendliest, most patient tone as I gave the man a smile. "I'm not asking for business details. I just wondered if anyone in the firm noticed anything suspicious surrounding Lady Hale. Anything that might point to the danger that led to her murder."

"I have nothing to say to you. Good day."

CHAPTER SEVEN

WELL, that was unequivocal. The scowling expression and cold tone of the man in the Forsyth and Summerhaye office made his words clear. I sighed and tried another path. "Are you Mr. Forsyth or Mr. Summerhaye?"

"Neither."

I stared at him as if he'd committed a great lapse of good manners.

He relented slightly. "My name is Kirkman. I'm clerk here."

"Mr. Kirkman, can you verify for me that the late Lady Hale did business with the firm of Forsyth and Summerhaye? The late Lady Hale who was recently brutally murdered?"

"No, I will not."

"What about Mrs. Gregory?"

"Mrs. Gregory wouldn't have had anything to do with Lady Hale's murder!" He started to rise as he exclaimed over my question. As his mistake sank in, he sat back down heavily.

"You obviously know Mrs. Gregory. I take it you know Lady Hale, too." I gave him a smile.

He refused to divulge anything else by the simple expedient of keeping silent and glaring at me. He refused to speak even when I asked to make an appointment with either of the two principals. Looking about the room, I decided Kirkman was a disaster as a clerk. If his only task was to keep people from learning anything about his employers, however, he was a success.

I wandered over to the second desk and idly shoved aside some of the documents with my hand. I could see yellowed patches where the papers had been exposed to the light and clear lines that separated those parts from the protected, white sections of the papers. Those papers hadn't been touched or rearranged in a very long time.

Despite Mr. Kirkman's intransigence, I left knowing one thing. There was something very odd about this company.

Despite supposedly doing a great deal of business, Forsyth and Summerhaye's office was shoddy, their clerk was sloppy, and the papers had yellowed where they lay. It was as if Forsyth and Summerhaye wasn't a business at all, but a stage set.

Wherever Mr. Forsyth and Mr. Summerhaye conducted business, it wasn't in their office.

When I left, not much wiser than when I entered but very much interested, I gave a long sigh. I was so exhausted from the encounter I might as well have walked the length of London.

There was more than one way to get the information I needed.

I'd learned Mr. Wylie's address from Jacob and made my way there as dark clouds spread a blanket across the sky. I discovered when I reached it that his office was one flight over a clock maker's shop.

When I knocked on the door, Jacob answered. "Georgia, what are you doing here?"

"Mr. Wylie kindly offered his help, should we ever need it. If we're to find little Teddy Hale, we could use his assistance."

I stepped inside and found Mr. Wylie's office to be cheery and home-like. Electric lights brightened the shiny wooden bookcases that lined the room with law texts. Both desks, Mr. Wylie's and Jacob's, matched the bookcases in quality and tidiness. A coal fire warmed the room. Lace curtains were pulled back to let in the watery winter sunshine.

Wylie rose as soon as he looked up from a heavy volume. "Miss Fenchurch, I'd be happy to give you whatever assistance you require."

I crossed to his desk, Jacob on my heels. "There is a young boy missing. His mother was recently murdered. Before her murder, she sold several of her properties to a firm called Forsyth and Summerhaye. This same firm bought a business from a woman named Mrs. Gregory. This woman then disappeared, but her body has not been recovered. I need to know as much as I can about Forsyth and Summerhaye."

"I'll be glad to assist. This will make a good learning experience for Jacob. But how will it help you find the missing child?"

I yanked off my gloves in frustration. "I don't know. I'm grasping at any possibility. But I believe Lady Imogen Fielding is mixed up in this somehow."

Wylie's eyes widened. "Oh, my. She's a formidable woman. I've only heard tales, but oh, my."

I remembered our last encounter. "Yes, she is formidable. Teddy was last seen in her custody, and I'm certain she knows where he is. She wouldn't put the child in any danger, I'm certain of that, but she has him hidden and until she decides otherwise, she won't help us return Teddy to his father."

"Why won't she?"

"Originally, she was keeping both mother and son secure and away from a husband the wife couldn't stand. Now that the wife is dead, I think she's judged the father guilty of her murder and is protecting the son."

Wylie smiled as he escorted me to a chair. "So you want to know everything possible about Forsyth and Summerhaye in the hope that it will tell you who might be hiding the boy. Now, supposing you tell me what you do know."

Both Wylie and Jacob sat at their desks and Jacob began to write as I told them what I'd learned. Wylie interrupted me a few times to make certain he was clear on all the facts.

"Since Lady Hale's wealth was from property, we can check at the Stamp Duty Land Tax office of the Inland Revenue. Sellers need to pay the stamp duty on their deed of title of property before they can complete a sale. We can compare your list of properties with what we find taxes paid on, and from there perhaps learn more about Forsyth and Summerhaye's dealings."

When he finished explaining what they planned to do, I said, "Sunday afternoon we need Jacob to return to Manchester and follow Sir Edward. He'll be leaving you on your own for a day or two. Will you have time to look into this?"

Wylie rose as soon as I did. His smile reached his bright blue eyes as he took my hand. "We'll do what we can before Sunday, and after that, I'll try to make time. Don't worry, Miss Fenchurch. You can count on me as you can on Jacob."

"Thank you." I returned his smile and tugged slightly on my hand.

After a moment, he released my fingers and blushed. "Excuse me. I didn't mean to be forward, but I feel as if I've known you forever from the stories Jacob tells."

"He's very impressed with you," I told him. Now that I'd completed my errand, I was anxious to get back to the bookshop. I pulled my gloves on as I moved toward the door. "Good luck with your searches."

I was glad to see Mr. Wylie didn't detain me any longer as I bundled up and headed out of the building. On the way to the bookshop, I had reason to curse under my breath as snow flurries began to slick the pavement. Everyone walked slowly and carefully, particularly uphill from the City toward Charing Cross. When I sped up my pace, I slipped, and found I had to grab a light pole to keep from falling. My face heated as I hoped everyone was so busy watching their own footing that no one noticed.

When I walked in, Frances said, "With this snow fouling traffic, if I leave for luncheon now, I won't return until almost closing time. Do you want me to stay longer or go?"

"You've had to stay far past your lunchtime. Go home and I'll see you tomorrow morning. Watch how you go. It's slippery out."

Frances immediately began to climb into her outerwear as I took mine off and shook it out. "Have we been busy?" I called out to her.

"We were until the snow began. No one's been in since." Frances walked over to the front door and paused. "Sir Broderick telephoned for you earlier. He didn't say why. The mail is on the counter. Nothing else has happened."

I glanced over at the bow window. No Dickens. "Have you seen the cat?"

"No. I thought he might be holed up at the bakery."

In Dickens's hierarchy of shops on our road, the bakery ranked nearly as high as ours. They didn't feed him like we did, and they didn't let him in their front window to sun himself, so I decided they must have a good supply of mice. Or maybe this was another example of Dickens's contrariness.

Once Frances left, I was alone. I wondered how things were going between Frances and her son's wife. Her son hadn't been married long when Frances's husband was murdered, supposedly in a street robbery. But what Frances was told by the police didn't add up. She contacted the Archivist Society and we eventually learned one of the guests at the family's hotel was a notorious smuggler. Her husband had overheard a conversation that made him a danger to their current illegal operation and so was silenced.

After the killers were hanged, she sought us out to join the Archivist Society. Years of practice in dealing with every sort of person in their hotel made her excellent at questioning neighbors and family members.

Unfortunately, her son's wife felt that as a widow, Frances should now let her son run the hotel unimpeded. The younger woman kept trying to send Frances away from her native London to the countryside, where the son's wife had relatives living on a farm.

Frances vehemently opposed every effort to ship her away from her home and her grandchildren while trying to stay on the good side of her son's wife. Apparently, even with Frances helping in the bookshop and aiding the Archivist Society, her son's wife felt she was underfoot.

I was glad of Frances's help. What I wanted at that moment were customers, but no one passed by our door. That made this the perfect time to call Sir Broderick. I picked up both halves of the telephone and held one to my ear as I spoke into the other. It didn't take long before I heard Sir

Broderick's booming voice come over the line.

"Frances said you called the shop. What can I do for you?" I knew ordinarily Sir Broderick would have told Frances why he called.

"Lady Monthalf sent a note here saying Lady Westover wants to see you immediately."

That didn't sound good. I pressed the speaker harder against my ear. "Is she getting worse?"

"Lady Monthalf says she's about the same."

Lady Phyllida Monthalf had become adept at organizing a household over the years, and she'd always been a good companion. When his grandmother became seriously ill with pneumonia, Inspector Grantham had come to ask Lady Phyllida to take charge of both Lady Westover's care and her staff. With Emma on her honeymoon, Phyllida had been bored with only me to fuss over in our home. This situation had been a godsend for her.

But this had left me with a cold, dirty flat. I was grateful for the chance to move into Sir Broderick's home where I once again didn't have to be responsible for household duties.

"Can she wait for me to come over as soon as I close the shop today?"

"Can you leave now?"

"No. I just returned and sent Frances home for the day."

"Then perhaps that would be best. I'll ask Dominique to hold dinner for you."

There was something in Sir Broderick's tone that made me uneasy. "What's wrong?"

"This is the first time since Lady Phyllida took over the household that she's sent us a message from Lady Westover."

"True, but that could mean this is very good news." It

was gloomy and snowy outside. There was a little boy missing. I wanted to look at the bright side of this request.

Sir Broderick smashed any chance of that. "Or very bad news."

I admit after our conversation I did a great deal of clock watching. We only had one customer once the snow made travel treacherous and I couldn't interest myself in any of our myriad books or weekly journals. Even the scandal rags couldn't hold my attention.

At the appointed time, I closed up the shop and made my way to Mayfair. Between the wind-whipped flurries and the slick pavement, I made slow progress. When I arrived, I was glad to see there was no funeral wreath by the door or straw on the pavement. Lady Westover still lived.

I rang the bell and the butler answered. I gave him my social "Georgia Fenchurch" card that contained only my name and said, "I received a message that Lady Westover wants to see me."

"Yes, miss." He handed off my outerwear and escorted me upstairs. Tapping on a second floor door, he opened it and stood aside.

I walked in to a well-heated but weakly lighted room. Lady Westover was propped up on pillows, looking pale and frail. Inspector Grantham stood on one side of her bed, Phyllida on the other. I walked over and stood beside Phyllida, giving her an eyebrow-raised glance.

"Lady Westover called for you." Phyllida leaned over Lady Westover and said in a firm voice, "Amelia, Georgia is here to see you."

"I can see that," she said in a feeble whisper. "Georgia, I want you to do something for me."

"Anything, my lady."

"Marry Blackford."

My eyes and mouth widened before I stopped myself. *Marry Blackford?* Lady Westover must have been delirious.

The inspector turned his guffaw into an implausible cough.

"Eddy, don't laugh. You're next on my list." Lady Westover might only be able to speak in a whisper, but there was steel in her tone.

"Inspector, are you getting married? I had no idea," I said brightly. I hoped to win myself some time before I had to respond. Marry Blackford? Even Lady Westover couldn't talk him into wedding me.

"Not that I knew about," Inspector Edward Grantham muttered.

Her faded eyes bore into mine. "I don't have much time, and I need to make sure I have this world running smoothly before I leave for the next. You must marry Blackford."

"Shouldn't you be telling this to Blackford?"

"He's not here." She sank back further into the pillows and shut her eyes.

I decided to be honest. "I admit I've thought about marrying him, but I suspect he'll come back from America with some heiress." I still had doubts about the two of us having a future together. As a duke, he'd been born to expect deference and instant agreement. I was a middle-class bookshop owner. Well read, with a natural curiosity and a stubbornness born of becoming the boss at seventeen. I never gave him agreement without first being certain he was right.

Worse, he'd been raised with the expectation that he marry a fellow aristocrat. Only someone raised with wealth and a title could understand the requirements of his class.

"No, he won't." She paused as her body was wracked with coughs. "He loves you. You need to convince him you'll make a good duchess." Then she closed her eyes as if wearied of looking at us.

"How do I do that?" If I knew, I'd have done it before now. And convinced myself as well.

She opened her eyes and looked directly at me. "Don't be foolish. You're a woman. Let him think it's his idea."

"All right." It seemed better to agree with her than to upset a deathly ill woman. "Now, will you tell me who Eddy's going to marry?"

Both Lady Westover and her grandson glared at me.

She declared herself tired and sent the three of us out of her room with a single wave of her hand. We went downstairs to the parlor where Phyllida ordered tea and sent a housemaid to sit with Lady Westover. The staff, by now accustomed to her running the household, did as she commanded.

I waited until we were alone. "Is she hallucinating? Me? Marry Blackford?"

"Her mind is as clear as a bell, Georgia. And why not?"

I started to pace. "Lady Phyllida, Blackford has gone to America. He'll probably come home with some beautiful heiress as his duchess."

"I liked it better when you called me Aunt Phyllida. You seemed to have more confidence then." She gave me a steely stare.

Spending time with Lady Westover had certainly renewed in Phyllida some of the aristocratic assurance she would have learned in the nursery. "Where did you and Lady Westover get this mad idea, Aunt Phyllida?"

"And when did you decide to include me in your plans?"

the inspector asked.

Phyllida faced him. "Your grandmother and I have been talking. Both of us are looking at the latter stages of our lives, and we'd like to straighten out the world before we leave it. Neither of us has named a satisfactory candidate for you yet, so you'd better get busy and look around for yourself before we do it for you, young man."

Just as she returned her gaze to me, a maid entered carrying the tea tray. I was safe only as long as Phyllida was busy with the tea.

I tried to think of reasons why I shouldn't marry Blackford, but my heart wasn't in it. I knew he'd never ask me, so there was no purpose in fending off her silly request. I sat and accepted a cup of tea.

"There's no reason you two should not wed, except Blackford's foolish ducal pride. Now, what are we going to do about it?" Phyllida pinned me to the chair with her gaze.

I found it hard to believe this was the same timid, shattered woman we rescued from her mad brother a dozen years before. I'd taken her home with me when the police took the earl to prison for murdering prostitutes, and Fleet Street descended on her doorstep. She slowly took over as my housekeeper, but it was years before she'd go outside our home. While she had trembled at the thought of our investigations, she appeared to have finally reclaimed her aristocratic authority.

"I'll let you two figure it out. I have a bookshop to run and a missing boy to locate."

"What has happened?" Phyllida asked.

The inspector set his cup and saucer down. "What missing boy?"

"Has Sir Edward Hale reported his son Teddy missing?"

"Not that I'm aware of. I'll check again in the morning. Sir Broderick made me aware of the case."

I told Inspector Grantham what little I knew about Teddy's disappearance and his visit with Lady Imogen Fielding.

"Do you think she'd hurt the child?"

"Not after watching her entertain him. She knows where he is and I'm sure she's made certain of his safety. I have no idea why she's keeping him away from his father now that his mother is dead."

"Isn't Lady Imogen..." Phyllida began.

"The one involved in the attempted drowning of Lady Wilcox," the inspector said.

"Oh, yes, that. No, I was thinking of something I heard later. Smuggling women. It sounds so absurd, but that's what it was. Lady Imogen was smuggling women." She glanced from one to the other of us, looking quite puzzled over the idea.

Inspector Grantham spluttered, "But surely. You must know more than that. What women? Where?"

"Were any children mentioned?" I asked.

"Not that I heard," Phyllida said. "I'm afraid that's all I remember."

"Who told you about this?" I hoped to jog Phyllida's memory and when I learned who had mentioned this to her, I would pay them a visit and demand the details. Or beg for them. I couldn't help but worry about the boy.

"I have no idea. It sounds so preposterous that no one could believe the story. It was probably some spiteful tale begun by Lord Wilcox."

I studied Phyllida. "And yet this lie stayed with you. I wonder why."

"I have no idea," she said, sounding defensive. "I don't have a sharp mind like yours, Georgia."

"Something made it stay in your memory. You thought it sounded like something Lady Imogen would do, or someone made a comment about the story that was so extraordinary that it made the tale stand out." This might be our first clue to Teddy's present whereabouts. My eagerness rang in my voice.

She scrunched up her face for a moment before relaxing and opening her eyes. "I'm sorry, Georgia. There's nothing else that I can remember."

She looked so sad I told her, "Don't think about it, and when you least expect it, something will come to you."

"I hope in time for that little boy."

One way or another, I was determined we'd find the child. "We'll be in time. We have to be."

CHAPTER EIGHT

THE worried expression left Phyllida's face. "Now, back to the subject we were discussing. How are you going to convince Blackford that he should marry you?"

"I don't believe it's possible."

"Nonsense. Everything is possible if you work at it. Especially when someone is as smitten with you as the duke is." She gave me a benign, motherly gaze. "Amelia is right. Blackford loves you."

I set down my teacup and crossed my arms over my chest. "He admires my brain. No one ever married a woman for her brains."

"Then use those brains, Georgia, and find a way to convince him he can't live without you. Because he can't, you know. He'll never be happy with anyone else. And neither will you."

Phyllida was right about me. I felt sure, however, that she was wrong about the self-assured duke. He'd been gone for several months and I was certain he was doing fine.

Inspector Grantham offered to escort me home, but I saw no reason for anyone to go out in the cold and ice who didn't have to. By the time I reached Sir Broderick's door, I was chilled by the wind, my clothes were stiffened by the icy flakes falling from the sky, and I was coughing from the smoke spewing out from millions of chimneys.

Mrs. Hardwick helped the butler pull my outerwear off

and then had me stand in front of the fire in the dining room until the soup course was served. It was hot and wet and heated my insides enough I thought I might warm up. Some day.

"Any idea where the child is?" Sir Broderick asked.

"None."

"Sir Edward leaves for Manchester the day after tomorrow. You must go there tomorrow and tell him we've had no luck so far, but we won't stop looking." He sounded quite firm, but he kindly let me sit nearer the fire than he was.

"I don't think I should tell him about Lady Imogen hiding Teddy and refusing to give us his location. A father might do something out of desperation."

"Do you think it's time to bring in the police?" Mrs. Hardwick asked.

I was glad to find her making suggestions in an Archivist Society case, and I saw a pleased expression cross Sir Broderick's face. "I mentioned this case to Inspector Grantham tonight. He's going to check on it at Scotland Yard in the morning."

"Is it time to bring in the whole Archivist Society?" Sir Broderick asked after the soup dishes had been exchanged for a course of spicy fish. One bite and I knew the snow was making Dominique homesick for the islands of her childhood.

Was Teddy homesick, wherever he was?

"Let's see what Mr. Wylie comes up with," Jacob said. "Georgia came by and asked him to look into a company called Forsyth and Summerhaye."

I set down my fork. "They bought several pieces of property from Lady Hale shortly before her death. I'm hoping to find a connection between Lady Hale and a Mrs. Gregory who did business with them shortly before she disappeared. I don't know how Forsyth and Summerhaye are involved in this, but I think they will lead me to Teddy."

"Are they the only lead you have?" Sir Broderick asked.

"For now."

"Perhaps tomorrow will be luckier," Mrs. Hardwick said, giving me an encouraging smile.

I needed it.

I OPENED the bookshop in the morning, not certain when Frances would arrive. Snow was a few inches deep in places, and everywhere pedestrians were slipping. Horses kicked up slush with each step. I swept a clear spot on the pavement in front of my door in the hopes that customers would come in and not track snow all over my shop. The effort made me sweaty and in need of a new broom.

Then two young boys came by with a coal shovel and offered their services to clear the walkway. I decided it was worth a halfpenny to clear the whole area in front of my shop. They shoveled the snow into the road and earned curses from cabbies and wagon drivers steering their horses through the mess.

Two customers were in the shop when Frances arrived. As she opened the door, she looked behind her and said "Oh, my."

I came around the counter in time to see Charles Dickens squeeze in the door in front of Frances, leaving little bloody footprints on my wooden floor. Icicles matted his fur. "Oh, dear."

"We must warm him up immediately. Do you have a towel somewhere, Georgia?"

Certain Frances would be better at this than I, I hurried

to do her bidding. When I returned with a stack of clean dust rags, Frances already had her outerwear off. She grabbed a couple of cloths off the top of the pile and picked Dickens up, cocooning him as she cradled him in her arms.

"You'll be more comfortable in my chair in the office," I told her and followed her in with the dust cloths. Once I was certain Frances was comfortable with a sleeping Dickens on her lap, I went into the shop and cleaned up the floor. Where had he been that he was frozen and bloodied?

Dickens frequented all of the shops on our street. I'd not known him to stray far from home. Surely he had a safe spot if he were caught outdoors in bad weather until someone opened their shop. And the bakery was the first to open on any morning. How very strange that he had to wait until we opened.

I was kept busy until luncheon, when Frances was due to go home and join her family at the hotel. Walking into my small, cramped office in the back, I found Frances still cradling Dickens. "How is he?"

"He was drenched, but I've managed to dry him off. He's warm now, but we need to look at his paws. I'll hold him if you'll look."

Dickens didn't try to hurt Frances, but with every paw I looked at, I got a nasty scratch from the claws of a different foot. He kept his eyes narrowed as he gazed at me, and I could picture him planning my demise.

"The bottoms of his feet look like they've been rubbed raw, with several small cuts on each one."

"We'll have to keep him indoors and as immobile as possible until they heal," Frances said firmly. "We'll have to keep filling his food and water dishes."

I glanced at the dishes under my desk that Emma had

kept filled. "I have nothing here," I told Frances. I suspected Dickens's feet would heal before my scratches. Next time I'd wear gloves to examine him.

"I'll bring some things back with me after luncheon."

"All right. I have to go out this afternoon to speak to Sir Edward again, but it will certainly wait until you return."

"Any news on the little boy?"

"None. And that's what I have to tell his father."

I was dreading it. I continued to dread it through waiting on customers and checking on Dickens, now sleeping in the bow window. While my mind said Teddy Hale was someplace safe and warm, my heart would look at poor, battered Dickens as Frances tried to coax him to take a little food and water and think if a street-wise cat could be injured so quickly, what chance did an innocent little boy have?

After Frances finished feeding Dickens and cleaning his paws, I told her, "I have to go face Teddy Hale's father now."

"Good luck, Georgia. I know you'll find the lad."

I made my way through the crusty, sloppy London streets, melting where the sun struck the ground, icy in the shadows of buildings. A cold breeze made me wonder how any of the snow could melt as the air stung my cheeks.

Arriving at Sir Edward Hale's townhouse, I barged in as soon as the butler, Johnson, opened the door. I refused to stand on the unprotected stoop in this wintery air.

"Do you have an appointment?" the butler asked.

"Sir Edward asked for progress in the hunt for his son before he leaves for Manchester tomorrow."

"I'll see if he is available." He made it sound as if he were condescending to do me a favor for which I should be grateful.

He came back in a few moments to lead me upstairs

along that dark, unwelcoming hall. For a change, Sir Edward had the draperies pulled open and he stood by the window. The additional light made the room and Sir Edward look more inviting, more approachable.

"Well, where is he?" The way he snapped out his words wiped away any thought that Sir Edward might be easier to get along with that day.

"I don't know yet. We've begun several lines of inquiry-"

"You were supposed to have located him and returned him to me by today. Why have you failed?"

I wanted to say, *Not for lack of trying.* I'd hoped to have the child home to his father by now, and it worried me that we hadn't succeeded so far. But Sir Edward seemed to be the type of man who only wanted results. Never excuses. "There are people hiding the child for motives we've not yet ascertained. Since you don't appear to have received a ransom request, finding him will prove more difficult."

"Who are these people?" Sir Edward was turning a deep, unhealthy shade of red.

"I only know of one so far. She no longer has him in her care. We are investigating her friends and acquaintances."

"Her? Prudence had him and you didn't tell me?" Sir Edward shouted at me.

"No. She's as worried as you are. She's never had him in her home. That was an obvious place to check."

"Then who?"

"It won't do you any good to call there now. Teddy isn't there."

"You won't return my son. You won't tell me who had him. You're fired." He marched over to stand behind his desk.

"That won't get you your son back."

"Are you threatening me?" I didn't realize anyone could

turn that red.

"No. We know where he was and that he's being taken care of. We will find him."

"Who had him? By God, I'll get the law after this woman."

"Oh, she'd like that."

On the verge of shouting, he shut his mouth and blinked. "She'd like that?" came out in a surprised voice.

"This woman enjoys notoriety, and she knows how to destroy her opponents. If you start a battle with her, you'll never see your son again. Leave this to the Archivist Society. We'll bring Teddy home without causing an uproar."

He began spluttering like a steam engine. "You haven't done a very good job so far. You're fired. I'm finished dealing with the Archivist Society. I'm not paying you a cent."

"We won't stop looking for your son. Of that you can be sure."

"It won't gain you anything," he snapped at me, walking back to the window to pull the draperies closed.

In the darkened room, I watched him sit behind his desk. "We'll get the satisfaction of seeing you reunited with your son."

"Good day, Miss Fenchurch."

I doubted this would go well, but I had to try. "Before I leave, I need any addresses you have for Miss Forbes."

"Miss Forbes?" He was shouting again. "Does she have something to do with Teddy's disappearance?"

"We don't know."

"You don't know where my son is. You don't know if Miss Forbes has him hidden. Well, what do you know?"

"We want to bring Teddy home safely to you, and for that, you need to cooperate. Miss Forbes's address please."

"Oh, all right." He dug around in a desk drawer, finally

pulling out her references. "Will this do?"

He slapped two sheets of paper in my hand. One contained her sister's address. "Yes. Good day, Sir Edward." I turned on my heel and strode out of the room.

Mr. Johnson was waiting by the front door to show me out, a look of satisfaction on his face.

"Your master leaves for Manchester tomorrow afternoon?" I asked.

"And what business is it of yours?"

"I'm sure Sir Edward will wonder why you won't acknowledge what he has already made public." When Johnson wouldn't help me, I swept my cloak over me with vigor.

"He's taking the two o'clock train, since you seem so concerned about his comings and goings. You should show more interest in little Teddy's whereabouts." He opened the door and cold air blasted my face.

I stepped out onto the landing. "We'll find him, Mr. Johnson."

The door shut firmly against my back.

SUNDAY WAS a most unsatisfactory day as I waited for news from someone. Anyone. There was no reason to expect to hear from Mr. Wylie, Grace, Inspector Grantham or Phyllida unless something terrible happened. But while they all kept still, a child was somewhere, separated from his father, and a murderer escaped justice.

I kept busy, going to church, reading, talking to Sir Broderick and Mrs. Hardwick about the issues of the day, but I was only going through the motions. In the back of my mind, I carried an image of the missing little boy with large, serious dark eyes.

And then I'd think of Blackford's serious dark eyes. Had he looked like that as a child?

I wished for another letter from him, but he was also keeping quiet. What was he doing in America? Was he safe? Had he found a lady in New York to make his duchess?

AS SOON as Frances returned from luncheon Monday, I hurried to the neighborhood of Sir Edward's home, hoping to find Molly. I didn't want to be seen by Mr. Johnson, so I didn't walk past their house. Instead, I waited in the cold at the corner where their lane met a busier street near an omnibus stop.

I paced back and forth, listening to the church bells to mark the passing of time. One o'clock. Then one fifteen, and no Molly. Had she been delayed or had her afternoon out been cancelled? Had she changed her mind about speaking to me? I decided to wait until at least one thirty.

The bells rang for half past one. My feet were numb, my fingers tingled, and my patience was wearing thin. I lingered, curious to discover what Molly could tell me about the household and the missing jewelry if she ever showed up.

A few minutes later, I saw her red head hurry up the pavement toward me. Every few steps, she would look over her shoulder.

When she reached me, I saw her coat was even thinner than she was. She was sturdy from hard work, but she wore an outdated lilac dress more suited to spring than winter and a straw boater that wouldn't keep her warm. She'd die of a chill if she stayed outside any length of time. "Molly, I'm glad you could meet me. Let's find a tea shop and get something warm inside you."

"Thank you. I didn't think Mr. Johnson would ever let me

go. With the master gone, he rules the house. Finally, Rose told me to slip out and she'd cover for me." She gave me a cocky smile. "There's a tea shop with wonderful cakes at the next corner."

"Let's go then."

"Rose insists we help you find the mistress's murderer. She's been ever so frightened since we heard."

Why? I wondered. "Does she have anything specific to worry about? Did Sir Edward or Mr. Johnson threaten either of you? Or make advances?"

"No. Nothing like that goes on, with the master or Mr. Johnson. You'd think we're just machines from the way they treat us. But that's all right. We do our work, get fed and get paid," Molly said.

"And Lady Hale?"

"She was nice."

"Which one of you acted as lady's maid to your mistress?"

"Rose did."

After we'd settled down with our tea and cakes and Molly had finished off hers and half of mine, I asked her, "What can you tell me about Lady Hale's missing jewelry?"

"Rose said the mistress said it was all very mystifying. The pieces taken were all given to her by the master. She was just glad none of the pieces from her parents were taken." She looked at the remains of my cake.

I nodded.

After it disappeared, she added, "Lady Hale thought Miss Forbes took the jewelry."

"Why?"

"Dunno. She did see her in her room."

I thought I understood what Molly meant. "Did Miss

Forbes say why she was in Lady Hale's room?"

"She said she was looking for the mistress. Lady Hale said she wouldn't find her in her dressing table."

"And Sir Edward wanted Miss Forbes to stay?"

"Yes, but that was just to annoy Lady Hale. Teddy is to go away to boarding school for Easter term, so Miss Forbes would be leaving soon, anyway."

"Did Lady Hale mind Teddy being sent away to school?"

"Yes, she wants—wanted him to go locally. But the master said he has to, because he wants Teddy raised to be a gentleman."

"Did they fight like this before Teddy was to leave for school?"

"They've always been very cool, very silent with each other." Molly gave me a knowing look and added, "And he never goes to her room."

"Did anything odd happen the day Lady Hale and Teddy left?"

Molly sipped the last of her tea. "Her ladyship put on all her good jewelry. That morning, before she left. She never wore some of it before dinner. It was more jewelry than she ever wore at one time."

"Are you sure?" It sounded odd, unless Lady Hale was planning to disappear.

"Yes. Rose commented on it in the morning before Lady Hale went out. Before she disappeared."

"Does Sir Edward seem glad Lady Hale is dead?"

She shook her dark head. "No. He's worried about Master Teddy, so he doesn't seem to be happy about anything."

"Anything else you can think of? Anything, no matter how trivial? And why is Rose frightened?"

Molly leaned forward in her seat. She pulled out a packet of papers tied up with string and handed it to me. "This is what was worrying Rose. She said to give them to you if I thought you could be trusted with the mistress's secret letters."

Secret letters. "Thank you for trusting me," I said as I glanced at the top envelope. It was a masculine hand, firm and neat. I resisted the urge to open it that moment to learn the identity of Lady Hale's secret admirer.

"The master had Rose clean out the mistress's room after he heard she died," Molly told me. "Rose knew where she kept her secret letters, so she put them in her apron pocket right away. She's been afraid ever since that the master would discover she had them and throw her out without a reference." The thought made the normally cheery Molly shiver.

"Have either of you read them?"

Molly shook her head. "Rose wouldn't, and she wouldn't let me, either."

"Did Sir Edward know about these letters?" I asked, weighing the stack in my hand.

"No. I'm sure he didn't. We'd have heard a good dustup then. 'Twas interesting, though," Molly said, looking at a point over my shoulder. "Rose said when the first few came the mistress would read them and then hide them. She seemed pleased with them. Rose would see her glance at the drawer where she hid them and smile. Then one day, Rose came in to fix her hair for dinner and found the mistress with the letters clutched in her hand, crying. She said she sounded like her heart would break."

CHAPTER NINE

I felt like I'd finally learned something useful, but I had no idea what it meant. "Did she receive any letters after the time Rose saw her crying?"

"Two or three."

I flipped through the stack. "The postmark shows these were all mailed between Easter and the New Year."

"Rose said the mistress was surprised when she saw the first one. They continued to come until about a month or six weeks ago. Then they just stopped. Except for the last one. That came just a couple of days before Lady Hale left."

I searched for the last envelope and saw the postmark was very recent. "Does Rose know what day she found Lady Hale crying? Or know which letters arrived after that day?" This had to be a clue to her murderer.

Molly shook her head, knocking a strand of hair loose. "No. She just knows two or three came after that day. Oh, and it was shortly before Christmas that Rose found her crying. Seemed wrong to be so sad at Christmastime."

"I need to keep these letters and read them," I told Molly.

"If it'll help you find her killer, then please, read them. Lady Hale was a nice woman. She shouldn't have been killed." She turned the cup around in its saucer. "The last note, well, Rose saw that one and it frightened her silly."

That grabbed my attention. "Why?"

"It was threatening, and then two or three days later, the

mistress just disappeared."

"What did the note say?"

"I'll never forget the words Rose showed me after the mistress's death. 'If you continue to seduce my husband, I will kill you.'"

"Was it in Lady Hale's handwriting? Did she write it?" What was going on in that household?

"No. Rose and I both knew her handwriting. This was different. More rounded. Loopy. You'd almost expect little flowers to pop out of the letters if it wasn't such an awful message."

"Do you have any idea how it ended up on her dressing table?"

"No. The postman had been by the house twice already that day, so it would have arrived on one of his rounds."

I watched her closely. "Neither you nor Rose were asked to deliver any messages for anyone?"

"No. We really weren't supposed to know about these letters. Lady Hale kept private things private, if you know what I mean." She pushed the cup away from her. "Can you find her killer?"

"Don't worry. We will." I felt more certain now that I knew about these letters and could read them.

Molly rose and said, "I'm late getting to my aunt's. Take good care of those. They meant the world to her ladyship. For all I know, her killer might want them."

He might, indeed. "Take care of yourself, Molly, and thank Rose for these." I gave Molly a few coins and said, "Give these to Rose so she can have a nice tea on her afternoon off."

We split up outside the door, and I went back to the bookshop, hoping to get a chance to read the letters before tonight.

I returned to find Mr. Wylie in the bookshop. Frances waited on our only customer while I led the solicitor into my office. "What have you learned?" I asked the moment the door was shut.

"Quite a bit. Forsyth and Summerhaye is a relatively new corporation, so finding their articles of incorporation wasn't difficult. The business is owned by Mrs. Bernice Forsyth Coghill, a widow, and Lady Julia Summerhaye Spencer, Lord Justice Spencer's wife."

"What?" Whatever I'd been thinking up to that point was thrown out the window.

He nodded.

"Whatever are they doing, buying Lady Hale's properties? And does this have anything to do with where Teddy is?"

"I don't know. Do you want me to write them and ask?" He seemed so very solemn I knew this wasn't the task for him.

"No. This will be better handled in person. By the Archivist Society." I planned to visit them that afternoon. "Do you have their directions?"

He told me where both ladies lived and I thanked him. Then he said, "Jacob and I learned something odd while we were looking at the list of properties you gave us. None of them are still in the hands of Forsyth and Summerhaye. Most of the sales were cancelled and the properties put into the trust for her son. A few had been sold on to other buyers. I don't know if you can make anything of that."

"It is odd."

As I opened up the door, he added, "If there is anything else you need, you have only to ask."

"I appreciate it, but I imagine the calls on the time of a

busy solicitor are many."

"Not so many that I can't help Jacob's friends find justice. I hope in time you'll find me to be a friend, too." There was an eagerness in his expression as he looked into my eyes that made me wonder if he wanted the friendship of the Archivist Society, or mine.

I hoped he meant the Archivist Society. I stared into his bright blue eyes and saw a friend. An ally in this case, and hopefully for many investigations in the future. But that was all.

My new acquaintance with Mr. Wylie was nothing compared to my deep esteem, fascination and love for Blackford. I tried not to admit it, even to myself, but Lady Westover's words were bothering me like an itch inside my corset.

I lingered in the doorway to my office. "Jacob has spoken highly to all of us about you. It sounds a bit like hero worship."

He laughed a pleasant baritone sound rich with enjoyment of the world. "I'm not a hero, I'm afraid. Just an ordinary mortal. But please don't tell Jacob. He'll pay more attention to my teaching if he sees me in that light."

I smiled in return. "Your secret is safe with me. And thank you again for the information."

As soon as I saw him safely away I told Frances where I was going. I locked the letters in my desk and left the bookshop. The remains of our snowstorm had melted and sun was peeking out from behind fast-moving clouds. The illusion of the sunshine made it a pleasure to be outside despite the cold. Mrs. Coghill's home was further away, located near Holland House, so I decided to enjoy the break in our dreadful winter weather and travel there by omnibus.

The trees were all bare branches and the lawns looked dead, but I could imagine what a lovely area Mrs. Coghill lived in during the other seasons. The houses were large and well kept, with small, neat gardens in front. I guessed the back gardens were extensive.

As I approached from one end of the street, I saw a nurse and a young, light-haired boy turn at one of the gates and go up the path to enter the house. When I reached the spot where they'd left the pavement, I realized they'd gone into the widowed Mrs. Coghill's house.

I was too far away to make out his face, but I was certain I'd once again found Teddy.

I walked up to the door and rang the bell. When the butler answered, I handed him my Archivist Society card and said, "I'd like to speak to Mrs. Coghill about her guest, Teddy Hale."

"If you'll wait here in the hall, madam, I will see if Mrs. Coghill is receiving visitors."

He left me in the hallway furnished with a coat tree and a bench while he disappeared in a room down the hall. A moment later, a maid appeared to dust the hall, keeping a close watch on me while she worked.

"Pleasant weather we're having," I said to engage her in conversation.

"Yes'm."

"I'm sure Teddy enjoyed his outing."

She turned frightened eyes on me for a second but didn't utter a sound. Then she turned to her work and began dusting faster.

I heard something clatter upstairs and the girl jerked her head to look at the ceiling. The hand using the feather duster was now moving so fast the feathers blurred.

The butler returned and said, "If you'll follow me to the morning room, Mrs. Coghill will receive you there."

I followed him down the hall and into a lavender room. Despite the sunshine outside, the draperies were drawn and the gaslights were on. A cheery fire was burning and I immediately walked over to enjoy the warmth. The mantelpiece was painted white and supported a variety of porcelain figurines and decorative plates, all painted in lavender, violet and white. Everything was lined up in precise order.

Once I warmed up, I glanced around. Frilly and lavender described everything in the room, from the draperies to the sofa pillows to the stitch work hung on the walls. The wallpaper was a pattern of lavender flowers and vines growing up white trellises. But the pillows rested squarely against the back of the sofa and each pleat in the draperies was sharply creased. Nothing dared be out of line.

I doubted anyone ever sat in that room.

Only a minute later, a thick set, buxom woman with brown hair liberally streaked with gray entered the room. I realized with a shock her gown was pink, not lavender. "I'm Mrs. Coghill. How may I help you?"

"I'm here to collect Teddy Hale."

"I think not."

"His father wants him home."

"His father," came back at me as a well-modulated sneer.

"He's the only parent Teddy has left now."

"But not the only person who loves him." Mrs. Coghill lifted her head in a stately pose.

"That may be, but the law says he must be returned to his father now that his mother is deceased. Unless you are a relative?" I waited to see if she'd lie and say she was his aunt or grandmother.

Instead, she ignored my bait as she raised an eyebrow and gazed on me as if I were a particularly incompetent servant. "And how do you think Alice came to be deceased?"

"We're working to discover who's guilty of her murder." My voice was filled with determination. We might be searching for Teddy, but Alice needed someone to hunt for her killer. To give her justice.

"You'll find Sir Edward is the culprit."

"Do you have any proof?"

"I don't need proof. I know Lady Hale was terrified of her husband. He was a bully and a philistine. He was the only one who wanted her dead." Mrs. Coghill sounded certain.

Certain enough that I asked, "Did you speak to Lady Hale in the days before her death?"

"Yes."

"What role did Forsyth and Summerhaye play in Lady Hale's plans?"

The woman stared at me in silence for a moment. She opened her mouth and then shut it. Finally, she asked, "How would I know?"

"You're half owner, Bernice Forsyth Coghill. Surely you know what Lady Hale's plans were when she started selling her properties to you."

Mrs. Coghill lifted her chin and said, "You have no proof."

"Yes, we do. Now please, tell me all and then I'll return Teddy to his father."

There was a tapping on the door and then Lady Imogen Fielding walked into the room, dressed in a fashionably cut hunter green dress. She glanced around the room, saw me, and her lips thinned.

"She knows about Forsyth and Summerhaye," Mrs.

Coghill said.

"She may know, but she's a middle-class spinster. She wouldn't understand." There was a sneer in Lady Imogen's voice.

"But an aristocratic spinster would?" I asked.

A smile flittered across Mrs. Coghill's face. "She has you there, Imogen."

Lady Imogen gave me a stare intended to put me in my place. Unfortunately for her, such things rarely worked on me. Too much time spent with Blackford, I decided. "Tell me what is going on. You might consider me to be on your side."

"You want to take Teddy back to his murdering father. That's hardly on our side," Lady Imogen said.

"I want to find out who killed Lady Hale. I think we all agree that's a worthy cause." I looked from one woman to the other.

"It was Sir Edward," Lady Imogen said.

"Can you prove it?" I asked.

"No, but it stands to reason."

"I am going to prove who killed Lady Hale. And when I do, if her murderer is not Sir Edward, his son must be returned to him." As I studied their faces, I could see an unwilling acceptance of my words on Mrs. Coghill's face.

Lady Imogen looked mulish. "Never."

"Then what do you propose? To keep the child in hiding forever? That's not fair to him. Teddy deserves a steady home life. With his father if he's innocent; with his aunt if his father is guilty."

"She's right, Imogen," Mrs. Coghill said. "I didn't get mixed up in this business to keep the child in limbo forever."

Lady Imogen appeared to swallow hot coals before she said, "Yes. All right. When you prove beyond a doubt the identity of Alice's killer."

"Good. Now explain what you're doing with Forsyth and Summerhaye." I couldn't imagine what they were doing with Lady Hale's properties.

"It has nothing to do with Alice's death. We had nothing to do with her murder. You'll have to be satisfied with that." Mrs. Coghill took half a step back and gestured toward the door.

I recognized a brick wall when I saw one. We'd have to learn more about Forsyth and Summerhaye before I approached Mrs. Coghill again. "Please don't keep moving Teddy around. Just leave him here until I have the answers I need." I curtsied to the ladies and turned to leave.

"Too late," Lady Imogen said. "My carriage has already taken him away to another safe location. Don't worry about the boy. Worry about catching a killer." There was a note of triumph in her voice.

I believed her. There was no point in searching the house. I'd learned my lesson the first time. I strode to the front door, both ladies following me. Before the butler reached for the door handle, I faced the women again and said, "Take very good care of Teddy. We don't know who killed Lady Hale or why. The boy may be in danger now that his mother is dead. He is her heir. He has inherited a fortune. If anything happens to him, you both will have to answer for the crime."

Lady Imogen gave me a defiant look down her nose, but Mrs. Coghill looked worried.

"Is there something you wish to tell me?" I asked the older woman.

"That wasn't something we'd considered," Mrs. Coghill admitted. "We will be sure to take precautions."

As soon as the door was opened I stepped outside, glad to be out of a house where I wouldn't get any more answers. The door was shut so quickly it nearly hit me.

It was time to approach Mrs. Coghill's business with Lady Hale from another direction. And Adam Fogarty was just the person to do it.

I hurried back to the bookshop. Waving to Frances where she waited on a customer, I tossed my cloak on the coat tree as the telephone rang. I answered and heard Sir Broderick's booming voice come on the line.

"Lord Barnwood is coming in today to see the Jacobean manuscript you acquired. Deal gently with him, particularly if Grace indicates he's letting her investigate this case during her work hours."

"Grace is coming with him?"

"Supposedly."

"That's good. I'll give a discount for every piece of information Grace has for me."

Sir Broderick's rumbling laugher came over the line. "Old Barnwood will enjoy the haggling that will cause."

I had just a minute to tell Sir Broderick what I wanted Adam Fogarty to check for me before the bell over the door rang, announcing customers.

With the good weather outdoors, business was brisk. We were so busy that it seemed we always had another customer waiting.

Fortunately, Lord Barnwood and Grace didn't arrive until near closing time, when business slowed down.

I'd only seen Lord Barnwood on a few occasions recently, since he preferred to haggle from the comfort of Sir Broderick's study, but Grace didn't need to be present for me to recognize him instantly. He still wore his high collar with a cravat, his frock coat was decades behind the times, and his muttonchop side-whiskers stood out in gray and yellow tufts. There was not another in London who looked like him.

He'd been a customer of my father's when I was a little girl, and I think he still thought of me that way. His appearance hadn't changed in the intervening years. Maybe, for him, time hadn't moved forward.

He walked over to the counter and as I curtsied, said, "I understand you have a marvelous manuscript from before the Puritan uprising."

I could picture Cromwell rolling in his grave over Lord Barnwell's dismissal of the Commonwealth. "Yes, I do," I replied very quietly and pulled on my white cotton gloves.

Lord Barnwell and Grace did the same while I brought out the manuscript from inside the locked grille cabinet behind the counter. Barnwell examined it for a minute, and then rubbing his hands together, said, "Sir Broderick said you would give me very favorable terms."

"Your discount depends on how much Grace has learned on our new investigation." I smiled, knowing my statement would pique his interest.

"I'm sure she's learned a great deal. Tell her, Grace."

Grace's eyes widened as she glanced from one of us to the other. "I hope I've done well."

"I'm sure you have, girl. Don't keep us in suspense."

"Well," she looked pleadingly at me, "Lady Hale had only her sister, Prudence. Both parents are dead. A cousin's family was wiped out by typhoid. Two other cousins traveled by sea and were reported lost in a storm off the Spanish coast. I could find no one living on her side of the family. Sir Edward has no near relatives. His parents are dead. No living siblings. There's no one to take in Teddy but his father or his aunt."

"There," said Lord Barnwell, "that should be worth a thirty percent discount."

"I think not," I said, making my voice sound as cold and forceful as possible.

"Wait. I have more," Grace said, giving her employer a nervous glance.

"Well, go on, girl."

"I went to Mrs. Gregory's business."

"How did you find it? No one at the house would tell me anything." She had my full attention.

"I spoke to a shopkeeper at the end of their block. She knew Mrs. Gregory and missed her. Apparently, her husband isn't as good about paying his bills on time. She told me Mrs. Gregory owned a quality furniture factory she inherited from her father. They turn out finished pieces using carved and decorated hardwoods. And she gave me the directions to find the building."

"What did you learn?" I was as eager for this information as Lord Barnwell was to obtain the old manuscript.

"A Mrs. Williams owns it now. They told me at the factory she's a relative of Mrs. Gregory. I couldn't learn anything else, however."

"Let me have the name and address of the factory, and I'll try to learn more about her a different way. What about the other woman? The one you inquired about originally, who disappeared after her daughter's wedding?"

"Mrs. Matthews. I've not had time to follow up on her."

I turned to Lord Barnwell and raised my brows.

"Perhaps I've been remiss in not allowing Grace to follow up on everything you asked for."

"I think perhaps a ten percent discount might be commensurate with the time Grace has put in so far."

"But I was planning to let her follow up on this Mrs. Matthews tomorrow. I think that's worth twenty-five percent."

"Fifteen percent. We don't know if Grace will learn anything of significance."

"Twenty percent, with enough time off to guarantee results."

"And an interview with the sister of Miss Susanna Forbes, the fired tutor?"

"For an extra five percent off."

I really needed Grace's help. "Provided she has enough time to learn something of use." And then I held my breath, waiting for his answer.

Barnwood could just as easily say no, at least in the short term. He knew there weren't that many antiquarian book collectors who could afford a truly rare book such as this. And I needed Grace's help now.

I pressed my fingers into the countertop, standing as still as I possibly could. Grace glanced from one of us to the other, turning pale as the silence lengthened. Lord Barnwood stared at the manuscript so hard his gaze could have set it on fire.

CHAPTER TEN

LORD Barnwood stared at me for a moment and then nodded his head.

I released the breath I was holding. "You have a deal. That will bring the price down to forty-five pounds."

"What? You have the unmitigated gall to charge me sixty pounds for this little manuscript?"

"Anyone else would pay that, Lord Barnwood. You are getting a bargain price thanks to your generosity in allowing Grace to help us safely reunite a young boy with his father and save him from peril while discovering the identity of his mother's murderer." I spread it a little thick. If I had to, I'd spread it with a shovel.

"Oh." Lord Barnwood's eyes widened and his muttonchops wiggled. "Well, in the interests of saving a young lad, I'm glad to do my civic duty. Forty-five, you say."

"Yes, milord." I'm sure anyone else would have bargained my sixty-pound price down to fifty, so I wasn't as generous as Lord Barnwood might believe. But he was happy, and I liked to keep my customers content.

While I wrapped up the manuscript, Grace wrote out the name and location of the furniture factory. "Mrs. Williams seldom sets foot in the factory," Grace told me, "but Mrs. Gregory apparently spent a lot of time there."

"Who manages the business in her absence?"

"A Mr. Rannold. He's a middle-aged man who spends as

much time on the factory floor as he does his office."

I stared at Grace, the confusion I felt carried in my voice. "It seems odd that if the business was sold to a relative, that it would have been sold to Forsyth and Summerhaye first and then to the relative. Especially since Forsyth and Summerhaye are a widow and a Lord Justice's wife."

"How do we know it was sold to Forsyth and Summerhaye?"

"Her daughter told me to go to them, since they had bought her mother's business. I need to have Mr. Wylie search the records for me. But first I'm going to see if I can locate Mrs. Williams." I looked at the clock. "But that will have to wait until morning."

I wrote out the name and address of Susannah Forbes's sister from her references and gave it to Grace.

"I'll check on this tomorrow," she told me. Lord Barnwood nodded in agreement.

It was full dark and bitterly cold by the time I closed the bookshop and headed to Sir Broderick's. Winter and this case were wearing me down.

I heard Jacob in the dining room when I entered the house, already telling Sir Broderick his news at full speed. I pulled off my outerwear and dashed in to learn what he'd discovered.

Sir Broderick spied me and said, "Wait. Georgia needs to hear this, too."

We sat down and tonight Dominique ladled out our soup. After we tasted the spicy, hot fish stew and told her how much we liked it, she left the room, a bright smile splitting her dark face.

Immediately, Jacob began telling us about his trip. "I had no trouble following Sir Edward. Apparently, he didn't think anyone would do such a thing. Once in Manchester, I followed him to that shabby commercial hotel. I expected to have to wait outside for a long time, but he was out again in fifteen minutes."

He took in two more spoonfuls of the fragrant stew before he continued. "He got a hansom cab immediately, and I was afraid I'd lose him. Fortunately, the next cab along was driven by a speedy fellow, and we soon caught up.

"I followed him to a row of houses in a genteel area where he got out, paid off the driver, and went inside one of the houses. I settled in to wait in an alley across the street. When he hadn't left by eleven, I went back to the hotel and booked myself in. I checked his room the next morning, courtesy of my lock picking skills."

He glanced around the table. "I was shocked when I discovered his bed hadn't been slept in and his suitcase was empty."

I had the sinking feeling Sir Edward had been robbed and Teddy was now an orphan.

I felt my chest tighten. Teddy couldn't have lost both parents so close in time to each other. My parents had died together and I knew it was a cruel fate for a child. My voice sounded as if I were being strangled when I gasped, "What happened to Sir Edward?"

Jacob said, "That was my question, too. I went back to the house where he'd gone the night before, planning to discover what I could there. Instead, I arrived in time to see Sir Edward leave by the front door and walk down to the corner where he caught a hansom cab."

My breath left my lungs in a whoosh. Sir Edward was alive.

"Once I followed him to one of his factories, I came back

to the street where I'd seen him that morning. I knocked on the door of the house I'd seen him enter and a maid answered. I asked to speak to Mr. Hale. The girl told me Mr. Hale was out, so I asked to speak to Mrs. Hale." He gave us all a triumphant smile. "The girl said she'd have to see if Mrs. Hale was at home."

I was aghast. Another Mrs. Hale? With the first one barely in her coffin?

"Did you speak to her?" Sir Broderick asked.

"What did you tell her?" I asked at nearly the same time.

"I was shown into the parlor and a lady entered a minute later wearing a bracelet that matched the one in the picture of Lady Hale wearing her missing jewelry. The lady is small, quiet and quite pretty."

"How old is she?"

"Older than you, Georgia. Maybe thirty-five. Light brown hair. Pretty brown eyes. Anyway, I said, 'Mrs. Hale?' and she said yes. I said 'I don't think so.'"

"That must have been uncomfortable," Mrs. Hardwick said.

"She denied it at first, but finally she admitted her real name is Emily Barrow. She'd met Sir Edward through friends in Chester a few years ago, and they'd been living as a married couple for more than a year. She moved to a new neighborhood, actually to a new town, so they could pass themselves off as husband and wife. Sir Edward had told her the previous night that his wife was dead, and all she could think about was marrying him."

"She's a brave girl," Sir Broderick said. "She doesn't know if he murdered his wife or not."

"Did she seem to have any hesitation about marrying him?" I asked.

"No. She's certain he's innocent."

Sir Broderick frowned. "Does he stay with her every time he's in Manchester?"

"Yes. And he told her he'll be able to move to Manchester to be with her all the time once they are truly married."

"Then why check into that grubby hotel if he's not going to stay there?" I didn't see the point.

We remained silent while Humphries changed out our empty fish stew plates for roasted chicken and stewed apples.

Once we were alone again, Sir Broderick said, "So anyone from London or anyone from his factories will think he's staying there. So no one will find out about Emily Barrow." He shook his head. "The next time you call on Sir Edward, Georgia, you'll have a great deal to talk about."

"And I have a project for Jacob and Mr. Wylie. If you can, investigate the recent sales of a certain London furniture factory. Supposedly, it changed hands from Mrs. Gregory to Forsyth and Summerhaye and then to a Mrs. Williams. I'll give you all the particulars after dinner."

"We'll be glad to, Georgia. Still chasing down Forsyth and Summerhaye?" Jacob asked.

"Mr. Wylie was busy while you were gone. Forsyth is the maiden name of a widowed Mrs. Coghill, and Summerhaye is the maiden name of the wife of a Lord Justice of Appeal. I visited Mrs. Coghill. She was keeping Teddy in her home until I arrived. I was shown into the parlor. The next thing I knew, Lady Imogen was there and Teddy had been sent away in her carriage."

"So he's missing again?" Mrs. Hardwick sounded aghast.

"Yes," I admitted. "But I impressed on them that Teddy could be in danger and to stop moving him all over the city.

We won't try to return him until we can prove who killed Lady Hale."

"You had no right to speak for the Archivist Society on this matter. What you proposed is against the law." Sir Broderick looked most stern.

"But it will keep Teddy safe until we can convince the ladies to hand him over. I don't want to drag him out of someone's house."

Sir Broderick met my look. "No. That is for the police to do."

I knew I wouldn't win that argument. Changing the subject, I asked, "What did Fogarty learn from the tenants of Lady Hale's former properties?"

"Nothing. Most of them are still paying their rent to the same man. Her business manager. Nothing changed as far as they are concerned. A few others have new landlords, different people in each case." Sir Broderick shook his head. "Look, Georgia, we can't allow—"

"Georgia, did you see the letters for you on the table in the hall?" Mrs. Hardwick broke in.

"Letters?" I abandoned my chicken and nearly knocked over my chair in my hurry to reach the hall. There was a letter from Emma as there was every day. Under it was another I recognized by the firm, masculine hand on the envelope as belonging to Blackford. I stood in the hall trembling, clutching the letter to my chest. What if I opened the letter and learned he'd found his duchess?

I slid both letters into my pocket with the letters addressed to Lady Hale and went back to the dining room.

Three faces looked expectantly at me from around the table.

I took a calming breath and said, "I'll read them after

dinner."

Mrs. Hardwick studied my face for a moment before she asked Jacob how his journey had been. Conversation came in fits and starts. I toyed with my food. My appetite had left me the instant I saw the letter from Blackford.

I should have immediately read his words and stopped the churning in my stomach. Delaying now wouldn't change what he'd put on paper.

Dinner finally dragged to a halt with coffee and cheese. I excused myself and went upstairs to my room. Shutting the door, I ripped open his letter with my paper knife and dropped into the chair.

> *Dear Georgia,*
> *I've traveled across the continent and*
> *visited all of my investments from Pittsburgh*
> *to Vancouver to Texas. I leave San Francisco*
> *in the morning for New York. If all goes well,*
> *I shall be well on my way home by the time*
> *this reaches you.*
> *Home. That word has a wonderful sound.*

He went on to tell me about the rough and tumble world of San Francisco and the hazards he expected to face on his rail journey back across the vast continent. He ended with

> *I hope you have an interesting investigation*
> *to keep you busy and that I can help you with*
> *it upon my return. I have much to discuss with*
> *you when I see you next. I don't dare put any*
> *of my thoughts on paper for fear you would*
> *mistake my meaning. Indeed, you may find my*
> *thoughts distasteful. Just know I look forward*

to our next meeting with great trepidation.
Sincerely,
Blackford

Well, that was cryptic. Distasteful? And I certainly didn't like the "great trepidation." I put the letter neatly into its envelope and set it with the other two I'd received from him.

And then I tried to put his message firmly out of my mind.

I opened Emma's letter. She wrote at length about the wonders of Constantinople and added Sumner had gathered all the detail he could use for his Mrs. Hepplewhite stories. I was relieved to read they would start home shortly and would make their journey a quick one. Even though her life had changed, I looked forward to spending time with beautiful, sensible Emma again. For ten years, she'd been my little sister in all but name. I missed her.

I heard a tap on my door. "Come in."

Mrs. Hardwick opened the door and stepped into the room. "Is everything all right?"

"Emma is enjoying Constantinople, and she and Sumner will soon begin their return journey." The news of the other letter forced its way out. "Blackford is on his way back and looks forward to our next meeting with great trepidation."

"Oh, dear." Her normally placid face furrowed with worry. "What could he possibly mean?"

"He also looks forward to helping me on my current investigation."

She wrung her hands. "That makes no sense. If he looks forward to helping you, why would he face it anxiously? He doesn't know what you're working on, does he?"

"I wouldn't think so."

"Perhaps he's had lessons in detection." There was hope

in her voice. "Or perhaps someone here has written to tell him about your newest case."

"I doubt it." I didn't mean to be so crushingly negative, but I wouldn't be jollied along with platitudes and silly guesses.

"No. I suppose not. Well, hopefully he'll soon return and you'll be able to question him directly." Mrs. Hardwick swept out, her tone dry, sounding every bit as stuffy as I had. I remained in my room with my misery.

I stared at the top letter addressed to Lady Hale. It appeared to be in a man's hand, and I wasn't in the mood for a love letter. I told myself I had finished work for the day, but that wasn't true. I didn't have the heart to read someone else's happiness. And I couldn't face anyone else's sorrow.

FRANCES AND I kept busy in the bookshop the next day. I barely had time to think about Blackford's letter except every other minute. If Frances realized something was wrong, she didn't pry. I made fast work of dusting, sweeping, and shelving books and periodicals, and let Frances be the face of the shop. That day hers was friendlier.

I was glad of a diversion when Grace entered. "I'm sorry I'm so late," she said, and I glanced at the clock. I was shocked to see it was mid-afternoon.

"You're not late," I told her. "What have you learned?"

"I spoke to Susannah Forbes's sister, Mrs. Young, who considers Lady Hale to be evil incarnate. Firing her sister and not giving her a reference seemed to her like a nasty way to react to a misunderstanding. She said her sister would show 'that hysterical woman.'"

"Good heavens, Grace. Did she say how her sister planned to do that?"

"No, but Mrs. Young finally gave me Miss Forbes's address and told me to ask her myself. For awhile, I didn't think she'd even pass on a message for me, until I assured her I'd never met Lady Hale, had no idea what she was like, and that the lady was dead. Mrs. Young had to hear all the details before she'd give me any information about where Miss Forbes was."

I smiled at the prospect of asking Miss Forbes her plans for Lady Hale. "I'll do that if you don't mind. I want to hear her impressions of the household. It'll be a nice balance to all those who think Sir Edward is a killer."

It was late afternoon before I could get away from the shop. By then, I had finished everything around the shop and had managed to catch up from my neglect of the accounts while working on our investigation. All Frances needed to do was turn off the lights and close the door.

I knew I was taking a risk trying to learn something at a factory at this time of day, but at that moment, Mrs. Gregory seemed our best chance to learn what Forsyth and Summerhaye were up to. And she seemed to be a better lead than Miss Forbes.

It was fully dark by the time I reached the neighborhood of the furniture factory. All around me were large, brick buildings with empty, gloomy windows, like sinister eyes watching me walk down the street. There were few people about, moving furtively in the shadows, and I could hear the rustle and scratch of small animals hunting food.

I was glad to find the furniture factory, but it appeared to be as closed for the night as all the others on this road. Unlike the others, there was a light in a window near a side door in an alley. I suspected the window, high up, was in the office. Someone must be working late.

I walked down the narrow alley between the furniture factory and the building next to it, holding my skirt up and trying to avoid patches of ice and frozen mud. At least the buildings cut down on the cold wind biting any exposed skin.

Turning when I heard a sound behind me, I skidded on some ice.

I cried out as I wrenched my back. Fortunately, my corset didn't allow me to twist to the point of pulling all my muscles. Even more fortunately, I found the alley was empty. Whatever frightening creature I imagined sneaking up on me had disappeared.

Limping a bit, I knocked and then tried the door handle. The door opened silently. I walked in and found myself in an unlit area. The only light came from a window above my head that must look out from the office over the shop. A good way, I imagined, to keep an eye on what was happening on the factory floor from the boss's perch.

Since the office window provided enough light to see my way, I avoided some barrels and a stack of boards as I walked forward. When I came to a short staircase that led up to a door, curiosity pushed me onward.

Was the manager, Mr. Rannold, still here, or had he gone out for a little while? I doubted he'd waste the money to leave a light on in the office all night. Would he think I was a robber? At the top, I knocked and opened what I suspected was the office door.

It was an outer office, unoccupied and unlit. On the far side of the room I could see light shining under a door. I walked over and opened the door without hesitating or knocking first.

I should have. The scene before me, of a man and woman in a tender embrace, was not one I should have burst in on unannounced.

The couple jumped apart and the man bellowed, "Who are you and why are you here?"

I stood my ground with effort. "Mr. Rannold?"

"Yes." He glared at me.

I took a chance. "And you must be Mrs. Williams."

The red-faced woman nodded.

"I can see why you wanted to buy the factory, Mrs. Williams, but what happened to your relative, Mrs. Gregory?" I watched them both, on guard for an attack from the angry-looking man.

Then the woman sighed and looked ready to collapse. "I've been afraid of this day for so long."

"Hush, Margery. She knows nothing."

Margery was Mrs. Gregory's name. Mrs. Gregory spent a lot of time at the factory. This woman was obviously in love with Mr. Rannold. My dawning understanding must have shown plainly on my face.

"She knows everything," the woman said and sank into a chair. "How did you find out?"

CHAPTER ELEVEN

NOT everything, but I now knew Mrs. Gregory, the old owner of the factory, had become Mrs. Williams, the new owner. "I had no idea until just now. How long were you planning to disappear before you left your family?"

"I'd wanted to leave for ages. My husband is a bully and a sadist who believes women have no right to their own beliefs and their own money. Then Albert and I fell in love. We didn't plan it, but... He's a widower and had no impediment to our marriage, but I have a living husband and the divorce laws are impossible for a woman."

"What about your daughter? I met her when I went by your old residence. How could you leave her behind?" The girl I saw was about sixteen, younger than I'd been when I lost my mother. I ached for her.

The woman smiled sadly. "Fortunately, my husband adores both our children and treats them with love and kindness. They in turn adore him and twist him around their pinkie fingers. She'll be better off with him. Both of them prefer their father to me. And it was simpler to vanish on my own."

A sad story, and I doubted I'd been told the whole truth. Still, I reminded myself this was not the reason I was there. "What role did Forsyth and Summerhaye play in your disappearance?"

"I'll not say a word against them," Margery Gregory said

in a firm voice, the businesswoman in her showing through her determined tone.

"I have no interest in telling your family where you are. And I have no interest in publicizing Forsyth and Summerhaye's role in this or any other disappearance. I'm trying to learn who murdered Lady Hale, a woman who was in the midst of using the services of Forsyth and Summerhaye when she died."

I stared at Margery Gregory and couldn't keep a begging tone from my voice. "I only need to understand how this works."

"How are you involved in discovering who killed this woman?"

I gave her my Archivist Society card.

She showed it to Mr. Rannold and said, "I've heard of your group. You're known for your discretion."

"Please tell me. What services do Forsyth and Summerhaye provide?" I hoped this was the clue that would explain Lady Hale's death.

She looked at a point above my head. "They provided, for a fee, for the title of my business to be transferred from my old name to my new one, with their company appearing as the purchasing firm. If anyone looked in the records, they probably wouldn't go further and so wouldn't find the second sale at a slightly later date. They also set up a haven for me to disappear to while the hunt was on. Since I was staying in London, they created a record of Mrs. Williams's existence for years prior to the date of my disappearance."

"I suppose they would transfer title on any property you own as well."

"Yes, although the only property I own is this factory." She glanced out the window toward the factory floor.

"Did you by any chance stay with Lady Imogen Fielding while you were in hiding?"

She peered into my eyes. "How on earth did you know that?"

"That's where Lady Hale was staying when she was murdered."

"Someone broke in and—"

"No." The case would be so much easier if her death had been part of a burglary. "She saw someone she recognized and went out. It was very foggy that morning. When she was next spotted, it was to pull her body out of the river with a stab wound to her heart."

Margery Gregory turned pale, her eyes widening with shock. "How awful. Have they arrested her husband?"

I shook my head. "No. There are other possibilities."

"Mr. Gregory would have killed me if he'd caught me. He still will if he finds me. Please, keep my secret." Her tone was so heartrending I couldn't help feeling sorry for her.

Mr. Rannold put a hand on her shoulder. "I used to see the bruises she wore from that brute. She tried to hide them, but long sleeves and high collars can only hide so much."

"I will discuss what you've told me with Mrs. Coghill, but no one outside of the Archivist Society will know of your new identity."

Margery Gregory held my gaze. "You think someone has figured out what Forsyth and Summerhaye are doing? No man is supposed to learn their secrets."

"Mr. Rannold knows," I pointed out.

"Only enough to praise them and to keep quiet about their existence." He stood proudly, his hand still protectively on Mrs. Gregory's shoulder.

"Lady Hale left with her young son. The boy will

eventually have to be returned to his father if the husband didn't murder his wife. Someone knew where they were and was watching Lady Imogen's house, but didn't try to take the boy."

"A reason why you don't believe the husband is the killer." Margery Gregory nodded. "Good luck with your search for that poor woman's killer, Miss Fenchurch."

I gave her a smile. "Good luck to you, Mrs. Williams."

Both Rannold and Margery smiled at my use of her assumed name.

"And what of your plans now?" This was pure curiosity on my part.

"We live very quietly in the outskirts. No one knows our real names or about the factory. And we pray every day not to be discovered." Mrs. Gregory took Mr. Rannold's hand and I noticed the wedding bands on both of them.

I'd pray for their lives to stay secret, too.

They saw me off as I hurried away from that dark and forbidding neighborhood of brick palaces, now empty with the end of the workday. I caught an omnibus and soon reached Sir Broderick's home. Once more, I walked in after they'd begun their soup.

I sat down and Dominique brought me a fragrant chicken and potato broth. The heat and the spices warmed my chilled heart.

"What have you learned?" Sir Broderick asked.

I told them how Forsyth and Summerhaye worked and requested their silence.

"There is a need for such a service," Mrs. Hardwick said. "Especially since the costs of a divorce are so onerous for a woman. And because so many men still think of wives as chattel."

"May I tell Mr. Wylie?" Jacob asked.

"He doesn't need to know," Sir Broderick said. "He isn't truly a part of the Archivist Society. I'm sure someday we'll have reason to share sensitive details, but not today."

"He's worked hard on this case," Jacob said. "And he's let me travel to Manchester without a word of complaint."

"Then I'm sure someday he'll be a part of our work," I said.

"Of course, it might all be to impress you," Jacob said with a grin.

"Oh, I don't think so." Of course, his courtship, if there ever were one, might be looked at with more favor after my conversation with Blackford that he faced with trepidation. Why might I find his thoughts distasteful? I was beginning to face his return with fear.

"Don't sell yourself short," Mrs. Hardwick said. "You're an impressive young woman. Bright enough to run a shop and work on complex investigations. Plus, you're pretty."

"Thank you, but I don't think so. When I stand next to Emma, no one notices me."

"Next to Emma, no one would notice the queen," Jacob said. I gave him a sour look and he sobered immediately. "I suppose you don't need us to look into anything now."

"Not at the moment. I'm going to talk to Mrs. Coghill again in the morning and have her explain exactly what services they performed for Lady Hale. Then I'll speak to Sir Edward about his lady friend, and Miss Forbes, the fired governess, about whether she knows anything that will help us solve Lady Hale's murder." Sometimes solving investigations was easy once we sliced our way through all the untruths people told us.

I hoped that was the case this time. Somehow, I didn't

think we'd be that lucky.

After dinner, I went up to my room and pulled out the stack of correspondence I'd received from Molly. It was time to face Alice Hale's joy and grief.

Untying the string, I opened the first letter. Signed only by the letter H, the missive professed his undying love. The second letter read nearly the same. The third was equally sappy.

Growing bored, I opened the bottom letter in the stack and my eyes widened. I studied the handwriting, which was clearly different than those written by H. This message was unsigned and very different from the others.

If you continue to seduce my husband, I will kill you.

I stared at the letter, trying to figure out who H was. And whose wife had threatened Lady Hale.

H could not be Sir Edward Hale. While sending his wife love letters to win back her affections was a touching thought, he didn't love Alice. I felt sure she wouldn't kill herself, and especially not with her child so close by. Would Emily Barrow call Sir Edward her husband? She did so in Manchester, but would she to his lawful wife?

Who else could it be? Count Heinrich Reinler? It wouldn't be the first time one sister went after the other's husband. Or George Howard? Alice worked closely with her business manager. I'd have to find out if he was married. The neighbor, Sir Henry Carstaire? He approved of his wife's friendship with Lady Hale. Could it be he wanted more than a friendship with her?

Or could it be someone I'd not heard of yet?

THE NEXT day rained heavily, the wind blowing water under my umbrella and keeping anyone indoors who didn't need to be out. At least all the snow and ice had already melted.

Once Frances was settled in the bookshop, I traveled my long and soggy way to Mrs. Coghill's house in fashionable Holland Park.

I washed up on her doorstep, feeling cold and miserable and probably looking like drowned rags. Her butler let me in as I asked to speak to his mistress. He left me in the hall to drip on the carpet as he went to announce me.

When he returned, it was to remove my wet outerwear and then to take me to the morning room where we'd met before. I was so miserable I looked past my hostess to her welcoming fire.

"Please," she said, stepping aside so I could stand in front of her hearth.

As the heat made the bottom of my skirt steam, I turned to her with a sigh of relief. "Thank you." Then I turned solemn as I said, "I came to tell you I spoke to Mrs. Gregory yesterday. She calls herself Mrs. Williams now."

The woman nodded as she walked to her desk to lay down a letter and her pince-nez. "Yes. I know what she calls herself now. Her company made this desk," she said, running a hand lightly across the surface. "They do fine work. But how did you possibly find her?"

"The Archivist Society is resourceful."

"Apparently. We tried so hard to make sure she'd be safe."

"Mr. Rannold is watching over her safety now."

"Yes. I thought that might be the case, but we don't pry into other reasons once the women tell us they are being mistreated by their husbands."

"Divorce is possible now."

"Not without great cost to the wife if the husband isn't willing. Sometimes at the cost of her life." She sat down on a sofa near the fire and said, "You want to know about Alice, don't you?"

"Yes." I noticed she sat without disturbing the rigid formation of the decorative pillows. As soon as she gestured for me to sit, I lowered myself onto the other sofa as near to the fire as I could and as carefully as possible so not to ruffle any of the pillow lace or frills.

"Sir Edward would have agreed to a divorce, but only if Alice would have admitted to adultery. Which would mean giving up all claims to Teddy."

"And she wouldn't do that?" I asked.

"She's his mother. A young boy should remain with his mother. She was very firm on that. That's why she came to us."

"Except now she's dead, and Sir Edward is the only parent the boy has left."

Mrs. Coghill studied me closely. "Strong motive for murder, wouldn't you say?"

I thought of the letters I'd read the night before. "But not the only one."

Mrs. Coghill looked directly at me, her brows knitted. "What do you mean?"

"I now know Lady Hale received a death threat. The postmark showed it arrived within a week of when she was killed."

She considered my news. "She never told us about it. It would have made a difference in how we'd handled things if we'd known her life was in danger from a third party. What did this threat say?"

"Did you know of a man other than Sir Edward that Lady

Hale was involved with?"

"Lady Hale? Goodness me, no."

"You're positive she wasn't running away with a man?"

"No. Of course not. I can't imagine..." She shook her head.

"What happened to Mrs. Matthews?" I asked, pressing my advantage now that I'd surprised the indomitable woman.

"You think she was murdered, too?" Mrs. Coghill asked, eyebrows raised. A touch of scorn filled her voice.

"She had a husband who sounded as intractable as Sir Edward."

"But her children were grown. Her daughter was married, regrettably as far as the father was concerned. No, Mrs. Matthews lives. Since you already know so much, I might as well tell you. We sold off her properties and gave her the money from the sales. She left for America, where her daughter had moved with her husband."

"A happy ending for her, perhaps. What services did you perform for Lady Hale?"

"We were in the midst of selling Lady Hale's properties when she was murdered. We stopped the process and changed everything over into a trust for Master Teddy."

"Is her solicitor and man of affairs aware that her properties were placed in trust for her son?"

Mrs. Coghill drew herself up as she faced me. "Of course. You seem to be questioning our honesty. I find that offensive. We only take on those clients we can help, and then take a fee that will cover our costs. None of the board draws a salary." She crossed her arms over her chest and stared at me, daring me to continue.

"You have a board?" I was surprised at the news. And wondered which one of them was hiding Teddy.

"Yes, we have a seven-member board whose identities

we keep confidential."

"All must be women of influence who help hide these women, find buyers for their properties, and help them create new identities." Quite a task, but I decided it wouldn't be difficult for a group of determined women.

"Yes. We run this like a business." Mrs. Coghill sounded proud of their accomplishments.

"With account ledgers, minutes of board meetings and the like?" Amazement coupled with approval leaked from my voice.

"Of course. We know what we're doing. Several of us are businesswomen. But please don't expect us to show our records to you."

I nodded my understanding. "Had any of these women escaped from their husbands taking their children with them before Lady Hale?"

"Only once." Did she believe Lady Hale's murder was tied to Sir Edward's determination that she not leave with Teddy? It seemed to be a favorite motive at the moment. "And that transition was successful."

"Where did Lady Hale plan to move with Teddy? Surely she didn't think she could stay in London with Sir Edward here?"

Mrs. Coghill sighed and said, "It can't make any difference now. Canada. A friend moved there last year, which put the idea into her head."

"Has anyone associated with your group been visited by Sir Edward or seen him lurking outside your homes?"

"Absolutely not. We keep our association with this organization secret from everyone, including our families."

I saw a problem with this secrecy. A problem the Archivist Society ran into on occasion. How did we reach potential clients in need of our services? "Then how did Lady Hale find you?"

"Through Imogen. She'd heard a rumor that Imogen helped women of property disappear from their husbands."

Similar to how the Archivist Society was discovered by clients. I'd played Imogen's role several times. Then I wondered if this was the same rumor Phyllida had heard. And that made me ask my next question. "Does Lady Hale's sister, Countess Reinler, know about Forsyth and Summerhaye?"

"We have an agreement with each of our ladies that they will contact no one from their former lives, nor will they tell anyone about their plans. We keep them incommunicado while they are with us. Once they leave, it is possible they may contact loved ones, but we strenuously discourage that."

There was one more question I had to ask. "Before Lady Hale, have any of your clients been murdered while staying with someone from your organization?"

Mrs. Coghill looked scandalized. "Of course not. But then, Alice left the safety of Lady Imogen's house to meet someone on a foggy street. She knew it was against the rules, but she deliberately broke them. And now you tell me she'd received a death threat." She shook her head sadly. "Alice slipped out while Teddy was having breakfast and Imogen was otherwise occupied."

"That someone was there to kill her means someone knows the secret of Forsyth and Summerhaye."

Mrs. Coghill shook her graying head. "No. It only means someone knows Lady Imogen's part in this business. For everyone's safety, we've decided for the time being that no one will stay at Imogen's residence."

I had to satisfy my curiosity. "How long has Forsyth and

Summerhaye been in existence? And why did you start this? It must require a lot of work." I didn't hide my admiration. These women provided a valuable service.

"Forsyth and Summerhaye is quite new, but we've been helping women escape domestic slavery for over four years now. And all because Julia Summerhaye's sister couldn't legally get away from her sadistic husband, despite the efforts of her brother-in-law, the Lord Justice of Appeal."

After I left Mrs. Coghill's home, I made my way to Sir Edward Hale's gloomy townhouse. Dark skies and water-drenched bricks made the house even more unappealing than usual. Mr. Johnson, a sour expression on his face, answered the door with "You again?"

"I'd like to see Sir Edward, please."

"And the nature of your business?"

"Is with your master."

"Wait here." He shut the door in my face, leaving me fuming in the deluge.

I would have left, but I wanted to see Sir Edward's face when I presented him with the evidence of his adultery. I wanted a family, and here was a man who'd thrown away the very thing I longed for.

The butler reappeared quickly, but not quickly enough to prevent me from getting even more soaked. As soon as he opened the door, I was inside, shoving wet clothing at him. "Where is Sir Edward?"

"I'll show you the way."

We followed the same dim trail as before to Sir Edward's study. I walked across the room to stand by Sir Edward's desk so he was forced to look up at me.

That brought him to his feet, and I realized he wasn't any taller than I was. "Why are you here? Have you found my son?"

"No, but we've found your mistress. Emily Barrow. She says you've promised to marry her. An excellent motive for murdering your wife."

"I did no such thing." Sir Edward Hale bellowed the words across the desk, his face transformed by fury.

"Promise to marry Miss Barrow or murder your wife?" I asked. I seriously doubted he'd tell me the truth.

He looked as if he'd bitten into something sour.

I kept pushing. I wanted him to answer not for the sake of the Archivist Society, but for his wife and son. "No one will believe your innocence, and you will hang for her murder. The only way you can avoid a death sentence is to start telling the truth. Otherwise, you'll die without ever seeing your son again."

Then I threatened him with what I thought was the worst possible outcome for his child. "And he'll grow up an orphan."

CHAPTER TWELVE

SIR Edward stared at me for a long moment. I could see the war going on inside him. Slowly, the bluster seeped out of his body as his shoulders drooped and he hung his head. Finally, in a low volume he said, "It's *Mrs.* Barrow. She's a widow. About a year and a half ago, I began staying at her home whenever I was in Manchester."

Then I saw how another piece of the puzzle fit. Jacob saw Mrs. Barrow wearing a piece of jewelry given to Lady Hale. "And Lady Hale's jewelry that was missing wasn't really missing, was it? You couldn't call the police because you took those pieces to give to Mrs. Barrow."

He nodded. "I couldn't tell Alice that, and I was afraid one of the servants might have seen me go into her room to take back my jewelry."

His jewelry? I looked heavenward for an instant. "Why not just buy Mrs. Barrow something new?"

"And leave all that expensive finery with Alice? She had plenty from her parents. Jewelry that she wore and didn't scorn like she did my gifts. Why let her keep my gifts if all she wanted to do was spurn them? And reject me. Emily doesn't scorn my presents. She knows they were once Alice's, and still she doesn't reject me." Sir Edward smiled. "She loves me."

"Why do you live in London if your business is in Manchester?" The whole Archivist Society wondered why he lived here.

"I had businesses in both cities when I met and married Alice. When my London business floundered and I had to sell out, I wanted to move to Manchester, but Alice wouldn't leave her father and sister. If I'd gone to Manchester without her, her father let me know he'd ruin me. He would have, too." Some of the bluster returned. "I was stuck here. I wish someone had warned me to marry a Newbury at my own peril."

"Did you know your wife knew Lady Imogen Fielding?"

"No. Really?" His surprise quickly fled from his face. "But then I paid little attention to Alice's friends."

That sounded familiar for some reason. Not Sir Edward, but someone else had said something similar. The harder I tried, the less I could reach out and grab the words he'd made me think of.

"Where is Teddy?" he demanded.

"He's being kept safe by people who believe you killed your wife. They fear you are also a danger to your son."

"Why would I kill Teddy? I love him. I'll never see a shilling of his money. I have no reason to harm him, and every reason to want him home."

For the first time, his sincerity shone in his words and on his face. "Please, bring my son back to me."

Exactly what Sir Broderick wanted us to arrange. And all I could do at that moment was say "We're trying to safely return him to you as quickly as possible" as I left.

My next stop, York Street off Baker Street, was the home of Miss Susannah Forbes, a residential student at Bedford College for Women. The college fit in with the mixed character of the buildings on the street, filled with offices, shops and residences. I walked, confident but soggy, up to the door and rang the bell.

The door was opened by a young woman who, without looking up from her book, said, "First door on your left," and walked off.

Bemused, I gaped at her even as I sought the shelter of the hall. I turned around to furl my umbrella so most of the water went outside and then put it in the umbrella stand. I walked over on squeaky, wet shoes and knocked on the first door on the left.

"Come in."

I opened it to find a young woman making a typewriter clatter at a good pace and another, older woman standing near the desk reading from a book. The older woman took off her spectacles and said, "Hang your cloak on a peg in the hall. You don't need to drip all over the house."

I did as she said and returned a moment later.

The older woman looked me over and said, "Good. May I help you?"

"I'm looking for Miss Susannah Forbes."

"If you'll have a seat, we'll summon her. I'm Miss Clayton, the principal here. And you are?"

"Miss Fenchurch." I gave her one of my Archivist Society cards.

She studied it through her glasses. "What is the Archivist Society?"

"A group of friends and acquaintances who solve cases Scotland Yard is unable to unravel."

"Crimes?"

"Yes. In this case, murder."

Miss Clayton took off her glasses and studied me like she would a flower or an insect. "Yes. I see." She pulled a card out of a file and studied it. I walked around her to look over her shoulder. It listed various courses and was signed by Susannah Forbes. The handwriting wasn't like any of Lady Hale's letters.

"Do you mind?" Miss Clayton asked, turning her head to look at me.

I stared back, not moving. "What is Miss Forbes studying?"

"She's doing the teaching certification program at King's College and a degree in Languages here."

That made sense. She'd been a governess to young Teddy. "Are all the students here studying to be teachers?"

"About half of them. All are studying the university curricula associated with London University. Were you a college student, Miss...?"

"Fenchurch. No. I was orphaned at seventeen and went to work."

"I'm sorry." Whether she meant because I was orphaned or because I didn't go to college, I wasn't sure. Putting the schedule card away, Miss Clayton went back to her book, ignoring me. I was left to sit on the only available chair, a hard wooden one shoved against the wall.

After fifteen minutes, the clattering from the typewriter stopped and the young woman took her sheets of typing and left the room. After another five, Miss Clayton abruptly put down her book and walked out of the room, saying over her shoulder, "I'll fetch Miss Forbes."

When the door opened again, a young woman with dark hair in a stylish knot and wearing a blue skirt and pale blue shirtwaist walked in. "Miss Clayton summoned me after French lecture and said you wanted to speak to me. I'm Susannah Forbes." Her tone didn't allow for nonsense. I suspected she'd make a good teacher.

I didn't know about "bold, brilliant and beautiful" as Countess Reinler claimed the woman described herself, but Miss Forbes was attractive enough. I rose and said, "I'm Georgia Fenchurch, a member of the Archivist Society."

"Miss Clayton told me. She also said you were investigating a murder." She looked at me levelly.

"Yes. Lady Hale."

"Well, well. And you suspect me because she threw me out without a reference." A smile hovered on her lips. "Let's hear your case against me."

She was certainly living up to the bold label. "She died a few weeks after she fired you."

"By then I was here. The Lent term began two days after I was summarily thrown out by Lady Hale."

"Did you already have a plan in place to attend here?" This woman didn't seem the type to do anything without a plan.

"Yes. I have a wealthy uncle. I'd asked him for the funds to attend university to get my teaching qualifications. He finally agreed over Christmas. I'd already taken the entrance examinations. I thought I'd have to wait until Easter term to begin, which is when Sir Edward planned for Teddy to go away to school, but Lady Hale did me a favor. She timed things perfectly for me."

"Perhaps you timed things perfectly for yourself, by getting fired in time to begin the new term?" Miss Forbes would no doubt become a good teacher, but there was something about her I didn't trust. I couldn't put my finger on what I found lacking in her character. Yet.

She leaned against the desk and stared at me, thin-lipped with disdain.

"So you just paid your fees and moved in?" My

amazement must have shown.

"Obviously you're not a university girl." She sounded smug. "Everything was in place, and they had an opening. I just showed up and registered. I moved in and began classes the next day at the beginning of term."

"No, I'm not a university girl. I didn't realize it was so easy to get in." I let my pique show, understanding Lady Hale's annoyance with the governess.

"The hardest part is to get someone to pay for it," Miss Forbes said with pride in her tone. "As long as you're relatively bright and paid attention in school, you can pass the entrance examination. What do you do, when you're not asking people questions?"

"I own and run my own business. A bookshop. It has proven to be an education."

"Inherited?"

"Yes."

She let annoyance show in her voice. "You have the advantage of me. My sister and I were the offspring of the wastrel branch of the family. We needed either a husband or an education for our daily bread. My sister chose one, I the other. I suspect my sister was the person who told you where to find me."

I nodded. By now I was certain I'd learn Miss Forbes was clear of any involvement in Lady Hale's murder. I gave her the date of Alice's death. "Where were you that morning?"

"That's easy. Tremulov, the Russian historian, was in town and gave a lecture that was open to all university students in London, male and female. We all went."

"What time did it begin?"

"Ten o'clock."

"And before then?"

She sighed with evident boredom. "I rose at seven, dressed, and then joined everyone for breakfast at eight. When we finished, I helped another student with a Latin translation. Latin has always been easy for me."

She could have added boastful to her description of herself. "Where did you work on the translation?"

"I'll show you."

Miss Forbes led me across the hall and opened the door to a large parlor furnished with secondhand furniture. Several young women were working alone or in groups, sprawled on the chairs with papers spread on tables and over the thin rug. Books were scattered everywhere. "This is where we worked on the translation that morning. There were probably half a dozen women in here at that time studying one subject or another. There usually are."

She waved across the room to one young woman who set down her book, paper and pencil, and walked over to join us.

"This is Anne Cook. Anne, please tell Miss Fenchurch what we were doing before the Tremulov lecture."

The thin girl with mousy brown hair looked from one to the other of us before she shrugged. "Susannah helped me with my Latin. It took us from breakfast until it was time to walk to the lecture hall."

I gave her the date.

"Yes, that was the date Tremulov spoke. I didn't know the Russians were such a bloodthirsty race." She smiled at us. "I need to get back to my botany."

I returned her smile. "Thank you, Miss Cook."

We left the parlor and Miss Forbes shut the door behind us. With a certain amount of glee she told me, "Obviously, I didn't kill Lady Hale, but I wish whoever did do it the best of luck."

"That's unkind," I told her.

"So was her shoddy treatment of me. I have no reason to wish her well." Miss Forbes didn't sound the least bit concerned that the woman had been murdered. In fact, she sounded indifferent to the loss of her former pupil, Teddy, or the suffering of his mother.

"She was a human being and she was murdered. She couldn't have always been cruel to you, or I don't believe you'd have stayed as long as you did," I said.

Miss Forbes checked her reflection in the hall mirror. Then she shrugged and faced me. "She'd been perfectly normal for the first few weeks I was there, but then she seemed to grow crazier by the day."

"Was that when she learned of her husband's plan to send Teddy to a boarding school? That couldn't have pleased her."

"No, she had already begun doing strange things, but that certainly made her worse."

This was the first time anyone said Lady Hale behaved strangely. "What did she do that was so odd?"

"Besides throw me out for no reason and without a reference?" Another long sigh of what, boredom? Disinterest? "Rose, her maid, was helping her remake some of her clothes when she noticed a stain on a skirt. This was an old dress, I think, one she hadn't worn since early autumn, but Lady Hale burst into tears and couldn't stop crying."

She loosed a giggle, for what reason I couldn't fathom. "A week or two later, when she learned about Sir Edward's plans for Teddy, she started hitting him and sobbing. She was normally so calm, so aloof. So cold."

"What was Sir Edward's reaction?"

"He was shocked. He defended himself, but he didn't try to hurt Lady Hale or even stop her."

I thought that spoke well of Sir Edward. "What happened the day you were fired?"

"I went into Lady Hale's room since I couldn't find her anywhere. She wasn't there, but there was a note on her dressing table. I went over to see if she'd left a note saying where she'd gone when she came in and started screaming at me. She fired me on the spot. Never gave me a chance to explain."

"Did you see what the note said?"

She snickered. "Indeed I did. It was a love letter, begging Lady Hale to meet him again. A love letter to a dried-up old prune."

"Do you know who it was from?"

"No."

Her answer was too quick. I didn't believe her. "You weren't asked to deliver any notes to your mistress?"

"Why would I? I wasn't a servant. And I didn't know the nasty trick she was going to play on me when I found the note." Miss Forbes was sneering at me now. "Who'd have thought the snotty woman had it in her to cheat on Sir Edward?"

I ignored her evil smile.

Alice's threatening letter arrived as little as two days before she walked out the front door of her house and never returned. And we still had no clue as to who sent it or who sent her love letters. "Tell me about Lady Hale's missing jewelry."

"There isn't much to tell."

"Try anyway."

Miss Forbes shrugged. "One day she called us all

together and asked if anyone knew about the jewelry missing from her dressing table. No one admitted to taking it. Sir Edward came in looking for Mr. Johnson and asked what was going on."

Miss Forbes looked at a point over my shoulder. "Lady Hale told him exactly what was missing, which turned out to be items he'd given her. He said she pawned them; she said she hadn't. He said if she was so careless as to mislay them, there was no point in us looking for them and not to bother. She went hysterical and chased him out of the room."

Then she turned her attention to me. "I think the maids looked for the jewelry out of loyalty to their mistress. I'd already taken her measure and didn't bother."

I believed she wouldn't bother if it didn't bring her gain. "Thank you, Miss Forbes. I wish you well in your studies."

She smiled. "When I finish here, I'll never be at the mercy of a crazy woman like Lady Hale again. I'll have a career teaching in an actual school, not struggling with some little brat with wealthy parents and a lack of brains."

I took my umbrella and headed back out into the weather, glad to have escaped the obnoxious Miss Forbes. Thank goodness she had an alibi. I didn't want to interview her again, possibly because I suspected she'd never find her students worthy of her time. I remembered with distaste those teachers during my schooling who had shared her attitude.

Lady Westover's Mayfair townhouse wasn't too far, but after one omnibus ride down Baker Street and another along Oxford, followed by a walk, I was soaked.

I arrived on her doorstep and was immediately shown in by the butler. With his face scrunched in distaste as he took my dripping cloak and bedraggled hat, he said, "I'll tell Lady

Phyllida you're here. If you'll wait in the parlor, you'll find there's a fire."

I went up to the parlor, grateful someone had taken pity on my waterlogged self. My skirt was steaming around the hem when Phyllida entered. "Good heavens, Georgia. Have you stood outside all morning? You look—oh, dear—positively dreadful."

"I've been traveling around London in pursuit of learning who killed Lady Hale. Have you remembered who you heard talking about Lady Imogen Fielding helping wives escape their husbands?"

"I think I may have. Let me ring for some tea and we'll see if we can work it out."

I drank my hot tea while sitting on the sofa across from Phyllida. My clothes slowly dried and my skin warmed from the heat of the fire. As soon as I felt recovered from the storm, I was anxious to discover what she could tell me about Lady Imogen. "What have you remembered?"

"The conversation had to be shortly after the Duchess of Callkirk disappeared. There were so many rumors."

"I remember." It had been a sensation in the papers for weeks. Her body was never recovered. Eventually, another scandal replaced it and we heard no more about the missing duchess.

"I ran into Lady Ormond whilst walking in Hyde Park. Everyone was discussing the duchess's disappearance in those days. I tried to avoid her—Lady Ormond, not the duchess—but she exclaimed at seeing me after such a long time. The only thing I could think of to tell her was that I'd come over from the continent to see my man of affairs and would be leaving shortly."

Phyllida shook her head and looked down in her lap. "I

couldn't tell her I was living with you and Emma. I couldn't. She'd want to visit, to pry into every corner of my life. She's such a busybody. Never takes no for an answer. And gives her opinion on everything and everybody."

I'd met Lady Ormond. I nodded my heartfelt agreement.

"She'd tell everyone that I was living as a housekeeper to a middle-class spinster. I love you and Emma dearly, but some wounds to our vanity are to be avoided at all costs." Phyllida looked guilty.

She had nothing to feel guilty about. She was a lady, the daughter of an earl. If her life had been unusual, she had finally found contentment, and Emma and I loved her. We'd made our own family. "No one should be forced to endure Lady Ormond's scathing, unfounded remarks. You did the right thing. Now, tell me what happened." My voice rose with eagerness.

"She insisted on my going calling with her that afternoon. And when she decides something... Finally, I went along just to quiet her. And who did we call on? The Countess of Everham."

Phyllida peered into my face. "You must remember. The countess was another of those American heiresses and a very good friend of the missing duchess. They'd known each other as girls in New York. So of course the conversation kept drifting back to the duchess's sudden disappearance."

I must have looked blank, because she said, "You know the sort of comments those ladies make. 'Thank goodness she produced an heir and a spare before she vanished. The duke must be frantic, but at least he doesn't have that worry, too.'"

"And someone said something about Lady Imogen making the duchess disappear?" Perhaps a questionable thing to say in the home of a friend, but I was glad they had and Phyllida heard it.

"Yes. That had to have been where I heard Lady Imogen's name, because ordinarily, I avoided making those terrible calls full of teacakes and reputation assassination. I still stay far away from them. Unless it becomes necessary for the Archivist Society."

I nodded. Her help had been invaluable a year and a half before when we searched for the killer of her cousin. Then I recalled how often I'd relied on Blackford's help and felt depression weigh me down. Dragging my mind back to business, I asked, "Who mentioned Lady Imogen?"

"I don't remember. Someone said something about 'It's a good thing the duchess doesn't know Lady Imogen, or we might guess she's disappeared.' Then someone else, I think it was that silly Lady Foxbottom—she's dead now, poor dear—said, 'But she does know her, they met at some musicale.' Then someone behind me, I never saw who, said, 'Then we might wonder why she ran away. And with whom.' It was as if all the ladies present shared a secret. Or different pieces of the same secret."

Phyllida studied me over the rim of her teacup. "There was a slyness in their voices. As if they knew the truth, but wouldn't come out and say so. They were being so polite and yet so cruel. Does that make sense?"

CHAPTER THIRTEEN

I peeled my still-wet hem away from my ankles. "Yes. I can't imagine any of them wanting to come right out and say what they were thinking. I never guessed there was another man in the equation with the Duchess of Callkirk." Like Mrs. Gregory, now living under the name Mrs. Williams.

"There were rumors she ran away with some completely unsuitable man, a writer or painter or something, and they escaped to the continent. Or America. Somewhere foreign," Phyllida said.

"And these women seemed to know something about it? What about Lady Ormond?" I dreaded the possibility of having to question her.

"She always assumes an attitude that says she knows everyone's secrets. I doubt she knew any more about it than I did. Don't waste your time talking to her."

"Has the duchess been seen since?"

"Not that I know of. Of course, I avoid making calls on anyone who would know." She set down her teacup. "Now, would you like to go up and visit with Lady Westover? I'm sure she'd love to see you."

"And ask me about the duke." That might prove to be the most difficult of my morning errands.

"Of course." Phyllida gave me a knowing smile.

She led me up to Lady Westover's room, where the old lady was propped up on pillows, looking more like herself.

Then her slender body was racked with deep coughs and I thought she'd break into pieces.

"Ah, Georgia. So good of you to call," she was finally able to gasp out.

"You're looking much better."

"Liar. I don't have much breath, so I'll come right to the point. What have you heard from Blackford?"

"I received another letter. From San Francisco. He was leaving then to cross America, spend a few days in New York, and afterward sail home. He may well be on the ocean by now, so you'll have to stop malingering."

A spasm of coughing showed she was not faking her illness. Finally, when she caught her breath, she said, "When you see him, ask him to visit me."

"Of course, but you must promise not to tell him to marry me." I gave her a stern look, but I knew it would do me no good.

"I, child? You were the one who brought up the subject. But now that you have, I think it's a splendid idea." Her eyes glittered with amusement. "I think a vase would be a good wedding present."

I didn't have the heart to tell her about the contents of the duke's letter and our upcoming conversation that he was facing with trepidation. Or his "distasteful" thoughts. She looked too frail to hear that her dreams, and mine, could come to naught.

"I've known his family since his grandparents' time. Good people, if a little stiff. They're all gone now and Blackford is alone. That's not good for him. He needs an heir to the title. Even more, he needs a family. What he needs is you, Georgia, and what's more, you need him. Don't forget, I introduced you. I knew what I was doing." Another coughing fit spared me anymore of her lecture.

She'd seated me next to the duke at a dinner party where I was playing the role of her poor relation. I'd needed to question everyone at the dinner with the exception of Lady Westover and her grandson, Inspector Grantham. Blackford had deflected my questions back at me so skillfully that I knew I'd met my equal at detection.

Lady Westover and I discussed the weather and everyone's health for a few minutes before coughing robbed her of any breath. I took my leave as Phyllida raised her up on more pillows.

After drying out at Lady Westover's, I washed ashore at the bookshop, once again looking drowned. But not as drowned as Charles Dickens, who was huddled by the door. As soon as I opened it, he stumbled in. He opened his mouth, but no mewing sound emerged.

"I wondered where he'd gone," Frances said, rushing forward to pick up the cat and wrap him in dry dusting cloths. "You poor thing."

I was left to peel off my wet outer garments and hang them to drip on the floor. Frances didn't seem worried about the state of my health. Of course, I'd chosen to go out in a downpour to search for a killer. I needed someone to knock some sense into my head, not worry about my health.

"How is he?"

"He can't make a sound and he's completely soaked. And he hadn't recovered from his last adventure." She pulled one foot out from the cloths and studied it. "Just look at this. The bottom of his paw is all bloody again. Who let him out?"

"I don't know." I was so used to Dickens coming and going as he wanted that I hadn't given his whereabouts a thought. And I doubted I'd notice if he slipped out with a customer or with me.

"We're going to have to keep him indoors, warm and dry, for quite some time if he's to recover. You'll have to take care of him while I go home to luncheon. I'll bring some salve for his paws when I return."

Frances handed me the bundle of wet fur and muslin and walked over to put on her cloak. "I'll be back as soon as I can," she called as she walked out the door.

Dickens and I glared at each other. When he didn't scratch me, I knew he was very ill.

I sat on a stool behind the counter, holding Dickens and trying to find another motive for Lady Hale's murder besides her husband's anger at her taking their son away with her. There was the money, which only benefitted Teddy and Alice's sister.

No, it could also benefit George Howard, who would have control of Teddy's money for all those years until Teddy was grown. Mr. Howard and the solicitor. Balancing Dickens on my shoulder, I opened a drawer under the counter and pulled out a sheet of paper with the information I needed. Lady Hale's solicitor's name was Sir Bernard Hall.

Someone else Lady Hale worked closely with whose name started with H.

However, this case might not rest on who received custody of Teddy or control of the money. The motive could be jealousy, pure and simple, if the very attractive Alice had become too friendly with another woman's husband. Someone had sent that threatening message.

Or Sir Edward could be jealous of her relationship with this man H.

Tonight, I'd ask Jacob to question Mr. Wylie on everything he knew about Sir Bernard Hall's and Sir Henry

Carstaire's private lives. And when Frances returned, I would go to George Howard's office to get a sample of his handwriting. With any luck, I would learn if he was married.

However, when Frances returned, I learned just how deadly a sick cat with injured paws can be. She held him and each paw in place while I administered the salve. That left three paws free to take his wrath out on me.

Once Dickens's paws and my injured hands were dealt with, I headed back into the city to visit Mr. Howard's office. At least the weather was improved. I arrived and rode up in what I still thought of as a shaky metal cage.

George Howard was the right age to be Lady Hale's mysterious Mr. H, and he'd gain by her death. I still hadn't thought of an excuse to examine his handwriting or his marital status.

His clerk showed me in after a few minutes wait. I entered and gave Mr. Howard a curtsy, my gloves staying on to hide my wounds. Once we were seated, I heard the clerk slip into a chair behind me.

"What can I do for you, Miss Fenchurch? Is this still about Lady Hale's murder?"

"No. This is a private matter. Countess Reinler speaks highly of you, and I wondered if you would be interested in taking on a small commission for me."

"That depends on the nature of this small commission."

"I am anticipating my wedding..." In my dreams, perhaps, but I believed in keeping my tales as close to reality as possible.

He nodded to me.

"Are you married, Mr. Howard?" It was a clumsy opening, but I'd only have this one chance.

"Yes, I've been happily married for a dozen years now." A

smile stretched across his face and his eyes softened as he looked at a photograph on his desk. I could only see the oval frame, but I was certain the picture was of his wife and children.

I smiled briefly at his words, but inside I was cheering. One detail checked. "I have a bookshop that will have to be managed by someone else once I wed. Would you be able to handle that agreement?"

"You should hire a solicitor for that. That's not the role I play in the countess's affairs."

"Oh, of course. How silly of me. I should see Sir Bernard Hall, I suppose."

"He'd be eminently qualified to carry out this work for you."

"I don't have his address, and because of a silly accident today, I can't grip a pencil with my hands." I held up my gloved hands with my fingers straight out. "Could you write it down for me?"

"Of course." Mr. Howard wrote out the directions to Sir Bernard's office in square, tight writing and handed the paper to me. His handwriting was nothing like that in the letters found in Lady Hale's room.

Mr. Howard might have designs on Lady Hale's money by controlling it as Teddy's financial guardian for the next two dozen years, but he wasn't the mysterious H.

"You'll have to excuse me," he said rising. "I have a funeral to attend this afternoon. Lady Hale's."

I rose as well and curtsied before heading for the door. "Such a sad occasion. And such a pretty woman."

"Very sad," he said, not commenting further.

Since I knew the funeral was to be held in the cemetery chapel, when I left Mr. Howard's office I headed in the same direction he was going. Being female, I couldn't attend the service, but no one would stop me from being in the cemetery at a discreet distance.

I waited in a nearby teashop while I guessed the service was in progress. Once they should have moved into the graveyard, I wrapped up in my scarf and coat and went out to brave the cold. At least the rain had stopped, leaving the bare branches and massive tombstones coated with water that would freeze during the night.

When I walked around the cemetery, I had no trouble finding the mourners because I recognized Mr. Howard standing to one side. Sir Edward Hale wasn't there. It was a small, pitiful-looking group made up mostly of paid mourners who rubbed their hands together and appeared ready to dash for warmer quarters the moment the final "amen" was uttered.

I edged as close to the group as I dared, staying hidden behind a well-placed obelisk. I hoped the actual mourners would bid farewell to each other by name when the rapidly read prayers were finished. That would be the only way I'd know who these men were.

Despite the speed at which the vicar read the prayers, the cold had crawled inside my coat by the time the graveside service finished. The paid mourners nearly ran from the cemetery and the vicar fled back to the chapel, leaving three well-dressed men behind.

"Well, Sir Bernard, it's a sad business."

I peeked around the granite monument to see the man Mr. Howard was addressing. Gray haired and bearded, Sir Bernard Hall was well past sixty years old, and I could see at once how he depended on his cane. Not likely to be the author of the passionate letters to Lady Hale. At least not recently, and the postmarks showed they had arrived in the past months.

"A sad business, indeed. Murder. Who would want to murder Lady Hale?"

"She'd just come into her inheritance," Mr. Howard said, settling his hat more firmly on his dark hair.

"You think Sir Edward killed her for her money?" the third man asked. He was thin and beginning to gray but good-looking, and I would guess no more than his early forties.

"He didn't come to his own wife's funeral," Mr. Howard said.

"Prostrated with grief, I imagine," Sir Bernard said. "And killing her wouldn't have put him any closer to her fortune."

Even at this distance, I saw both of the other men's eyes widen at the indiscretion. I knew it was true because of what her sister told me, but Lady Hale's solicitor should never have said that before the reading of the will.

"I'm sure that won't go any further," Sir Bernard said belatedly.

"Of course not," the third man said. "But won't he control her money until Teddy reaches his majority?"

I peeked out again to see Sir Bernard shake his head.

The third man continued, "I doubt Sir Edward is saddened by Lady Hale's death. The entire neighborhood knew they didn't get on."

"What's your interest in this, Carstaire?" Sir Bernard asked.

So that was Sir Henry Carstaire.

"We were neighbors. Our families have been friendly for years, and our children are fond of young Teddy Hale. Didn't seem right that no one would see her off, so to speak."

"There's nothing right about this business," Sir Bernard

replied in a tone as gloomy as the weather.

"Murder," Mr. Howard said as he glanced toward the cemetery gates. "I'm surprised it didn't bring out the ghouls and the curious."

I was glad I was off to the side. Otherwise, they might have thought I was one of the ghouls.

"The cold must be keeping them indoors," Sir Bernard said. "And I believe the weather is warning me it's time to leave as well. Good day, gentlemen."

He limped slowly away, his cane tapping on stone, forcing me behind a mausoleum so as not to be seen. A second set of footsteps made me peek past the granite wall to see Mr. Howard following. Where was Sir Henry?

I came out to find him, head bent, looking at the mound of soggy dirt. I waited, giving him time to say goodbye. When he walked away, setting his top hat on his gray peppered hair, I stepped out in front of him.

"Sir Henry Carstaire?"

His eyes were red. "Yes. And who are you?"

"Georgia Peabody. I was a friend of Lady Hale's." That was my usual alias when I worked on cases. I even had business cards made up for it. It meant juggling multiple cards for different situations, but it made my roles more convincing.

"I'm sorry for your loss."

I decided to jump in with both feet. "As I am for yours. You cared about her deeply, didn't you?"

"No. What do you mean? We were neighbors. What business is it of yours?" He glanced about fearfully, but there was no one to overhear us.

Taking very direct aim, I took a chance and said, "Alice told me about your—special friendship."

He jumped back a foot, stumbling into a large headstone. "No. She wouldn't have." Then he seemed to remember his legal training and changed his tone to one of gruff confusion. "There was nothing to say. You must be mistaken." A worried frown on his face, Sir Henry dashed away from me.

He darted between granite markers in his hurry. With each step, he picked up speed. An ancient headstone, now crooked, tripped him up in his desire to reach the road and escape.

He grabbed for a stone angel, saving him from a fall into the mud and slick moss. Turning, he glanced back as he righted himself. Then he strode out of the graveyard.

I reached the cemetery gates in time to see him leap into a hansom cab and ride away.

I immediately gave up the idea of chasing after Sir Henry Carstaire. I was too cold and wet. After time spent outdoors in a cemetery during the afternoon, I was looking forward to closing up the bookshop and heading to Sir Broderick's for a hot, flavorful dinner cooked by Dominique.

It wasn't long after my return before Frances said, "Make sure Dickens doesn't escape tonight," as she pulled on her coat and set her hat above her large topknot.

"He's sleeping under my desk. He should be all right for the night," I told her.

"If you're sure..."

"Yes. Go home. Enjoy your evening," I told her as Mrs. King, the jeweler's wife from the next shop, came in, jingling the bell over the door.

"I don't mean to spread gossip," Mrs. King began, slipping off her coat and rubbing her hands together.

Oh, yes, she does.

"But have you been to Foster's bakery since we last

spoke?"

"No. I'm staying with friends while Aunt Phyllida is nursing a dear friend through a long illness. I've had no reason to go over there." *If she gossips about an unassuming baker, what does she say about me?*

The thought froze me in place for a second. Did Mrs. King suspect my connection to the Archivist Society? Better not to ask.

"Good night," Frances called as she pulled on her gloves and opened the door. I spied a smile hovering on her lips. She'd been cornered by Mrs. King before.

"Good night," I called back.

"The bakery has gotten worse. Since Mr. Foster's been ill with influenza, Mrs. Foster has cheated on the measures to bake her loaves, she's used inferior ingredients, and she snarls at anyone who asks her a simple question. The woman is positively uncivil."

"She must be under a lot of strain with Mr. Foster being ill." *And dealing with your criticism.*

"I'm sure she is, but calling Mrs. Whitcomb, the barber's mother, a witch is going too far." Mrs. King was warming to her subject.

"A witch?" Now she had my attention. I admit to listening to occasional gossip, especially when it sounds improbable or spiteful.

"Yes. Nellie Whitcomb has a habit of talking to herself. Plus, she has that old dog that follows everywhere after her. Mrs. Foster says old Mrs. Whitcomb smells like the dog, and she doesn't want the old hag in her presence. Says she's an affront to the decent people on our street. And Mr. Whitcomb does try so hard with his mother. Worse of all, Mrs. Foster hates animals. Positively despises them."

"She sounds like a very unhappy person." As was anyone cornered by Mrs. King. At that moment, that was me.

"No Christian charity in the woman. None at all. Mrs. Foster can't stand a living soul, neither man nor beast. According to young Mr. Foster, who's been apprenticing with his father, his mother has always been like this. That's why she stayed home while his father ran the bakery. At least until he became ill. Then she had to come in and help out." Mrs. King planted herself between me and the door.

"The rest of us don't mind helping in a family business, but it's not good enough for Mrs. Foster." Mrs. King gave a weary sigh. I wondered what reason she had to be weary. I was the one stuck listening to her. "Fortunately, the boy says his father is on the mend."

"That's good news, but I have to get home. They don't like me to be late for dinner. It's been good talking to you, Mrs. King." I pulled on my coat and turned off the lights.

"Go over to the bakery some time, and you'll see what I mean."

"I'm sure." I put on my hat and picked up my gloves and my keys to the shop. "Are you ready?"

"Oh! Yes. Good talking to you, Miss Fenchurch. I hope the person hanging around outside last night doesn't come back. Made me fear a break-in."

"What person? What did he look like?" Had I rattled Alice's killer enough that he was studying my shop for an attack?

"Not a he, dearie. A she. Odd choice for a woman, being a burglar. It could just have been a housewife wanting a little peace. It's quiet out here at night. Still, you never know about people, do you?"

That was probably it. I couldn't imagine any of the

women involved with this murder lingering outside my shop at night in the cold.

As Mrs. King went back to the jewelry shop, I locked up and took in a deep breath of cold air. It was a bitter night out. I was glad Dickens was indoors.

I left, walking on the opposite side of the street from the shuttered bakery, glad I could walk away from the petty disagreements between the shopkeepers on my street. What I couldn't distance myself from was the knowledge that somewhere lurked Lady Hale's murderer. The lady was dead and buried, her son hidden away and possibly in danger because of his inheritance, and I didn't see any way to avenge one and help the other. I trudged on in the dark through the cold, wet weather.

CHAPTER FOURTEEN

THE next morning, I arrived to find Frances had already shown up at the bookshop. As she was busy feeding Dickens and making a fuss over him, I opened the shop and began dusting.

"Who will you be questioning today?" Frances asked as she let Dickens climb into the bow window while she picked up a broom.

"After that strange encounter with Sir Henry in the graveyard, I believe I'll visit his chambers this morning."

"What about the boy? Any more thoughts as to where he could be?" She glanced outside at our bone-chilling weather and pursed her lips together. I knew she had a soft spot for children, starting with her own grandchildren.

"I believe Lady Imogen and Mrs. Coghill are taking very good care of him," I assured her. "I think we'll return him to his father or his aunt faster if we concentrate on who murdered his mother."

Our conversation had to stop as our first customer of the day walked in looking for something light and humorous. Despite the cold temperatures, the weak sunlight encouraged people to get outdoors and brought more business into my shop.

When we finally got a lull in our work, I told Frances I was heading off to the barrister's office and made my way toward Holborn. Once there I climbed two flights of stairs up to Sir Henry Carstaire's chambers.

His clerk greeted me as soon as I walked in the door. I gave him my Georgia Peabody card and he asked me to sit while he learned if Sir Henry would be able to see me.

I decided this was what I expected of an old-fashioned barrister's office. The walls were covered with shelves holding large, leather-bound law books. The chair was uncomfortable, with a flat wooden seat that wouldn't welcome any bottom, and was kept in a corner of the room, away from the clerk's desk. The dark wood and rows of heavy, impenetrable-looking books sucked the light and heat out of the room.

I looked over to see a figure dressed in black dart away from the crack in the doorway where the clerk had left the door ajar. Then I heard hushed voices and a moment later, the clerk returned. "I'm very sorry, but Sir Henry won't be able to see you. He's very busy at present."

"Perhaps I can make an appointment for tomorrow."

"I'm afraid tomorrow won't be convenient, either."

I felt my cheeks heat. "Then when would be convenient?"

The clerk, a man in his early twenties, pursed his thin lips together and glanced away. When he looked back at me, embarrassment leaked from his pale brown eyes. He twisted his long fingers and said, "Apparently it won't be convenient for Sir Henry to handle any matters for you. He's a barrister. He only takes pleadings from solicitors."

If Sir Henry, second son of Lord Carstaire, thought he could avoid me, he was mistaken. "That is most unfortunate, since I am anxious to speak to him. On a private matter."

"That won't be possible."

"Oh, yes, it will happen. The only question is where and when. Good day." I turned and made a dignified exit, making certain my hands didn't fist until I was in the stairwell.

Sir Henry knew something. What? And how would I get him to talk to me?

Perhaps Mr. Wylie could find a way for the two of us to meet.

I made my way along the few blocks to Mr. Wylie's office. Jacob looked up in surprise when I walked in.

"He's not here right now," Jacob said in answer to my question. "He's briefing a barrister for one of his clients. What do you need?"

"I want to speak to a barrister, Sir Henry Carstaire. He won't see me, but perhaps Mr. Wylie could arrange something so I could have a few minutes of his time. And it needs to be private. I think something might have been going on between Sir Henry and Lady Hale."

Jacob raised his eyebrows. "This investigation gets murkier by the day. I'll ask Mr. Wylie to see if he can arrange something."

"If he gets a hand written note from Sir Henry, please ask him to save it for me. It's important."

He nodded.

I asked him to find out what Mr. Wylie knew about Sir Bernard Hall, Sir Henry Carstaire, and George Howard. Then I thanked him and left, trying to dream up an action that would require Sir Henry to speak to me. I decided that if I spoke to Lady Lydia Carstaire again, he might feel obligated to speak to me, if only to tell me to stop harassing his wife.

I returned to the Hales' fashionable neighborhood and walked around the corner from the Hale residence to that of the Carstaires. The butler answered my knock, glancing up at the sky as he did so. The weather was less cold and windy than on my first visit to this house, which might be the only nice thing to say about this chilly, frustrating day.

"Is Lady Carstaire at home?" I asked, giving him a copy of the Archivist Society card I had used at the house before. "I'd like a quick word with her."

His eyebrows rose as he looked at the card. "If you'll wait here, I'll check."

The butler shut the door and reopened it a minute later. His face was so stiff I thought it would crack when he spoke. "Lady Carstaire says she has nothing to say to you, now or in the future."

"Then please tell her I will go back to see her husband again. I'm sure he can be prevailed upon to be more forthcoming. He certainly was with Lady Hale."

Overhead, I heard a gasp and a crack. Glancing through the doorway to peer up the stairs, I saw a light green skirt swish out of view. Lady Carstaire was listening. Good. Maybe now I'd hear from her husband.

"That is your choice, madam," the butler said in a stuffy voice as he shut the door on me.

I spent the rest of the day in the bookshop with a number of regular customers coming in to pick up new volumes on their hobbies or from their favorite authors. Frances and I had a chance to spend pleasant moments talking to old friends about a variety of authors and topics as we found books and wrapped parcels. The weather was definitely better than a winter storm, but with the lack of wind, we could see the fog start to thicken.

Late in the day, a very old, unkempt man entered my shop. Frances shot me a puzzled look, but I recognized him immediately. Count Vicennes, the last of an ancient line of aristocrats run out of France at the time of the revolution, toddled up to my counter.

"Good afternoon, milord." I gave him a deep curtsy.

"Good afternoon, *mademoiselle*. How are you?" His voice sounded rusty with disuse.

"I am well. And you?" I knew he'd come to the point in his own time. And he truly didn't look well. A strong breeze should have been enough to blow him away.

It took a few minutes of chatter before the count reached into his filthy overcoat and produced a package wrapped in lambskin. He opened it with shaking fingers to show me a prayer book, gilt still visible in spots on the cover. The starting capitals were an extra large size, printed from blocks carved with vines that twirled and slithered around the letters. The pages were as dry and fragile as the old man's skin. The ink hadn't so much faded as grown old and weary.

I'd seldom seen a book so ancient and beautiful, probably printed on the Continent during the time of the Tudors. And with it in such beautiful condition, I could think of a few buyers who'd pay richly to own this.

"I think perhaps I can handle this for you." And then I began the long process of negotiating with the count.

When Frances was free, I asked her to send for tea and cakes from the tea shop at the end of the block. As she approached the counter to get my proffered coins, she jerked slightly as the smell coming off Count Vicennes and his filthy garments hit her nose.

When the tea things arrived, I carried them to my crowded office and set them down on my newly cleared desk. I'd already offered the old man a seat, and the room was beginning to smell of mold and filth. Fortunately, the book only smelled dry.

The old man ate and drank eagerly and enjoyed protracted haggling in the warmth of the room. I wondered if

I'd ever be able to get the smell out. Not, I was sure, without opening the window in this wretched weather.

Finally, we came to an agreement. I put the volume in my bag to bring home that night and saw him leave with enough money to live well on for months.

I returned to Sir Broderick's that night ready to dine on Dominique's fine cooking and cocoon myself in the comfort and fellowship of friends. After I left the prayer book in my room, I joined them in the parlor, glad to see Jacob had already arrived, and in a few moments we moved to the dining room, where Dominique's pigeon soup was immediately set before us.

"I asked Mr. Wylie about all of your questions, Georgia," Jacob told me when he'd finished his soup.

"Has he been able to find any answers? And can he get Sir Henry to speak to me?"

"He sent Sir Henry a note asking for a conference but not mentioning the subject. So far he hasn't received a reply. He says Sir Henry is very proper, unlikely to put a foot wrong. As a second son of the aristocracy, he's always concerned with status. And his wife is even worse."

We fell silent as Humphries came in to bring us the fish course and clear away the soup dishes. Once he'd gone, I asked, "What has he learned about Sir Bernard Hall and Mr. Howard?"

"Both are well regarded and have sterling reputations. Neither have money problems. Sir Bernard married wealth ages ago. She's now as elderly as he and an invalid. He's reported to be devoted to her and stays at home rather than pursuing any social life.

"Mr. Howard is very good at his job and Lord Newbury and others reward him handsomely for his work. He's married with three children, and he doesn't allow anything to interfere with his family time. He won't even travel on the weekends for his clients." As soon as Jacob finished speaking, he dug into his fish and peas.

"Well, I think we can eliminate them from our inquiries, at least for the moment." I began to eat, scarcely tasting Dominique's spicy fish as I thought about where this left the investigation.

My top suspects were Lady Hale's husband, her sister, and by extension, her brother-in-law, and Sir Henry Carstaire, who had become my best guess for author of the love letters. I was suspicious of his show of sorrow at the grave.

Having learned Count Heinrich Reinler left the country the day Lady Hale died and hadn't returned made him a promising candidate for murderer in my eyes. But if that were true, Teddy would be in danger because he stood between the count and countess and his newly inherited money.

I did see one way forward with the love letters. "Jacob, don't forget to have Mr. Wylie save any written replies from Sir Henry Carstaire. I want to compare the handwriting to something I have."

"What's that?" Sir Broderick asked, pushing his fish plate an inch or two away from him.

"One of Lady Hale's maids saved love letters from her mistress's room after her death. Letters she'd received in the past several months. They were signed H."

"Surely Sir Henry isn't the only H in this business."

"He's not, Sir Broderick, but it's a way to learn whether or not he was her mystery lover."

"And if he was?" His skepticism was evident in his voice.

"It would explain why he refuses to speak to me. And it might give him a reason to kill her."

Sir Broderick shook his large head. "Fogarty spoke to the pathologist. It wouldn't have taken a great deal of strength to stab Lady Hale with the sharp weapon that was used. He said even a woman could have done it."

"I'm including her sister at the top of the list for Lady Hale's killer," I told Sir Broderick. "And Lady Imogen Fielding. She has no discernable motive, but she's a sculptor, and therefore must be as strong as any man. I'd also include Lady Hale's dismissed governess if the woman hadn't had such a good alibi."

"Georgia's always ready to include women as suspects," Jacob said and grinned.

"But to look the person you're about to kill in the eye?" Sir Broderick shuddered. "Not something you'd expect from the weaker half."

"Perhaps something you should consider more often," Mrs. Hardwick said.

I couldn't hide my smile. Our housekeeper was growing more outspoken, and Sir Broderick was benefitting from her challenges. She was bringing him to life in a way I couldn't, even with the stimulation of the Archivist Society cases.

We stayed silent while the chicken course was brought in. Once we were alone again, I said, "Count Vicennes came to see me today with a very early printed prayer book in Latin. It's in beautiful condition for something so ancient. Know anyone who'd be interested?"

"Did you bring it home with you?" Sir Broderick spoke with such eagerness that for a moment, I thought I'd see him rise from his wheeled chair.

"Of course."

Sir Broderick was nearly salivating over the excitement of the newest treasure from Count Vicennes. "We'll look at it in the study after dinner. The count's collection is one of the most superb I've ever seen, and I've only seen the ones he's willing to part with."

"This will be a very short dinner," Mrs. Hardwick said, but she smiled at Sir Broderick when he glanced at her.

After a few minutes, he said, "Would you mind having coffee in the parlor after I've seen this book?"

We all agreed and I went up to bring the book to the study, picking up a letter from Emma on the way. When I reached Sir Broderick, I found Jacob and Mrs. Hardwick waiting with him. They all oohed and aahed over it and gasped when I said how much I'd paid for it, but Sir Broderick said I was right to pay that much for such a stunning specimen and would make money on its sale.

"I thought you'd want to buy it."

"I do, but if Lord Barnwood found out I didn't give him a chance to bid on it, he'd never speak to me again. I'll give him a call in the morning, if that's all right with you, Georgia."

"Of course." It was one less thing for me to concern myself with. I locked the volume up in his antiquarian book depository, designed to be fire- and theft-proof. I hoped the metal box was never put to the test.

After coffee, I went up to write a reply to Emma's letter. They'd stopped in Rome for a few days while Sumner talked to the publisher who put out Italian editions of his works. Emma planned to revisit all the ancient sites in the city.

I described how I was writing to her while wrapped in a woolen shawl and how jealous I was that she was seeing ruins that were two thousand years old.

I also filled her in on the latest developments in our

investigation. That part of the letter was short.

THE NEXT morning was gloomy, but the fog had only thickened a little. As cold as it was while I crossed London to the bookshop, the lack of a breeze made me sure it would be foggier by the end of the day. Bitter-tasting, still air had settled on top of London.

We had a few customers during the morning, and Dickens seemed to rally enough to lie in the bow window. By lunchtime, I worried about Frances trying to cross the roads to her family's hotel and back. Visibility was worsening. Dickens went back to the bed Frances had made him under my desk. I still hadn't heard him meow.

The day grew gloomier while no wind came to sweep away the fog. We could still see the shops across the street, but little else. Everything seemed to be tinted yellowish-gray. Traffic slowed and then vanished as more people gave up the effort to travel across London. Everyone was praying for a windstorm.

The postman grumbled as he handed over our afternoon mail, bringing a whiff of coal smoke in with him, and banged the door on his way out.

"Well, he certainly is cheerful," Frances muttered, looking up from the novel she was reading.

I flipped through the letters and invoices, stopping at an envelope of thick, expensive paper. Opening it, I found a short message.

*Miss Fenchurch, I will see you, but not
where we might be observed talking
together. Meet me in front of Lady
Imogen Fielding's house this evening*

at five o'clock. In the last place I saw
Alice.

Sir Henry Carstaire

"Yes," I squealed, causing Dickens to open one eye and glare at me. "Sir Henry Carstaire has finally agreed to meet me. In front of Lady Imogen Fielding's. If I'm going to make our appointment, I have to leave now. Will you be all right, Frances?"

"Of course. Will you be safe? It'll be dark by the time you get there."

"If I disappear, remember where I was headed." I was too excited about finally being able to talk to Sir Henry to worry about meeting him after dark. After all, we were meeting on a public street. In London, there were always other people passing by. Even in the fog. I pulled on my coat, pinned on my hat, and headed out the door.

At the last moment, I put the letter from Sir Henry in my bag. It was on plain stationery, probably because he didn't want his clerk to know about our meeting. I guessed he mailed it himself at lunchtime.

The streetlamps had already been lit when I climbed down from the omnibus and headed toward the river. The last flickers of daylight added enough light for me to cross the road with ease, but darkness descended and the fog thickened with every step I took towards the Thames. The smell alone, dampness mixed with the coal smoke, told me I was headed toward the river.

By the time I reached Cheyne Walk near Lady Imogen's home, I could scarcely see the road at my feet. Street lamps were few and far between and wouldn't be much use in that night's mucky air.

How would I ever find Sir Henry in this pea soup? I

called out, "Sir Henry? Sir Henry?"

The only answers I heard were the lap of the river against the base of the wall, wood scraping on stone and some footsteps.

I imagined they were stealthy footsteps. I shivered with fright before I told myself not to be silly. It was only someone as disoriented by the fog as I was.

I thought I heard a "hello," but it was muffled. Possibly only a boat scraping against a wharf, or the bark of a dog or the wind catching an unlocked gate.

"Sir Henry?" I called again and then coughed in the dank, foul-smelling air.

Again a muffled noise that sounded like a voice. Had someone said "hello?" Or had a distant cat struck at an adversary?

I turned around, trying to decide where the sound had come from. "Hello?"

I heard a small cry, or the call of a seagull. I listened, but there was nothing else. "Sir Henry?" Again there was no answer but the footsteps coming toward me.

The fog came in waves. One moment I couldn't see my feet. The next, I could see a section of a nearby house or part of a wall or a sliver of the road for a good distance. The fog played hide and seek with the world, and I was tired of this game.

I faced the direction I thought I heard someone walking and waited for someone to appear. And expected, despite warning myself not to be imaginative, to run away screaming.

The footsteps stopped.

Why was no one walking along this street?

I backed up a few steps into the fog. I could hear muffled footsteps start again, but I couldn't see anyone. I heard the lap of the Thames on the bank, but I couldn't see the river. Frequently, I couldn't even make out the low wall along the embankment.

I stopped, hoping the person would appear out of the mist. Instead, the footsteps stopped immediately after mine did. Whether or not it was Sir Henry, I was certain someone wished me ill.

If I could have figured out in which direction I'd find the main road and the omnibus, I'd have run there immediately. This dark, empty, riverfront street was the perfect place for an attack.

Well, I refused to be a victim.

I tried to tiptoe toward the houses, but confused by the thick fog, I seemed to go endlessly along the roadway. Fortunately, I didn't hear the clop of horses' hooves or the clatter of cart wheels warning of the approach of a vehicle to run me down.

I stumbled on a loose paving stone and a skittering rock gave away my position. The quiet footsteps marched relentlessly toward me again, but no one appeared out of the mist. I hurried forward, and the footsteps sped up. Shivers ran down my spine that had nothing to do with the weather.

Where was a side street to take me to the main road? I looked over my shoulder as I began to run, and smashed into something immovable.

"Careful, Georgia."

I whipped my head back to find the Duke of Blackford in front of me.

CHAPTER FIFTEEN

"MY lord," I gasped as I windmilled my arms to keep from falling backward. I hadn't heard him and didn't expect to collide with anyone or anything. My heart galloped from the shock.

Blackford was in London! Seeing him made my heart beat even faster. I hadn't expected him to reach London yet, and I certainly never thought I'd run into him on foggy Cheyne Walk.

He put his hands on my waist to keep me from tumbling to the damp paving stones. "Blackford will do," he said, misunderstanding my oath. "Frances said you'd be down here. Where are you going in this weather? Are you on an investigation?"

At least I was certain his weren't the stealthy footsteps. He'd appeared from the wrong direction. I looked over my shoulder and listened, but the footsteps were gone. I nodded, not wanting him to let me go. "Let's get out of this soggy atmosphere."

"My carriage is a street or two over. I wasn't quite sure where I would find you. Don't worry, the fog is much thinner there." He took my arm and led me unerringly through the soup.

"How can you find your way through this?" I thought it was a wonder. I couldn't find a single landmark.

"I keep on until I hit something, and then I adjust

accordingly." He grinned at what I knew was a shocked expression on my face. "I know this area intimately from my childhood. My father had a mistress who lived along here."

What a strange way to spend his childhood, in the company of his father's mistress. "But what will keep us from falling into the river?" seemed like a safer topic of conversation.

"The wall. Don't worry. I'm back now. I won't let anything happen to you."

"Is that what you face telling me with trepidation? I certainly don't think of your help with distaste." If he'd found a duchess in America, I needed to know while the fog might hide my tears.

"Perhaps trepidation wasn't the right word."

"Perhaps you should just tell me what's on your mind." I needed to know as soon as possible for the sake of my sanity.

"Not here. I'm too busy keeping us from falling in the river. Ah, good. Here's the cross street," he said as the fog thinned to show us a lane between the corners of two houses. "If we follow this to the King's Road, we'll find my carriage waiting."

We moved faster now that we found the fog much decreased as buildings blocked the mist from the river. The Wellington coach loomed out of the gloom, and I suddenly remembered something I hadn't missed while the duke was away.

A footman opened the door for us, and Blackford took me by the waist and lifted me into the coach. Now, there was something I'd missed. And something I felt certain I'd soon have only in my dreams.

I sat down as the duke sprang into the coach. "How long have you been in London?"

He pulled out his gold pocket watch and opened the lid. "Thirty-five minutes," he said, putting it away again.

I schooled my face into a semblance of polite interest, trying to hide how thrilled I was that his first goal in London was to see me. "It didn't take you long to find me, Your Grace."

In the silence, his dark eyes bore into mine as his face took on a granite cast. "It's a good thing I did, too. What were you doing wandering around the banks of the Thames on your own in a pea soup?" He sounded annoyed.

"I was supposed to be meeting someone who has vital information about the investigation I'm working on." I wasn't going to tell him I was being followed by a shadowy character.

"Who?"

"I don't see where that's any—"

"What fool wanted to meet you in such dangerous surroundings? The villain you're trying to capture?" He snapped out his words, but at the same time he gathered my hands in his and stroked my fingers with his thumbs.

For the first time since I'd entered Cheyne Walk, I felt safe. "I was to meet the man I believe Lady Hale planned to run away with at one time. He's a barrister. Sir Henry Carstaire."

Surprise flashed across Blackford's face before he said, "I can't picture Sir Henry leaving his prestige and his reputation behind to run off with a woman. Although I've met his wife, and perhaps it isn't so surprising a thought."

I needed to explain. "In the end, Lady Hale planned to run off to Canada with her son, leaving husband, sister and Sir Henry Carstaire behind. She'd been in hiding for only a day or two when she went out of the house where she was staying and met her killer."

Blackford gave me a thoughtful scowl and dropped my hands. "Where was she hiding?"

"Lady Imogen Fielding's."

"Good heavens. Did she choose all her friends for their outsized reputations?"

"Perhaps." I wouldn't share what I'd learned about Forsyth and Summerhaye with him. I considered it a secret not to be divulged without need. "Now, what did you want to tell me?"

"I want you to be my duchess." He might as well have been discussing the weather for all the emotion he displayed.

"What?!" My mind went completely blank with shock. The carriage hit a bump and I nearly fell off the seat. Shaken, I grabbed a strap and settled myself more firmly in place. Had I heard him right or was I dreaming?

"I realize I asked you to be my mistress when I couldn't see a way forward to make you my duchess. Please forgive me. Now that I've been to the United States and Canada, I've discovered a world where things like rank and title and ancestry don't mean what they do here." The words fairly tumbled from his mouth.

He took one of my hands again. "I saw a whole new way of looking at things. A way that makes more sense in this modern world. Where talent and intelligence and hard work are important. And you have all the characteristics that make you aristocratic, Georgia."

I was amazed at his lovely speech and nearly let my jaw drop.

"Characteristics I want to pass on to our children. I want you to bear the next duke."

He wanted me to be the mother of a duke? My heart

nearly jumped out of my chest. To Blackford's way of thinking, that would be the ultimate compliment.

It was also something I'd daydreamed about.

To my shock, he got down on one knee on the cramped carriage floor and said, "Please do me the honor of becoming my wife, Georgia."

A moment ago we were discussing an ongoing investigation. Now he was asking me to become his duchess. He was on one knee, giving me a proper proposal, here in the Wellington carriage that he was so proud of. My brain couldn't absorb his words or his actions. I had to be dreaming. This wasn't really happening.

I stared at him for a moment and then blurted out, "Are you joking?"

"Do I look like I'm joking? I've never been more serious." He scowled up at me.

No. He couldn't be serious. He was a duke. My ears must have been playing tricks on me. "Oh, Blackford, get up. You look so uncomfortable all scrunched on the floor. We need to discuss this sensibly."

He climbed back onto the seat across from me, dropping my hand and putting as much distance between us as possible. "What is there to discuss? I asked you to marry me. Now you say yes."

As if it were that easy. Part of me was screaming *Yes!* But even though he was proposing marriage, he still sounded like a duke and not a lover. "It's not that simple. You may have learned to overlook my humble beginnings, but what about your family and friends? They won't look with pleasure on your marriage to a middle-class shop owner. They won't like a duchess who doesn't always recognize the order of precedence."

"My closest relations are cousins I rarely see and don't care about. And my friends, if they are my friends, will welcome you with open arms."

"While the rest of society snubs us? I wasn't presented at court. No one in society knows my family back three generations. They won't know what to make of me, and you won't like that, Blackford." I certainly wouldn't, and I'd feel guilty every time Blackford had to endure an icy reception.

"I don't care." His voice rose to emphasize his point.

"Well, I shall. And will you allow me the freedom to hunt for murderers with the Archivist Society?"

"Of course."

"Alone?"

"Why wouldn't you want my help? I've aided the Archivist Society in the past." He folded his arms across his chest, a sure sign I'd ruffled his feathers. Oh, dear. This wasn't going well for either of us.

"Of course you may assist the Archivist Society. But I wouldn't want you interrupting every interview I'll have with a witness or suspect. Not like you did today."

He studied me with his mesmerizing dark eyes. "Leaving aside the more deadly aspects of the location, why would Sir Henry Carstaire meet you in such an uncomfortable spot? Why not in his chambers?"

"In his note he said he didn't want to be seen with me. The spot where he'd last seen Lady Hale would be private enough."

"Let me see." He held out one hand.

I pulled the message out of my bag and handed it to him.

He scowled at it for a moment as he held it to catch the light of a streetlamp. "This isn't Sir Henry's hand."

"How can you be sure?"

"I've seen his writing before. He's left-handed. His writing has a distinctive slope. This was written by a right handed person."

"Oh." I took the note back and studied it. Why hadn't I noticed Sir Henry was left-handed? I'd been so determined to speak to him after his rebuffs that I'd not considered how meeting him in front of Lady Imogen's on a foggy night could be dangerous.

"Let me help." He didn't sound like he'd take no for an answer.

"What do you have in mind?"

"I'll have my solicitor set up a meeting with him in chambers. Then we'll go along."

"I've already tried that. Jacob's master is attempting to set up a meeting for me."

"Jacob's master?" He raised his brows. "It seems I have been away a long time."

"Mr. Wylie is a solicitor. Jacob is studying under him while working on Archivist Society cases. It's an arrangement that seems to suit them both."

"Has he been able to arrange the meeting?" Fortunately, Blackford seemed to have forgotten his proposal while I had found a way to gain time to consider how much it would change my life.

"I don't know." A panicked voice inside my head said, unfortunately, Blackford might have forgotten it entirely. "I need to have time to consider your proposal."

Oh, dear. My tone gave away my anxiety.

The duke's lips quivered at the edges as if he were trying to hide a triumphant smile. "How much time will you need?"

"As much as it takes. This is a serious commitment. And we need to resolve a number of issues."

He nodded and reached across the carriage to take one of my hands. Then in a tone I'd never heard from him, a voice both loving and anxious, he said, "Please say yes, Georgia. I love you."

He said "I love you." My heart raced so fast I thought I'd faint. I never thought I'd hear those words from him, and I couldn't wait to hear them again. Speechless, the only reply I could give him was a sigh.

Blackford studied me for a long time with a sad face while I frantically tried to think of what to say. "Did you tell Sir Henry your real name? Walking along the river at night in a thick fog to meet him was taking an unnecessary risk."

"When we started, we thought we were looking for a missing woman and child. It wasn't until after we began searching that we discovered Lady Hale had been murdered." I looked at Blackford, and then held up one hand. "Oh. No, I didn't start trying to meet Sir Henry until later. I told him I was Georgia Peabody. Not Fenchurch."

"Whoever sent you that note knows your name is Fenchurch."

Sir Edward Hale and Countess Reinler both knew my real name. As did the women of Forsyth and Summerhaye. And Lady Hale's neighbors. "Those most involved in Lady Hale's life and the consequences of her death know me by my proper name."

Blackford shut his eyes and shook his head. "You take too many chances, Georgia," he told me when he opened his eyes and fixed me with a stare. "That note put you right where someone wanted you."

"I was just too eager to meet with him. I'm sure he was Alice's lover, but I can't get him to admit it. Or even to speak with me."

"That's not a thing a barrister would freely admit. And avoiding you makes it possible to ignore awkward questions." He gathered both my hands in his. "You look cold. Let me give you a ride to Sir Broderick's."

"That would be very kind, Your Grace."

He signaled his driver and then faced me again. "Perhaps now you'll start calling me Gordon."

I thought calling him Ranleigh, his surname, was forward. Who knew how long it would take me to call him by his Christian name. "In time. Right now, I'm more comfortable calling you Blackford."

"You may call me whatever makes you happy. As long as you say yes."

I decided to change topics. "I hope you'll come in and say hello to Sir Broderick and Mrs. Hardwick. Perhaps stay for dinner if you don't have any plans."

"I'd like that. Tell me, how are they getting on?"

"They've become great friends, and Mrs. Hardwick is beginning to speak out on Archivist Society matters. It's good to see her comfortable enough with us to say what's on her mind. Meanwhile, I've heard from Emma almost daily. She and Sumner had an enjoyable wedding trip and have now reached Italy on their way home."

"Will she go to work for you again and help with the Archivist Society?"

"Not in the bookshop. But I imagine she'll be as involved in Archivist Society cases as she has time for, now that she's a married woman. Her letters make me believe she and Sumner are very happy. Tell me, Your Grace, how was your trip?"

He raised his dark brows. "Your Grace?"

I gave him a smile that showed how much I enjoyed our

closer relationship, even if I hadn't given my answer. "Ranleigh, if you prefer."

He gifted me with one of the warm smiles that I'd missed. "Very much." He glanced out the window and then turned to focus on my face. "We're almost to Sir Broderick's. Why don't I save the tale so you only have to hear it once?"

Then he moved from his seat to mine, put his arms around me, and gave me a very satisfying kiss. "I've wanted to do that since the instant I ran into you on Cheyne Walk."

"I'm only sorry you waited so long." Then my cheeks heated at my boldness.

"I've missed you, Georgia." He nuzzled my ear, and warmth flooded through me.

I threw my arms around his neck and squeezed, knocking his top hat off. "I'm sorry, Ranleigh, but I missed you so much."

"You have nothing to be sorry for." He kissed me again before picking up his hat. "And now we need to go inside. We're at Sir Broderick's."

He helped me down the long distance to the pavement before Humphries opened the door to us. "This is Sir Broderick's new manservant, Humphries," I said as I climbed the steps and walked inside. "And this is the Duke of Blackford. Is Sir Broderick in his study?"

"Yes, miss."

"Good. Don't announce us. I want to see the surprise. Come on." After we handed off our outerwear, I rushed up the stairs with Blackford on my heels. "Sir Broderick..."

"Your Grace," he exclaimed as he saw us, rolling his chair in our direction. "So good to have you back." He and Blackford exchanged a vigorous handclasp.

"Any chance we could invite him to dinner and hear

about his trip?" I asked.

"Excellent idea. Mrs. Hardwick!"

A moment later, the woman came in wearing a deep lavender gown with ruffles over the shoulders that came to a point at her waist and showed off narrow sleeves. Very slimming and, I was almost certain, new.

"Mrs. Hardwick, will dinner stretch to feed His Grace?"

A smile broke over her plain face, making it beautiful. "Oh, Your Grace. We're so glad you've arrived safely. We'd be honored if you'd join us for dinner and tell us about your journey. Let me go see to it."

"That's very kind of you," the duke said with a slight bow.

She gave him a curtsy, raised her eyebrows at me, and left.

I knew she'd be questioning me later.

Once we were seated in the study, the men with glasses of port, Blackford said, "Sir Broderick, as the closest thing Georgia has to a father now, well, I want you to know..." He took a quick sip of port. "I want you to know that I've asked her to become my wife."

I glanced over and saw the hairs at the nape of Blackford's neck were curling. A sure sign he was nervous.

My palms were sweating. I guess we both were nervous.

Sir Broderick's smile couldn't have been wider. "My good man. That is wonderful news. My best wishes to you both." He set down his port so fast it was still sloshing in the glass when he reached Blackford to shake his hand.

"Not so fast," I said. "I've not said yes yet."

"I take it you've not said no, either." Sir Broderick studied me closely.

"I have to be certain in my own mind. And with this

current investigation..." Truly, I was still surprised. At his sudden arrival, at his proposal, at the possibility of becoming a duchess. My thoughts were in a muddle.

"What you need is a good night's sleep. Everything will become clearer in the morning." Sir Broderick glanced at the clock. "Now, I suppose we'd better wait to hear about your trip until Jacob gets home. He'll be eager to hear about your adventures, too."

At least no one was pressuring me. Yet.

As soon as Jacob arrived home, dinner was served. It was a lively affair, with much discussion about New York and the Rocky Mountains. In the course of visiting his investments, Blackford slept under the stars, rode on a paddlewheel steamer, traveled by train over mountains, sailed on the Pacific Ocean from Vancouver to San Francisco, and crossed the Atlantic during winter storms. His four months away were filled with adventure.

He'd ridden across fields of wheat and corn so wide he couldn't see the ends. He'd seen outposts on his way west that were small towns on his return journey. He painted so vivid a portrait of a continent we could see it from the dining room in London.

It all sounded exciting, but I was much more interested in the people he met. Irish, Chinese, natives, French Canadians, wealthy New Yorkers squeezed into tall, narrow houses on an island, while ranchers lived on huge tracts of land so empty and unspoiled that I could hardly believe it possible. And they all had their different customs and foods.

Blackford told his tales with the dry wit I had so missed. Mrs. Hardwick made him stop during the fowl course so she could have Dominique come upstairs and hear about the foreign dishes he'd sampled. Jacob stated at least three times that the next time Blackford underwent such a trip, he was going with him and no one better dare stop him.

Afterward, the duke began a lengthy discussion with Sir Broderick on American publishing. They discussed crime detection in New York and autopsies in San Francisco. Then Blackford told us about dining with Andrew Carnegie, the Scotsman who became wealthy in America, and the American financier J. P. Morgan as the three men discussed their joint business ventures.

He found so many riches from England and the continent had made their way to America that he frequently felt he was dining in London when he was in New York, Toronto or Chicago. He said the balls on the east coast of America were as glittery as any held in London.

Dinner took five times as long as usual, but it felt like five minutes from the time we sat down until we rose. I didn't remember eating a bite, and I doubted Blackford had a chance to more than sample any of the dishes for all the questions we asked.

We had settled in the parlor for our coffee when the footman knocked on the door and walked in. "Humphries," Sir Broderick said, "what is it?"

Inspector Grantham walked in behind him. "Miss Georgia Fenchurch, were you meeting Sir Henry Carstaire this afternoon on Cheyne Walk?" he announced in his formal tone.

"Yes, but he never showed up. And then I ran into Blackford and left with him." I set down my cup and saucer with a click when I saw how stiff his back and his facial muscles appeared. "What's wrong, Inspector?"

"You need to come to Scotland Yard with me to answer some questions. Sir Henry was found a little while ago on

Cheyne Walk. He was stabbed through the heart."

CHAPTER SIXTEEN

SIR Broderick and Blackford spoke over each other, telling Grantham he was wrong. I sat there, stunned into silence. I hadn't killed Sir Henry, but how did the police know I was supposed to meet him where they found his body?

"Are you arresting her?" Blackford demanded as he rose to his feet.

"No. I'm asking her to accompany me to assist in our inquiries." Grantham looked like he'd rather be doing anything else.

"Then you'll probably want me down there, too. We were together on Cheyne Walk." Blackford turned to Sir Broderick. "Call my solicitor and have him meet us at Scotland Yard. Sir Jeremiah Potts."

"Immediately." Sir Broderick began to wheel his chair toward the elevator. Mrs. Hardwick walked over and gave my hands a squeeze while she gave me an encouraging smile.

At least my friends didn't consider me a murderer.

"Is it all right if I bring Miss Fenchurch in my carriage?" Blackford said.

Grantham sighed. "Your Grace, it's not as if you two are married."

"I've asked her to marry me. We're as good as wed," Blackford snapped out. He seemed to be ignoring the fact I hadn't agreed. Yet.

Still, I could see the advantage of Blackford's protection.

I rose and walked over to the two men on shaky legs. "I'll need to fetch my coat and hat, Inspector," I murmured.

He nodded wordlessly.

In a few minutes, Blackford's solicitor was notified and we were dressed to meet the cold night. This time, when Blackford climbed up to join me in the Wellington coach, he sat next to me. "Did you bring your letter from Sir Henry?" he asked.

"Yes. I'm sure it will help, but I'm still frightened. In all our investigations, I've never before been suspected of being the villain."

"I would guess Sir Henry had a similar note on his body signed by you."

"I didn't write it." I couldn't hide the annoyance in my tone.

"I know that." Despite his dryness, he reached over and took one of my hands in his. "Georgia, it's going to be okay. And no matter what you eventually answer, for tonight we're engaged and you're under my protection."

"I shouldn't need to be under your protection. My work for the past dozen years should speak for itself. I had no reason to stab Sir Henry. I don't even know for certain if he was avoiding me or why he was afraid to meet me, if he didn't want to speak to me. This isn't fair." I found I was squeezing his hand as hard as I could and let go with an embarrassed gasp.

His expression didn't show that he'd noticed me mangling his hand. "But you suspect you know why."

"Yes." I took his hand again and held on with a gentle clasp. His warmth and strength seemed to pass into the cold, frightened core of my being. I began to feel more assured. He must have realized how much his presence helped me because he placed both of his hands around mine.

I was accepting his help and not being gracious about it. I took a shaky breath and said, "That wasn't much of a thank you, was it, Your Grace? Thank you. I appreciate your help even more so since you give it with no strings attached."

"None whatsoever. Although I hope it helps my suit." I gave him a quick glance at his final words and he returned it while wiggling his brows before his expression turned grave. "Georgia, I hope you know me well enough by now to know I'm glad to help the Archivist Society with their investigations. I consider this part of your inquiry. Who knows what we may learn tonight at Scotland Yard."

I squeezed his hand, lightly this time, and gave him what I hoped appeared to be a brave smile. In the poor light inside the carriage, I hoped he couldn't see my lips tremble.

We followed Grantham's carriage around to a side entrance of the massive red brick office block that was Scotland Yard. As we entered the gates, Blackford gave me a kiss that left me breathless and a little disoriented when the carriage door was opened and we were met by grim-faced constables.

We were led inside through a small ground floor doorway and then marched down tiled corridors and up stairs lighted by bare light bulbs. Constables flanked me as if I'd already been arrested. I was disheartened by the time we entered a small, bare room.

We were told to sit on the hard wooden chairs. Then we were left alone with a bobby standing immobile near the door. I was glad I still huddled inside my cloak since no draperies blocked the cold air from entering around the windows. Blackford wore a disinterested expression that said he was there to assist the police if they were smart enough to accept his help. He lacked the frightened look I knew must be evident in my eyes as my hands trembled.

"Blackford," I began.

He put his finger to his lips.

I fell silent.

In a few minutes, Grantham walked in with an older, rounder man with very thin hair and a sneer on his face. A second bobby took a chair in a corner and readied his notepad and pencil. "I'm Superintendent Marcum and I want to know which of you stabbed Sir Henry Carstaire."

"Neither," I told him.

"Are you sure?"

"Yes."

"Were you together the whole time you were in Cheyne Walk?"

"No." I hated admitting that.

He leaned forward, towering above me. I could smell a faint odor of onions and coal dust on his clothes and see the wrinkles in his skin. "Then how can you be sure?"

"We had no more reason to kill Sir Henry than you did, Superintendent. And neither of us are killers. I don't know about you," I added.

Grantham rubbed his upper lip to hide the beginning of a smile.

"I'd like you to give me a sample of your handwriting," Marcum said. He put paper and pen and ink in front of me.

"What do you want her to write?" Blackford asked, staring at the superintendent's face and not glancing at the paper.

"How about 'I know what you've done. Meet me on Cheyne Walk.'"

There'd been a note on Sir Henry. That's why they came

so quickly to question me. But figuring out what Scotland Yard was thinking was not going to help me. I wrote out the words in my best handwriting and handed it to Marcum.

The duke then reached over, took pen to paper and wrote out the words in the handwriting I'd come to love in the letters he'd sent me from America. "I don't want any misunderstandings," he said with ducal displeasure.

The superintendent examined both samples against a third paper that he produced.

"We found this note in Sir Henry's pocket." Marcum held the letter open in front of our faces. I leaned forward to read it. "Oh, you can pick it up. It's already been examined."

The note read: *Sir Henry Carstaire,*

> *I know what you've done. Meet me on Cheyne*
> *Walk in front of Lady Imogen Fielding's to*
> *discuss terms.*
> *Georgia Fenchurch*

"I didn't write this." The handwriting was nothing like mine.

"It bears your name. What terms were you going to discuss? Were you planning to blackmail him? Was he unwilling to pay the price for your silence?"

"It's not my handwriting. I know nothing about it. I was sent a letter from Sir Henry asking me to meet him there. Here." I pulled out the letter I'd received at the bookshop and held it out to the Superintendent.

"You could have written this at any time," he said as he took the note.

"It's not my handwriting either."

A stoop-shouldered, short man carrying a top hat and leaning heavily on a cane walked in and said, "Good evening, Superintendent."

Blackford said, "Georgia, this is my solicitor, Sir Jeremiah Potts. Sir Jeremiah, this is Georgia Fenchurch, my intended."

"Pleased to meet you, my dear," the man said without a trace of irony at our surroundings.

"And you, sir," I said with a nod.

The superintendent gave a mighty sigh. "Good evening, Sir Jeremiah. I suppose you'd like me to summarize what we've learned so far?"

"If you'd be so kind."

He ran a finger under his stiff, high collar and began. "Sir Henry Carstaire, barrister, was found on the river wall along Cheyne Walk this evening during a break in the fog. Two men on their way home found his body. He'd been stabbed in the heart."

He cleared his throat. "He was a neighbor of Lady Hale, who was recently murdered in the same manner and location, but her body was dumped in the river. It being low tide, her body couldn't float away. Due to some metal work there along the wall, Sir Henry's body was snagged. Otherwise it would also have fallen into the Thames, but at a higher tide when it could have been submerged in the water or floated off."

When he paused, Sir Jeremiah said, "Go on."

"In his pocket was a message signed by Miss Georgia Fenchurch, asking him to meet her at that location to discuss terms as she was aware of some deed he'd committed."

"Have you questioned Miss Fenchurch?"

"She has not been forthcoming," Superintendent Marcum said.

"She hasn't bowed down to his bullying," Blackford said.

"Your Grace…" the superintendent began, tugging at his collar once more.

Uncrossing his legs, Blackford sat up straight and fixed the superintendent with a stare. "If you'd asked like a sensible man, you'd have learned that Miss Fenchurch received a letter from Sir Henry in the post this afternoon, asking for a five o'clock meeting. She told her employee, Mrs. Atterby, where she was going and why, and the good lady told me when I called at the bookshop a few minutes later. I went straight to Cheyne Walk and bumped into Miss Fenchurch. Literally. The fog was quite thick. We went back to my carriage where she showed me the note."

"You've asked for samples of her handwriting?" Sir Jeremiah said.

"Both the duke and Miss Fenchurch gave us samples."

"And did either of them match?"

"No," Marcum said. His shoulders slumped slightly.

"At any time did either of you see anyone else on Cheyne Walk?" Inspector Grantham asked.

"No." Blackford gave a definite ring to his words.

"I heard footsteps. I thought they were following me. But I never saw anyone," I told the inspector.

"Convenient, these footsteps that belonged to a person you never saw," Marcum said.

"Convenient for you, perhaps. I found them ominous. I might have seen the person if Blackford hadn't come along. I was more than glad to leave with him since Sir Henry hadn't shown up and I had no desire to linger in that place. It seemed positively dangerous," I told him, sounding much stuffier than I would to Inspector Grantham.

"How long were you there before the duke arrived?"

"Just a few minutes. It had become completely dark as well as foggy just as I arrived, so I moved slowly. I hadn't gone more than maybe fifty feet before I bumped into

Blackford."

"And you, Your Grace?" the superintendent asked. "How long were you there before you found Miss Fenchurch?"

"Only a minute or two. I heard her footsteps as I reached the street and walked toward her."

"During this time, either of you could have stabbed Sir Henry," Marcum said.

"Do you have the murder weapon?" Sir Jeremiah asked.

"Well, no," Marcum admitted.

"Have you found it in the possession of either of these people?"

"They could have thrown it in the river."

"So could the real assassin. Without any more evidence than forged notes which don't match the handwriting of my clients, they are both going to leave here. Now." Sir Jeremiah craned his head up to look into Marcum's face.

"Your clients? Both of them?" Superintendent Marcum spluttered.

"Yes. And I believe you've taken up enough of their time. Good day, Superintendent."

Blackford stood and took my hand as I rose. Then he took back my note, the one supposedly authored by Sir Henry. "Let's return to Sir Broderick's and finish our coffee. Thank you, Sir Jeremiah," he added as we left the room.

"Quite a homecoming," the solicitor replied. "Call me if you need me later." Putting on his hat, the slight man walked away, tapping his cane on the worn wooden floor.

Inspector Grantham caught up with us in time to lead us downstairs. "We'll continue the investigation thinking of you both as suspects, but I imagine, Blackford, you at least are in the clear. I know Marcum. The fact Georgia's handwriting doesn't match won't slow him down."

"Give me some good news," Blackford grumbled.

"She's still free. And congratulations on your engagement. My grandmother will be pleased."

The inspector and I shared a smile. "Now she can put all her efforts into marrying you to a suitable candidate."

"Oh, don't remind me." The smile slid off his face.

"What's this?" Blackford asked.

"Lady Westover and Lady Phyllida have put their heads together and decided it is time for the two of us to get married and for Inspector Grantham to find a bride before they do it for him." I raised my eyebrows at Blackford.

"Then I suppose I need to visit Lady Westover tomorrow," Blackford said. From his dry tone, I was certain he would tell the two ladies the truth and then they'd both start badgering me to agree to his proposal.

I knew it wouldn't take much to convince me. I loved him. If only I was sure this equalitarian mood of his wouldn't quickly wear off, leaving him to regret his offer.

I couldn't imagine what he would be like if he were trapped with a wife he no longer wanted. He'd realized how terrible life would have been had he married his first fiancée. Her death had saved him that time, but I wouldn't want a repeat of that cure. I was certain he wouldn't be pleasant to live with if he married the wrong woman.

He helped me into his waiting carriage and climbed in after me. Grantham held the door open. "That was a near thing, Georgia. Marcum was determined to arrest you when you came in. Stay away from this investigation. Spend time in your bookshop. Or go plan your wedding instead."

BLACKFORD DIDN'T press his suit that night. At least not verbally. However, our carriage ride back to Sir Broderick's was slow and Blackford was a talented kisser. I was breathing hard and a little disheveled when he walked me inside. If Humphries noticed how flushed my face must have been when he opened the door, he showed no sign.

Sir Broderick and Mrs. Hardwick were waiting in the parlor with a fresh pot of tea. After we assured them everything was all right, Blackford took his leave. Exhausted, I went to bed.

It had been a long, grueling day, but the only thing I could think about was Blackford's proposal and his kisses. That alone kept me up half the night.

I couldn't imagine being called Your Grace, and certainly not by Sir Broderick, Aunt Phyllida, Emma or anyone associated with my bookshop or the Archivist Society. I couldn't imagine giving up my independence and freedom to be constrained by the duke's authority, duties and arrogance. He'd been so sure that we didn't have a wedded future together before he left on his trip.

Despite his change of heart, I would have to deal daily with the wives of peers who held to his former beliefs and would delight in letting me know my every failure as a duchess. How long could I bear to be mocked and scorned?

But I also couldn't imagine never seeing Blackford again, or not leaning on his strength when he offered it so willingly. Especially since I was at the top of Superintendent Marcum's list of suspects.

As I arrived at the breakfast table heavy lidded, Sir Broderick greeted me with, "Well?"

Mrs. Hardwick cleared her throat.

He gave her a quick glance before turning his full attention on me. "Have you made a decision?"

"No."

"Then it's a good thing the duke is a patient man. No man is going to wait forever while you dither."

"It's not that I'm unsure of my feelings. It's just..."

"You're uncertain of the duke's change of heart. Or your reception into society," Mrs. Hardwick said.

"Yes." Finally someone understood.

"Then I recommend the two of you have a long talk. Tell him about your doubts. Because your many friends think you would make a very happy couple." She gave me a small smile before taking a bite of her toast.

"We need to talk, but I have a bookshop to run, a killer to catch, and a Scotland Yard superintendent to avoid. Blackford has his many businesses to attend to."

Mrs. Hardwick shook her head slowly, her kindly eyes fixed on me. "Surely you'll find time after dinner tonight. Invite the duke to join us again so you two can talk in private. Discuss what's bothering you."

I gave her a conspiratorial smile. "I will. Thank you."

Sir Broderick watched me with narrowed eyes. "What happened last evening?"

I told him.

"Do you want me to hand this investigation off to other Archivist Society members?"

"No. Lady Hale's killer may have been targeting me last night as well as Sir Henry. I must be close. I'd like to see this through, both for Teddy's sake and for Lady Hale."

He nodded. "Please, promise me you'll be careful."

"Of course. I'm just going to the bookshop."

However, I soon found myself in a series of crises.

Dickens turned his nose up at the cooked bits of liver Frances gave him and demanded to go outside. At least he was meowing again. She was equally adamant that he was staying inside until he was better.

I discovered one of the publishers shorted us on the latest shipment of weekly magazines, requiring a long, frustrating telephone call to straighten out the matter.

And Lord Barnwood and Sir Broderick couldn't come to terms on the old prayer book I'd bought at a high price from Count Vicennes. With the two men bickering over terms while drinking myriad cups of tea, the phone didn't seem to stop ringing all morning.

I found myself with Lord Barnwood on the other end of the telephone line complaining, while in the background I could hear Sir Broderick saying, "She's going to agree with me." Frances was helping a customer when an old lady slowly toddled in the door.

A cold gust of air slid under my skirt and up my legs, making me glance over just as a multi-shaded brown ball of fur streaked out the open doorway. Frances saw him, too. "Go after him, Georgia. His feet still aren't healed. He can't be out there in this weather. It's supposed to sleet!"

"Oh, dear. I'll talk to you later," I said into the mouthpiece and hung up the phone. Grabbing my cloak, I rushed hatless and gloveless after Dickens.

The cold bit my cheeks immediately. Fortunately, the fog had dissipated into gloom in anticipation of the sleet. I spotted Dickens on the other side of the street. I dodged a wagon as I chased after him. At least my efforts kept me from shivering.

Dickens ran down a passageway between two buildings and I squeezed in, following without thinking about where the brick-sided passage would lead. My only concern was catching him and bringing him back to the bookshop before Frances gave us both a tongue-lashing.

When I reached the end of the passage, my shoes damp with leaves and bits of newsprint sticking to them, Dickens was two shops ahead of me, crouching on a puddle of ice in the alley and eyeing a plump mouse. At least he had stopped. My corset was pressing on my lungs and any air I could pull in froze in my throat.

I'd nearly sneaked up on him when Mrs. Foster, the baker's wife, came out of the back of her bakery with a pail, shouting, "Go away, you devil." She tossed the water, hitting me, Dickens, and the mouse.

The cold water soaked my hands and my skirt, leaving me shaking with chills and anger. Dickens tried to run, but one foot slid down into a crack between paving stones. I bent down over him and grabbed hold of his middle while trying to loosen his back foot, but the paving stones were frozen together and I couldn't get him free. "What do you think you're doing?" I snapped at her. "You soaked me in this freezing weather."

"Get that filthy cat away from here," she screamed at me.

"You're mad," I shouted. "You attacked me. If I catch pneumonia, I'll send the law after you."

"I'm sorry about that, but I can't abide cats. I've been trying to run him off for days and days, but he keeps coming back. Even cold water on a cold day like today won't keep him gone for long. Filthy animal."

"He's not filthy. He's a very clean animal, and he keeps down the vermin on our street. Vermin you seem to have in plenty. That mouse was huge. You probably have rats." Not a nice thing to shout at a baker, but I was chilled and furious.

I ended with, "Don't ever let me catch you throwing water on him again." My lofty tone was ruined by my position, outside without a hat or gloves like a common trollop, crouched down, clutching a struggling, scratching cat.

"Rats? I'll have you know I run a very clean shop. Keep that animal away from here." She went in and slammed the door.

I couldn't get Dickens's foot free. Icicles were forming on the ends of his fur and on my skirt. My hands and face hurt from the cold. The paving stones were frozen in place and wouldn't budge by a hair. I was bent over in an uncomfortable position, holding on to a wounded cat who didn't like me.

I sneezed and Dickens scratched me. I needed to get him back to the bookshop before we both froze in this shadowy alley.

Then the sleet started.

There was no one in the alley to help. My shouts brought no one outside. As much as I wanted to get under cover and out of the weather, I couldn't abandon Dickens, who was now meowing pitifully.

I'd rarely felt so alone.

CHAPTER SEVENTEEN

I heard the door open again and I looked up, shrinking back from the expected bucket of icy water.

Instead, young Mr. Foster came out and ran over to me, pulling his jacket up to cover his head from the sleet. "Are you all right, Miss Fenchurch?"

"Yes, but I can't free Dickens's foot."

He studied the situation for a moment. "You hold onto him good. I'll try to chip the stones apart." The young man pulled out his pocketknife and hacked at the ice between the frozen paving stones. In a minute, he was able to break the icy bond. He wedged a stone up and Dickens was free, despite ice hanging from his fur. He wiggled in my arms. I grabbed him by the scruff of the neck and around his middle and hung on.

"Thank you," I said, rising on stiffened legs. Dickens chose that moment to draw blood.

"I'm sorry about that. At least, Papa is improving and Mama will soon be free to stay at home where she'd rather be." He reached out and petted Dickens between the ears. "She's terrified of dogs and cats. She's sure they carry deadly diseases. I've never been allowed a pet." His last statement sounded wistful.

The traitor purred for the young man.

"I wish your father a speedy recovery. Thank you," I said, and he nodded to me.

I raced the hissing cat through the sleet back to the bookshop where Frances was waiting by the door, wringing her hands. "Oh, thank goodness. I was afraid he'd get away. Oh, you've got blood on your cloak."

"Dickens's feet. Or my hands. I know what's happened to him now." Asking the customers to browse for a moment, we went in the back, where I told her the story while we put salve on his feet.

"We'll have to keep him away from there," Frances said, finally letting him go.

"Good luck with that. They have the fattest mice on the street."

"No wonder, if Mrs. Foster can't stand cats. The place must be overrun."

Leaving Frances to feed Dickens the liver he'd turned his nose up at before, I went out to wait on customers and ignored the ringing telephone. By the time I'd finished with the second customer, Frances answered the telephone.

"Oh, hello, Lord Barnwood. How are you...? No, Georgia isn't available right now. We've had a bit of a crisis... Of course I'll have her call you at Sir Broderick's the moment she's free... No, we're not having a fire. Nothing so drastic as that... Good day to you, my lord."

She hung up the phone and gave me a triumphant smile.

"Thank you, Frances. That will give us peace for a few minutes."

Once the shop was empty of customers, I called Blackford House. Stevens, the duke's butler, answered and said, "His Grace is in a meeting right now. May I give him a message?"

"I was hoping to invite him to dinner at Sir Broderick's tonight if he's available."

"I'm sorry, Miss Fenchurch. I know His Grace is dining with some business associates tonight."

"Then perhaps ask him if he's available tomorrow night."

"If you'd care to wait for a reply?"

"Thank you, Stevens."

But it was Blackford, not Stevens, who came on the line a minute later. "Georgia, I'm sorry. I've been asked to Lord Thompson's tomorrow night, and Lord Cavendish's the night after. After being away so long, there are a number of people I need to see and arrangements to make. Until we announce our engagement, I can't impose on my hostesses to invite you, too."

"That's quite all right, Your Grace," I told him, remembering the beauty I'd seen who was Cavendish's daughter and wondering if Thompson also had a marriageable child. "Please let me know when your schedule can accommodate us."

"Georgia, I would love to have dinner with you. But I've just returned and—"

"Perhaps another time when your social calendar is less busy," slid out between my clenched teeth.

"Georgia! It's not like—"

"Good day, Your Grace."

I heard "Georgia!" before I hung up the telephone with a little more force than necessary.

As soon as I ended the call with Blackford, I was ashamed of my jealousy and furious at him for making plans that didn't leave room for assuaging my fears.

Frances walked over and said, "That didn't go well. Tell me what happened."

Fortunately the shop was empty, because I burst into tears. "Blackford asked me to marry him. I told him I had to think about it, because who'd believe Blackford would change his mind on the subject of who was aristocratic enough to marry a duke. I want to talk to him about it, but he's running around London with his blue-blooded social engagements every night."

"Oh, dear." Frances gave me a hug. "And you with an investigation and a young boy's life to worry about. And Lord Barnwood."

I laughed through my tears. "Oh, yes. Don't forget Lord Barnwood. I suppose I'll have to call him next and listen to his laments."

I picked up the phone and called Sir Broderick. When he answered, it was to say, "What's wrong?" with panic in his voice.

"Dickens escaped and I had to track him down. His foot was wedged between two frozen paving stones and we were hit by a bucket of water thrown at him by a neighbor and had to be rescued. Then we had to dress his wounds and deal with customers. I hope Lord Barnwood isn't too upset."

"He pictured a bigger catastrophe." Was that a chuckle I heard from the other end of the line?

"And Blackwood has dinner engagements the next three nights at least, so I can't talk to him." I nearly wailed my words.

"Then talk to him during the day. Leave Frances in charge and track Blackford down."

"I don't think he'd appreciate it."

"He might appreciate it a great deal."

I huffed out a sigh of aggravation. "I'll see you at dinner tonight. Let me know what you and Lord Barnwood decide."

"He's already left. We'll resume discussions when his desire for the book overcomes his willpower."

And while they debated, I was out the money I'd paid Count Vicennes. Just one more grievance in a day full of frustration.

More customers came in and we were busy for the next hour. Once the shop was empty again, I told Frances about Sir Henry's death. "And now that he's dead, I don't know how I'll get a good specimen of his handwriting. He might still have been Alice's lover."

"I'd hope you'd be more concerned about a police superintendent thinking you're the killer."

"I know I didn't do it. So there's no reason to worry."

"Georgia, I saw how many mistakes they made trying to find my husband's killer. Every case the Archivist Society has taken on is because Scotland Yard made an error. They may not have hanged the wrong person in any of our cases, but they've jailed a few. I don't want to see you go to jail."

I refused to show the fear her words stoked inside me, growing like a fire in my mind. "I don't want to go to jail, either. Now, we need to see something we know was written by Sir Henry to compare to Lady Hale's letters."

"You have a man's letters to her. But how do you know she reciprocated his affection?"

"I don't, except that she kept all the letters. She wouldn't have if she'd thought him a nuisance. There's also some neighborhood gossip linking them, at least as friends."

"Then I doubt he killed Alice." Frances began dusting as we talked.

I preferred to pace. "They were killed the same way in the same place. That argues for the same murderer. But what was the motive? Money? Fury on Sir Edward's part that his wife was cheating on him?"

"He was cheating on her with Mrs. Barrow. He'd hardly

kill her for that reason." Frances's tone was dry.

"Unless he wanted her out of the way so he could marry Mrs. Barrow as he's promised to do." I threw my hands in the air. "Which gives him no reason to kill Sir Henry. And I feel certain they were killed by the same hand."

"Perhaps Sir Henry had evidence Sir Edward killed his wife. Perhaps he saw him do it."

"Why would he have cause to go to Cheyne Walk first thing on a foggy morning?"

Frances smiled. "What if they were going to run away together? If Sir Edward beat him there, Sir Henry would have been in the perfect position to see the murder."

I nodded my agreement. Frances had a good theory. "We don't know where Sir Henry was that morning, and we don't know whether he'd decided to leave with Alice. I need to visit Lady Imogen again. And I believe I want to talk to Lady Moffatt. She's the most observant person in Lady Hale's neighborhood. Maybe she'll have some insight for me." I pulled on my cloak. "I'll try to be back by lunchtime."

I hurried past the Carstaire home. Because of the sleet, the straw on the walkway and street out front was frozen and crepe hung stiffly above the door. Lady Carstaire was following the customs for her husband that Sir Edward had refused to observe for his wife.

Fortunately, I found Lady Moffatt at home and more than willing to talk. I was shown into her morning room, where a merry fire was burning. After she ordered tea and the maid left, she said, "Two murders in the neighborhood, even if the killings didn't occur here. I wondered if you'd be back."

I decided a willingness to share information might help me get more. "Two neighbors killed in the same way and in the same place at a distance from their homes. It makes me wonder what these two people had in common."

"I can see why. Lady Hale and Lady Carstaire had known each other for nearly twenty years, since they shared their first season together. And then for the past nine years they've been neighbors." She made herself more comfortable in her chair before she continued.

"We're a friendly neighborhood. We visit each other over the holidays and stop to chat in the communal gardens in good weather. Alice helped with the flowers, although Lydia, I'm afraid to say, found neither the time nor the energy."

The maid entered with the tea, and for the next few minutes, we were occupied with such questions as "one lump or two?"

Once we were settled with our cups and saucers, I asked, "Did you see both families at parties during the most recent Christmas season?" That would have been only two months before.

"Oh, yes. Lady Hale and Sir Edward ignored each other at these affairs. That hasn't changed in years, but at Christmastime this year, I caught Lady Hale snapping at Sir Henry Carstaire any time they thought they'd managed a moment alone. Otherwise, she greeted anything he said with icy indifference."

"Her sharp words to him. Did this happen more than once?"

She gave me a knowing look. "And at more than one party."

"Did you hear what they were arguing about?"

"Alice said Sir Henry had promised, and now he was going back on his word. This was shortly after her father died, and Sir Henry answered that she was well provided for. She could do anything she wanted. She didn't need him."

Lady Moffatt raised her eyebrows as she said the last.

"I wonder what she asked him to do. She didn't need him as a barrister, did she?"

"Only if she sued Sir Edward for divorce, and they'd been so cold to each other for so long, everyone around here assumed they'd go on like that forever. So many couples do."

"What were Lady Hale and Sir Henry like together before this Christmas?"

Lady Moffatt took a sip of tea. "Thick as thieves for the past year. I'd see them on summer evenings strolling in the garden. Sir Edward didn't have time for such things, and Lydia always said her health was too frail to spend time out of doors. As if anyone would believe that.

"You'd see them, standing just a little too close and finding little reasons to touch. A leaf landing on a sleeve. An insect flying past. Then... no, it didn't necessarily have anything to do with Sir Henry."

"What didn't?" This sounded like juicy gossip, even if it wasn't helpful.

Lady Moffatt leaned forward and lowered her voice, although we were the only two in the room. "In midsummer, I saw Lady Hale getting into a hansom cab at the end of the street."

Ladies frequently caught cabs on the main street. "Was that something she did often?"

She nodded. "After that, I'd notice that twice a week, Alice would walk out by herself toward the end of the street at the same time each day. A few times, I had to go out right after she passed by. She always got into a hansom cab and rode away. And she always returned home on foot."

"What time did she go out?"

"Half past noon. And she'd return between three and

four. This would be on Mondays and Thursdays, when Sir Edward was most likely to be in Manchester at his factories."

"I wonder where she went." Knowing that might explain a lot about these murders.

"I have no idea. I thought it odd she didn't ride the hansom cab the whole way home. It wouldn't have cost her more money."

"Was she still leaving on Mondays and Thursdays until her death?"

"No. It stopped shortly after her father died. Early December, I believe." She blushed and took a sip of tea. "At least that was when I noticed."

And she seemed to have made a point of noticing. "You've been most helpful, Lady Moffatt. Is there any other detail you recall?"

"No. People do such strange things. I just hope that little Teddy is all right."

"He will be as soon as we discover who killed his mother so we can reunite him with whoever will be his guardian."

"His father or his aunt. It's hard to tell which would be better for him." Setting down her cup and saucer, Lady Moffatt added, "I can't see Sir Edward killing his wife. He just didn't seem to care about her anymore. And you must have to care a great deal to murder someone."

As I left her house, grateful the sleet had faded away to a mist, I thought about what Lady Moffatt had said. You had to care a great deal. That meant you had to truly hate the person you murdered. Or love someone still living. Someone you want to protect.

And that led me back to Sir Edward Hale, who loved his son and wanted to protect him from his mother. In which case, Sir Henry Carstaire was dead because he knew something about the first murder and had to be silenced.

Or Count and Countess Reinler, who could have been working together or separately to gain Lady Hale's half of her father's estate and pin the blame on Sir Edward, whom Prudence Reinler obviously hated.

There was no reason to think the countess knew Sir Henry or he knew her. Had I missed something? Time to find out. Lady Imogen and her friends would have to wait.

I arrived at Countess Reinler's home only slightly damp from the mist and gave my card to the butler. After a surprisingly long wait compared to my other calls on this household, I was shown into the morning room. The fire was dying in the grate. I guessed she wasn't expecting visitors this morning.

A moment later, the countess walked in. "You have news of my nephew? Or my sister's murderer?"

Behind her, I heard the laughter of a young boy. She quickly shut the door.

"Your son has returned? Then I'm sorry to interrupt your time with him."

Her smile was brilliant. "Yes, my husband arrived surprisingly early. He knows how upset I am about my sister's death. He and Dieter returned only an hour ago." Then her mouth sagged. "With a house guest. He brought back a fellow countryman."

"You are busy. I won't keep you long. You told me you and your sister were close. Did she tell you about a special friendship she had? A friendship with a man?"

She began to pace across the room. "Does it matter now?"

"Yes. Do you know the identity of this man?"

She stopped, looking away from me and speaking softly.

"He was a neighbor who was quite infatuated with her. I'm sure there can't be more than one of those."

"And his name?"

She faced me, watching me as her hands clenched in fists. "Surely you've already learned his name."

"Please. I need confirmation."

Her shoulders drooped as if the ability to fight had left her. "I suppose it can't hurt now. Sir Henry Carstaire."

"Were they planning to run away together?"

"They talked about it, but Sir Henry began to get cold feet. In the end, Alice was going to leave on her own with Teddy."

"So you knew about Lady Imogen Fielding."

"No. I thought she was coming here. I was as surprised as anyone when I learned where she and Teddy had been." She walked over to the fireplace and put both hands on the mantel. "Did Sir Henry kill her?"

"Sir Henry Carstaire has been murdered in much the same way, and in the same place, as Lady Hale."

She swung around, a horrified look on her face. "Another murder?"

"Yes."

"Some madman must be lurking by the river."

"A very clever madman. A note was found in Sir Henry's pocket, asking him for a meeting at that location. The note was supposedly signed by me. I received a note asking the same thing, supposedly signed by Sir Henry. I've seen the note I supposedly wrote. The handwriting was nothing like mine. However, his killer must have been aware that I wanted to speak to him about your sister's murder."

We stared at each other as her jaw worked. Finally, she made her voice heard as she said, "You might have been marked for murder as well."

"I suppose so." I made the comment as offhand as I could, but inside, her words made me tremble. I might still be a target of the murderer. Adding this to my questions about the duke's proposal and the superintendent's idea that I was the killer, I doubted I would sleep a wink again that night.

I was certain Prudence Reinler had more she could tell me. "Would Sir Henry have gained in any way from your sister's death?"

"Not that I know of. She didn't leave him anything in her will. I know she gave him the house where they used to meet, but she did that when they broke off the affair."

"She gave him a house? What house?" I found it astounding. Why give something so valuable to a man with whom she'd just ended a relationship?

"It's a small house that served as a home in retirement to our old nurse. She died last spring and Papa gave the house to Alice. It's in a rundown area and contains old furnishings. The value of the building and furnishings isn't very much, and Alice said she had other reasons to give it to him."

"What reasons?" Was he blackmailing her?

"She told me she'd always be embarrassed seeing the house or the rents or anything to do with it." The countess began to pace again, studying the thick, patterned carpet. "It would remind her of a mistake she made. An error of judgment regarding another person's character."

"So she didn't give it to him in exchange for his silence about their relationship?"

Prudence gave a vague gesture. "It's possible. She felt Sir Henry had used her shamelessly, so he might as well be burdened by something tangible from the relationship. Something he might have to explain." Then, almost as if she were speaking to herself, she said, "She had."

I heard her whispered words. "What had she gained?" Jewelry, I guessed, or another property.

The countess gasped, then blushed and walked away from me. "What? No. She gained nothing but worry and heartache."

Lady Hale had gained something in return. Some physical item. Something I knew nothing about yet. I had to discover what Prudence Reinler was hiding. "Countess. You must tell me. This could have some bearing on her death."

She loosed a deep sigh. "I suppose it can't hurt to tell you now. Although I'm surprised it didn't come out at her autopsy."

Didn't come out...oh, dear Lord. I lowered my voice. "She was carrying a child. Sir Henry's child."

The woman nodded.

CHAPTER EIGHTEEN

I had to swallow a gasp before I could speak. "Depending on the coroner, they might not have gone much further than the obviously deadly knife wound to her heart. Time needed for other work, respect for her position in society, laziness. Your sister's secret went to her grave with her. How far along was she?"

Prudence Reinler sighed before she answered. "Four months. Possibly a little more. It would have been noticeable soon."

"Surely she could have passed it off as her husband's."

"Oh, you are an innocent, Miss Fenchurch." She emphasized the "miss." "Sir Edward and my sister would have needed to have marital relations for that. That hadn't happened in years. But it would have given Sir Edward grounds to throw her out, divorce her on grounds of adultery and take Teddy away from her. My sister couldn't have lived with that."

The shame and humiliation would have undone any woman. Society would cut her dead. Her son would be lost to her forever. "So her solution was to leave?"

"Yes. There was nothing else to do. Her life here would be in ruins. Completely destroyed. I told her I'd help her in any way I could."

"But she found Lady Imogen and her network."

"Apparently so. She didn't tell me, but I think that was so

I could be genuinely surprised when she disappeared." She gave me a weak smile. "Is there anything else you want to know? Any other secrets you want revealed?"

"Are there any more?" It was a brutal comment, but knowing all this earlier might have saved Sir Henry's life.

"No. And now I think you should leave."

"I won't share your sister's secret outside the members of the Archivist Society working to find your sister's killer," I assured her.

She grabbed hold of my arm before I could walk out of the room and looked at me through wet eyes. "You can't tell anyone. No one at all."

I patted the hand that gripped me. "I have to. You must see that. This is the reason she had to leave and may be the reason she was murdered. There's no way to gain justice for your sister if I keep this to myself."

"Oh, please. Her reputation—"

Her sister was murdered and the countess could only think of her reputation? I tempered my response as best I could. "Won't suffer in her social circles. The Archivist Society deals in facts, not in gossip. This is crucial for finding her killer. You do want her murderer caught and punished, don't you?"

She nodded and let go of my arm.

I was nearly at the front door when two men and a boy appeared on the stairs. I froze with what must have been a look of horror when I realized I recognized them all.

Dieter and his father were in the photograph I'd been shown by the countess. The other man, their houseguest, was Count Farkas. Also known as Mr. Wolf.

My parents' killer.

Their murderer was back in London. My breath became

rapid and my pulse banged in my ears. I swallowed down bile and hoped I wouldn't get sick on the countess's richly colored carpet. Farkas stared into my eyes, and for a moment, I thought I would faint before I steeled myself for the encounter.

He couldn't have returned just to torment me.

He walked to the bottom of the steps where he gave me a small bow. "My dear Miss Fenchurch. So nice to see you again."

"It would be nice to see you hang," I replied. My cheeks were hot. My vision narrowed until all I saw was the murderer.

I heard someone gasp. I suspected it was Countess Reinler.

"It was an unfortunate accident," Farkas said smoothly. He could just as easily have been discussing a rip in the carpet.

"It wasn't an accident. You tied them to chairs and set the building on fire."

"You could have rescued them. The outcome was your failure."

In an instant I was seventeen again. A seventeen-year-old who hadn't saved her parents. I could feel the flames and smell the burning wood. "I couldn't. The roof collapsed." I realized my voice was little more than a whisper.

"You lost your parents and I lost possession of my Gutenberg Bible. We both suffered." He sounded as if his loss of a book was equal to the deaths of two people and the terrible injuries to Sir Broderick. He showed no remorse.

With cold fury in my voice, I said, "Good. I hope you never hold your Bible again, since I can never hold my parents." Then it hit me. There could only be one reason why

Count Farkas had returned. I took a step backward to put more space between us as I asked in a suspicious tone, "What brings you to London?"

"I am enjoying a visit with my friend and countryman."

I didn't believe him. The look passing between the count and countess told me otherwise. "You're on the hunt for your Gutenberg."

He smiled. "I'm always on a hunt for my Bible."

"You think it's here in London." I didn't phrase it as a question. I was sure he'd returned on his quest.

His smile widened. "I now believe I know who Lupton sold it to. With your father's connivance."

"Who?" I believed Count Farkas would kill this unknown buyer in his hunt for the Gutenberg Bible. He'd killed my parents and a fellow bookshop owner named Denis Lupton within days of each other, certain they'd hidden his possession. My parents had nothing to do with the theft, but that made no difference to their killer. In the years since, he'd left a trail of bodies across the globe, from South Africa to the Americas to Europe.

Someone needed to be warned of the danger to his life.

"Ah, that does not concern you, Miss Fenchurch." His tone was still cordial. Refined. But his expression was deadly.

"I believe you've finished your conversation with my wife," Count Reinler said, glancing at his wife as he stepped forward to block the space between Count Farkas and me. "Good afternoon."

"Good afternoon." I gave him a curtsy, then turned to his wife. She stood to one side, keeping a protective arm around a boy of about ten. Her lips trembled below frightened eyes. Again I curtsied. "Good afternoon, Lady Reinler. Thank you for your assistance."

Ignoring Count Farkas, I turned and glanced at the butler who quickly opened the door. I escaped into the cold morning air and the damp wind blowing between the tall, elegant houses, not stopping to take a deep breath until I reached the corner.

I needed to talk to the Archivist Society. And I needed to see Blackford.

I returned to the bookshop, for once relieved that it was empty of customers. As Frances put on her coat and hat to leave for lunch, I went straight to the counter and picked up the receiver. In a moment, I was put through to Sir Broderick. I asked him to call an emergency meeting of the Archivist Society for that night.

Frances heard my words, nodded, and waved as she walked out the door.

Then I called Blackford's, where the phone was answered by Stevens, his butler.

"This is Georgia Fenchurch. Is His Grace in?"

"No, miss. He had business to attend to this afternoon."

"When he returns, will you tell him there's an Archivist Society meeting tonight? It's extremely important."

"I will, miss. And may I ask if you'll be continuing with the Archivist Society when you become mistress here?"

His words stabbed me in the heart. My dream to be mistress of Blackford House seemed ever more unlikely. "If I become mistress there, then yes."

"Very good, miss."

I hung up, unsure how Stevens and the rest of the staff felt about the possibility of gaining me, a middle-class bookshop owner and part-time sleuth, as mistress. I couldn't imagine making much of a difference in their lives. At least not as big a difference as they would make in mine.

The bell jingled over the door. I looked up, expecting to see a customer. Instead, I found Superintendent Marcum staring at me.

"Miss Fenchurch, I was hoping to find you alone."

"Then you'd better make it quick. One never knows when a customer will come in."

My warning appeared to be lost on him when he strode forward. "I want you to understand that if you killed Sir Henry, the protection of someone as powerful as the Duke of Blackford won't do you any good."

If my gaze could shoot bullets, the superintendent would be a bloody corpse on my bookshop floor. "If I had killed Sir Henry, Blackford wouldn't protect me. He believes in justice as much as I do."

He stood across the counter from me, glaring into my eyes. "If you believe in justice, then confess."

I was tempted to tell him what I'd learned about Lady Hale's delicate condition, but decided the information would be lost on him. The Archivist Society would be able to use the news to find the killer, so I kept my lips firmly sealed and my gaze steady.

"Come, come, Miss Fenchurch. We know you were there. We know how easily you could have faked your handwriting on both notes. It would have been the work of a moment to drop the murder weapon into the Thames. But it must have been a shock to have your fiancé appear out of the mists like that. Ruined your plans, did he?"

I summoned up my imitation of regal bearing. "Why would I have killed Sir Henry Carstaire?"

"We know you've been hounding him at his office and at home. You've been annoying his wife. You even surprised him in the cemetery after a funeral."

How on earth had the police learned about that? Perhaps Mr. Howard or Sir Bernard Hill saw me come out from behind a mausoleum. "I was trying to ask him about his relationship with Lady Hale."

"Were you jealous of her friendship with Sir Henry? And why were you using an alias while you followed Sir Henry around the city?"

The police had learned about that, too. There was no point in explaining how the Archivist Society worked. I'd only sound more guilty.

And he didn't like the interference of amateurs.

All I could manage was a denial. "You're wrong, superintendent. Wrong. I didn't kill..."

The shop bell rang, and a muffled-up, middle-aged woman walked in. She stopped and waited in silence, looking from the policeman to me and back again. She must have thought him a customer.

I turned away from him and said to the woman, "May I help you?"

"Are you sure I'm not interrupting?"

"He was just leaving. Now, what can I do for you?"

The superintendent slammed his hat on his head and stomped out of the shop.

DINNER DRAGGED on forever at Sir Broderick's that night. At least, I thought so. The clock never moved. But Mrs. Hardwick commented on how rushed dinner felt, and Sir Broderick and Jacob were unusually quiet, watching me while trying not to appear so.

I kept thinking about my conversation with Lady Imogen. Even after I bluntly told her what Countess Reinler told me, she denied any knowledge of Lady Hale's condition.

Finally I'd lost my temper and told her two people had died because of this secret and asked if she wanted any more blood on her hands. Only then did she admit the truth. Lady Hale had told her about the baby, about Sir Henry Carstaire, about everything. She'd known all along.

Keeping this secret inside me made me terrible company at the dinner table. How had Lady Imogen and Countess Reinler kept Alice's secret so serenely?

Finally, dinner was over and I hurried into the parlor. No one had arrived yet. I refused to admit to myself that I was waiting for one special guest. I paced back and forth while Dominique brought up tea and biscuits and Mrs. Hardwick set up the tea service. They moved around me, trying not to acknowledge I kept getting in their way.

"Are you planning to wear a path in the rug?" Sir Broderick asked as I nearly collided with him for the second time.

"I'm sorry."

"You must have big news, Georgia," Jacob said.

"It's the key to this investigation. It must be."

"She's been saying that all afternoon and pacing around the bookshop. That is, when she wasn't running off to see Lady Imogen Fielding," Frances said as she came in the parlor. "Oh, good, Dominique's biscuits."

Adam Fogarty and Grace Yates were the last to arrive. Once everyone settled in, I felt all eyes watching me, waiting for my news.

And still Blackford hadn't arrived.

Well, I supposed I deserved that, not immediately saying "Yes" to his proposal and taking a giant leap into the future, heart first. Still, it hurt.

I wanted to be sure of the duke's feelings. I wondered if

he was certain of them and didn't see any reason to discuss them once he'd made up his mind. The duke never seemed to have doubts. Never in all the time I'd known him.

With something as momentous as his proposal, I had nothing but doubts. I craved the security he'd give me, but I feared it was an illusion.

I stopped pacing and faced the room. The expectant faces staring at me brought me back to the reason they were all here. After a deep breath, I said, "Lady Hale was carrying a child by Sir Henry Carstaire. One she could not possibly pass off as her husband's."

Murmurs and exclamations circled the room, led by Sir Broderick saying, "Why wasn't it found during the autopsy?"

"That is a question for Scotland Yard. I discovered this from one source today, and then had it confirmed by another. Two different women that Lady Hale confided in."

"How long?" Grace asked.

"Four months. At least."

"That was why you ran off to Lady Imogen Fielding's this afternoon," Frances said, "but where did you learn it this morning? From Lady Carstaire?"

"No, I haven't spoken to her. Alice's sister finally admitted it."

"I can see why she had to disappear now, since it would soon be obvious that she was carrying a child. Her husband would certainly know if it wasn't his," Fogarty said.

"And he could have legally taken her son Teddy away from her when he divorced her as an adulteress. Alice didn't sound like the type of mother who would easily give up her son," Frances said, shaking her head.

"Hiding until she could get out of the country with the money from her properties to start a new life for herself and both of her children. Well," Sir Broderick said, head bent, "we understand why she did what she did. But I don't see where it gets us any closer to her murderer."

"We can rule out Sir Henry. I believe he was killed by the same person who murdered Alice. We can rule out Sir Edward. He didn't need to kill his wife, provided he knew why she'd run off. And in talking to her sister, I just can't believe she'd kill Alice." I started to pace again.

"Then who did?" Grace asked. "You ruled out the governess, Miss Forbes."

"I don't know. I've run out of suspects." The words died on my lips as I looked over to see the door open.

Blackford appeared, his evening suit as dark as his eyes and his cravat and collar as white as newly blown snow. He strode in, bringing with him enough cold air from outside and his own dominating energy to fill the space. "I can't believe you've run out of suspects, Georgia."

My heart banged in my chest loud enough to be heard across the room. When I caught my breath, I replied, "I have, Your Grace. Sir Edward didn't care enough to have killed Alice if he didn't know about the babe she carried, and he'd have been elated if he did know. The courts would grant him full custody of Teddy and a divorce from his adulterous wife."

I caught myself staring at him and glanced away. "I don't think Count and Countess Reinler need money so badly that the countess would kill her own sister. If Sir Henry wrote the love letters, he's been killed, probably by the same murderer."

"I brought a sample of Sir Henry's handwriting with me." Blackford smiled as he walked toward me, holding out a note on thick, white paper.

"How did you come by this, Your Grace?" Sir Broderick

asked.

"A business associate of mine was involved in a lawsuit. Sir Henry was representing one side before the court and required my testimony. He sent me a note giving me the date and time." He gave me an apologetic smile. "I'd forgotten I had this until I asked my business secretary about possible samples of Sir Henry's handwriting."

"Let me go get the letters." New energy at this good news sped my feet up the stairs to my room. I collected all the letters associated with this case from where I'd stored them in a drawer. Then I checked my reflection in the looking glass, re-pinned an errant lock of hair, and hurried back down.

When I returned to the parlor, Blackford stood in the same place as he'd been when I left. "Here's one, Ranleigh. Tell me what you think."

He took the letter with a broad smile just as I realized I'd once again called him by his surname, not his title or "Your Grace." While not exactly a declaration of intent, he must have seen which way my thoughts were leaning.

"I'm not an expert, but I'd say these were written by the same man." He handed both letters to me.

"I agree." I handed them to Sir Broderick.

Then I looked at Blackford and smiled. This is what I wanted: to be working with him, to watch thoughts cross his face, to hear him make connections and solve problems.

"How would anyone know Sir Henry was the father, even if they knew Lady Hale was carrying a child?" Fogarty asked.

"I'd bet anything Lady Carstaire knows plenty about this. She was his wife, after all. And they usually know when something's up. Even if they don't want to know," Frances said.

The room grew still. I looked at Frances, eyes and mouth open in shock. A woman stab two people to death and toss their bodies into the Thames? Well, not Sir Henry's. His was caught on the rail. He'd have been heavier than Alice. Too heavy for fragile Lady Carstaire to handle. "Oh, she wouldn't have. Would she?"

"Why not?" Blackford asked. "Women are capable of most things. I've learned that from you."

His hard stare made me wonder why he was angry with me. All I wanted was some of his time to pose my questions to him about his change of heart. "Thank you, I think. We are talking about a murderess."

"If Lady Carstaire did it, she certainly had the best motive of all. Her husband was having an affair with another woman, had gotten her with child, and might be leaving with her. An abandoned wife. Think of the scandal," Sir Broderick said.

"She's very conscious of appearances. I noticed that the first time I spoke to her," I said. I opened the threatening note Alice had received and something about the handwriting struck me.

"Wait a moment." I pictured the letter I'd received supposedly written by Sir Henry. I believed the handwriting matched Alice's frightening letter.

I passed it to Blackford, who handed it to Sir Broderick. "We can be sure the person who threatened Lady Hale sent the messages to you and Sir Henry to meet on Cheyne Walk, but how do we prove it was Lady Carstaire? No one saw anything," Sir Broderick said.

"I wonder if she was the one I heard following me on Cheyne Walk?" I said and looked at Blackford. "Those certainly weren't your footsteps. I'd know them anywhere."

"Georgia, are you planning to do what I think you're going to do?" Blackford asked.

"Of course. I'll send her a note and when she sets up a meeting, you can rescue me before she stabs me through the heart." I gave him a confident smile.

"It's a terrible idea." Blackford strode away from me.

"We need to involve Inspector Grantham," Fogarty said.

"Of course. The more, the merrier." I smiled at Blackford's back, wishing he'd look at me.

"Perhaps we should invite Superintendent Marcum. He's convinced you're the murderer," Blackford said, still facing away from me.

I wouldn't admit that Marcum had visited me at the shop. His accusations still annoyed me. More than that, they frightened me. Fogarty had said he had a reputation of being tenacious, whether he was right or wrong. "He won't think I'm the murderer if Lady Carstaire takes our bait."

Blackford spun around then to face me. "What if she doesn't, Georgia? You'll look guiltier than ever, not to mention ridiculous."

We stared at each other as I pictured my chances to become Duchess of Blackford slipping through my fingers. I had no idea what he was thinking, but the deep black of his eyes told me he was not happy.

"What are you going to say in the note?" Sir Broderick asked, looking from one of us to the other.

"I'm going to say there was a break in the fog and I saw her stab her husband. As it is, I may have heard her stab him, but I can't be certain. I'll tell her that either she goes to the police and confesses, or I'll go to them and tell them what I know."

"You'll immediately become a target of her insanity,"

Blackford said. His eyes pinned me in place, but the fury in them was gone. Instead, I saw fear.

"She's not mad. She's sane and calculating and evil." I shivered despite the heat from the fire that Sir Broderick kept burning, winter and summer.

"When will you send the letter?" Fogarty asked.

"Tomorrow, first post."

"I'll go around and see Grantham in the morning. Tell him what we know and what we plan."

I was glad to hear Fogarty say "we."

"Don't go out alone once you send the letter," Sir Broderick said. "Jacob, would you escort Georgia to and from the bookshop until this is finished?"

"Of course."

"Then I don't think there's anything else we need to do tonight. Thank you everyone for coming." Sir Broderick nodded to the group. "Your Grace, if you'd wait a moment."

Once it was just the three of us in the parlor, I said, "I saw Count Farkas today. He's a houseguest of Countess Reinler. And I think he has a new idea about where his Gutenberg Bible is. He said he suspects he knows who Lupton sold it to. And I believe that person is here in London."

"Just what we need at this moment," Sir Broderick said, smacking the armrests on his wheeled chair.

"He saw you? He spoke to you?" Blackford asked.

"Yes. We spoke. He still claims my parents' deaths were an accident that I was to blame for." I walked closer to the fire in hope of getting warm. Rubbing my hands together, I tried to drive the cold from my soul.

"They weren't, Georgia. Everything that happened was his fault," Sir Broderick told me.

"I know that, but he doesn't believe it. The loss of his

Bible is all he cares about." I swung around to face the two men. "I wonder who took that Bible originally and where it is now."

Sir Broderick glanced down at his legs and then gave me a level look. "We may never know. But it's not our problem at the moment. We have another killer to stop first."

"Sir Broderick, would you excuse Blackford and me while we talk?" I needed to have a frank discussion with the duke over his change of heart and how long it would last. I would have a terrible battle ahead of me trying to be accepted into aristocratic society. If I had to struggle to keep Blackford on my side, I'd never survive.

"I can't tonight, Georgia. I came over between engagements. We'll talk later. And I'll be glad to drop in from time to time to check on your welfare. Good night." Blackford bowed to Sir Broderick and then lifted my hand to his lips.

His skin touching mine warmed me more than the fire. His heated gaze held me in place as he lowered my hand but held on to it.

"I look forward to seeing you again, Ranleigh. We have a lot to discuss. Our engagement, to begin with." I squeezed his hand, wishing I could ask him the questions that still kept me in doubt. Ignoring Sir Broderick's presence, I blurted out, "I need to talk to you now more than ever. This decision will affect the rest of our lives."

He spoke quietly. "We will talk. Soon." Then he whispered, "I love you," into my ear before dropping my hand and striding out of the room.

CHAPTER NINETEEN

AS soon as Blackford left the room, I dropped heavily onto a chair. "Oh, Sir Broderick, we need to talk."

"About Count Farkas?"

"No. Blackford and I need to talk about what he asked me."

He bit back a smile. "I'm afraid I can't help you there."

"No one can except Blackford. I suppose I'll have to wait until he's less busy and I've led the police to a killer." With a sigh, I rose and went up to my room.

It was another night spent tossing in my bed. Every time I fell asleep, I dreamed I was in a ballroom in a daytime dress while all around me, fabulously dressed peers were laughing at me. And when I turned to Sir Broderick, Emma, Grace, Sumner and Jacob, they talked to each other and ignored me. Blackford was nowhere to be found.

I rose early and penned the note to Lady Carstaire before breakfast. When Sir Broderick came down to eat, he found the letter at his usual place at the table next to the roaring fire. He looked it over and said, "Yes, that should get her attention. You can mail it on your way to the bookshop with Jacob."

"He doesn't need to walk with me this morning." Lady Carstaire couldn't possibly know what we'd discovered.

"Nevertheless, this will be good practice for you. You're not always the most cautious of people."

Jacob came in the dining room and said, "You may not be cautious, but I've never known you to stick your neck out like this. It's going to take courage, Georgia."

Or insanity, I added silently. "I know," I told his back as he helped himself to breakfast. Suddenly, my eggs and toast didn't look appealing as my appetite fled. "Lady Carstaire stabbed two people in the heart while looking into their faces. One of them was her husband. How could she do that?"

"She's mad," Jacob said.

"No, I don't think so."

"Hatred," Mrs. Hardwick said, "can drive a person mad."

We finished breakfast in silence before Jacob walked me to Fenchurch's Books. I mailed the letter in the box we passed on Oxford Street.

Frances soon noticed I was clumsy and preoccupied after I knocked over the same display twice. "You've mailed the letter?" she asked.

I nodded.

We had to wait until mid-afternoon for a reply. I was on the telephone with Sir Broderick and Lord Barnwood, listening to them bicker over the price for the prayer book when the post came. Frances took it from our postman and glanced through the envelopes. Then she hurried toward me, waving one in the air.

"Hold on a moment." I set down the receiver, Lord Barnwood's voice coming through faintly as I ripped open the envelope.

The note read:

> *Dear Miss Fenchurch,*
> *You must be mistaken. I didn't kill my husband.*
> *I've not been near Cheyne Walk this winter, my*
> *health being ever so fragile. Do not repeat*

*these accusations to anyone or I shall have to
contact my solicitor.*
Lady Lydia Carstaire

"Everyone keeps saying her health is frail, but is it?" I asked.

"You don't trust her," Frances said.

"She killed two people and she knows I know. No, I don't trust her. I don't dare." I picked up the phone to discover Lord Barnwood was still talking. He must not have realized I hadn't been on the line for the past minute or two. "My lord, would you put Sir Broderick on?"

"Of course." The glee in his voice made me guess he thought I was in agreement with whatever he'd been rambling on about.

"You've heard from her?" Sir Broderick said a moment later.

"Yes. She denies everything and says if I repeat this to anyone, she'll call her solicitor. She uses her frail health as a defense."

"We need to find out if anyone in the neighborhood saw her out and about on either of the days in question. Not you, Georgia. She knows you. I'll have Lord Barnwood send Grace over and you can fill her in on what we need."

"Yes, sir. Tell him he gets an extra discount for loaning us Grace's services." I couldn't help but smile when I spoke. Lord Barnwood would be willing to have Grace participate in this investigation for weeks if it meant a good discount on his antiquarian purchases.

Grace arrived a few minutes later, smiling broadly. "You'd have thought Christmas arrived again when Sir Broderick repeated what you said about Lord Barnwood getting a special discount for giving me time off to investigate."

"I just hope Sir Broderick doesn't give away that prayer book."

"It must have cost you a fortune. It's beautiful," Grace said. When I nodded, she asked, "Now, what is it you need me to do?"

"Go to the Carstaire neighborhood. See if you can talk to any of the servants on the street about seeing Lady Carstaire out two days ago, particularly in the afternoon. She keeps claiming to be frail, so they might have remarked on seeing her out in cold, foggy weather. Also, ask Lady Moffatt. She seems very happy to tell us what she's seen, and she notices a great deal."

"And if I meet the Carstaires' servants?"

"With the death of the master two days ago, they may not be allowed out. And if you do talk to any of them, be very careful how you ask your questions."

"I always am. And Georgia, you'd better be careful." She gave me a grin and left the bookshop.

The afternoon grew increasingly gloomy and night fell early along with a new snowfall. "Be careful how you go," I told Frances as she bundled up to face her trip home.

"Those flakes are so big and fat, it won't stick. We used to say that's the kind of snow you get when spring arrives."

I looked out to see the snow melting into slush and puddles around the street lamps. "I hope so. I'm ready for spring."

I didn't have too long to wait after closing time for Jacob to arrive. We locked up the shop and walked home to Sir Broderick's.

Thankfully, no one came after either of us with a knife.

We'd just entered Sir Broderick's home when he shouted

from the study. We both ran upstairs, still in our coats, to find him holding the phone and looking pale.

"What's wrong?"

He waved the receiver. "This is Lord Barnwood. Someone is trying to break into his home and he's there alone."

"Where are his servants?"

"Grace and the couple who keep house for him all live out."

Jacob crossed the room toward the telephone. "Hang up and call the police."

"He doesn't want me to break the connection. He says he's frightened."

"It's not far," I said, rushing down the stairs. "Come on, Jacob. We'll find a bobby on the main road."

Humphries nimbly jumped out of my way as he yanked open the door. I ran out and down the pavement, hearing Jacob's faster footsteps gaining on me as I tried not to slip.

I was gasping in short breaths of cold air by the time I reached Lord Barnwood's street. Jacob and the constable both had longer strides and so had arrived ahead of me.

Lord Barnwood's house stood alone, a reminder of earlier days in London, with a side street on one side and an untamed jungle of a garden on the other. It looked dark, cold, and forbidding on this snowy night.

Jacob came to a stop on the slushy pavement in front of the house. "Do you think he left? The house looks empty."

"If he was so frightened he wouldn't hang up the phone, he'd be too scared to move." I hurried past Jacob and banged on the door with my fist. When that didn't get me any response, I tried the doorknob.

It turned in my hand and the door swung open, showing

the damage from being forced. I stood on the stoop and peered into the gloom.

"We can't enter, miss," the constable said.

"Look at the doorjamb. It's splintered here. Someone broke open the lock." Jacob said.

"This is Lord Barnwood's house. He called Sir Broderick duVene and said he was being attacked in his home. Jacob and I will go inside. You can wait here if you want. We'll call you when we find him." I marched about ten feet into the house and stopped. I really didn't want to go any further without a bright light and the support of the police.

Jacob walked past me, an oil lamp from the table by the door in his hand. "Which way, do you think? Down the hall or upstairs?"

"The entrance to his library is at the end of the hall. It takes up both floors of the entire back of the house. It's his refuge. He'd have gone there if he were afraid of a burglar."

Jacob lit the lamp and led the way as I followed him.

We were nearly at the door when we heard a crash. Jacob grabbed the doorknob and found it refused to turn. I faced the front door, waved my arms, and yelled, "Constable, we can hear a fight in this room, but the door is locked."

He blew his whistle three times and then came in.

"Hold the lamp, Georgia," Jacob said as he took three steps and slammed his shoulder against the door. It held. "Help me, constable."

They tried twice, but the door lock held. More crashing and shouting could be heard inside.

"It must be bolted," the constable said.

I coughed and looked down. Smoke was slithering out from under the door.

"Smoke!" I shouted and pointed at the floor. Gray fog

rolled up around our knees. Already I could smell the acrid stench of leather bindings burning. "The library's on fire!"

Count Farkas was in town and now there was another fire. I failed my parents. I couldn't fail Lord Barnwood.

"Oh, dear," the bobby said and rushed outside, blowing his whistle frantically. I heard him talking to someone and then footsteps running away.

"Do you have your lock picking tools with you?" I asked Jacob. "We have to get in there."

"No. I'd have used them already instead of hurting my shoulder," Jacob snapped back.

I deserved his annoyance, but I needed to find a way in. I ran to the next doorway along the hall that led back to the front door. Opening the door, I found there was no entrance to the library, but there was a fireplace with the usual tools for maintaining a fire. I grabbed the poker and rejoined Jacob. "Let's try to pry it open."

With both of us pushing on the poker handle and the damage Jacob had already done to the lock with his shoulder, we finally sprung the door open. I still had the poker in my hand as we stared in shock at the mayhem before us.

Part of the library was alight from a broken lantern on the floor by a bookcase. The burning oil had apparently splashed on old books, which immediately caught fire, spreading the conflagration. Lord Barnwood lay sprawled in the middle of the room on a rug that was smoldering on its far side. Count Farkas was tossing books aside as he searched the bookshelves on the library balcony.

I ran to Lord Barnwood and immediately saw the bloody gash on his bald head. Waving to Jacob through the wispy smoke, I shouted, "Help me get him out of here."

Jacob, one eye on Farkas, came over and picked up Lord

Barnwood by the shoulders. The old man groaned and I said a silent thank you. He was still alive. I tossed the poker aside and grabbed his feet. We struggled under the weight, but we finally reached the door and got into the hallway.

Two constables were in the hall and one helped Jacob take Lord Barnwood to the front door. I grabbed the other one by the sleeve. "The library's on fire—"

"We've called the fire brigade, miss."

"And Count Farkas is tearing the room apart. He's looking for one particular book he thinks was stolen from him."

The bobby gave me a puzzled look but said, "You get out, miss. He'll have to leave. The building might burn down at any moment."

He swung the door open and marched in. I peeked in to see where Count Farkas was and whether he now held his Gutenberg Bible. The bobby was a few feet into the room, moving cautiously as he stared at the flames and keeping one sleeve pressed over his nose and mouth. Suddenly, I saw the poker I'd dropped swing around and hit the bobby in the back of the head.

Even with his helmet, the young man went down like a rock.

"No," I screamed and ran in toward where I knew Count Farkas must be standing, hidden behind a bookcase. "Take your Bible and get out, but don't hurt anyone else."

Farkas gripped my arms. "I can't find it. Barnwood told me he has it in here, up on the balcony, but he wouldn't say..." He doubled over coughing. Soot and sweat poured down his cheeks from the heat of the flames. The air was thick with sparks and embers.

I could hear the clang of the fire brigade outside. Soon

water would be pouring over the library from their hoses, but I doubted in time to save anything. I tried to pull away. "Let me get the bobby out while you look."

He held on to me. "No. You know where it is. You're going to get it for me."

I struggled, but I couldn't get free of his grip. Panic made me fight. I didn't want to die in a fire like my parents had. Coughing, I said, "I haven't been in this library in years. Let me go."

"You know where his secret hiding place is."

He sounded so certain that I was sure Lord Barnwood told him Sir Broderick, Grace, and I all knew the location of his fire- and theft-resistant book safe. "We can't reach it. It's up on the balcony. It'll collapse into the fire." My voice came in gasps.

"Show me." While my strength ebbed in the heat, Count Farkas seemed to gain energy from the fire. With superhuman effort, he dragged me forward, pushed me up the circular steps ahead of him and then along the balcony. I fought every step, afraid of the fire and horrified by what he'd done to my parents. I might as well try to hold back the wind. I couldn't stop his relentless progress as he shoved me along.

The heat was trapped under the library roof and books were beginning to char from the high temperatures. Flames were licking up the shelves on the lower level, fed by burning antiquarian books printed on tinder-dry paper. My throat stung from the smoke and my eyes watered until I could barely breathe or see.

"It's there." I coughed. "Behind the painting."

Count Farkas pulled the painting of a girl reading a book, created by an Italian master, and tossed it down onto the flames. Fire whooshed up from the canvas. Another bookcase erupted in flames.

Behind where the painting had been was a good-sized safe. The heat from the fire would destroy anything inside, even if the fire never reached the books. "What's the combination?" he demanded.

Helping would be the fastest way out of this inferno. "Shakespeare's birth," cough, "year."

"What?" He yanked me closer to the front of the safe. Sweat was pouring down my face and my hairdo, never willing to stay up properly, hung over my shoulders.

"Fifteen - six - four. I think that's right."

"Do it." Then he began to cough, gripping my arm tighter and smashing me hard against the safe.

The metal singed my chest through the fabric of my dress and shift. I cried out and jumped away. Soon no one would be able to touch the safe.

"Open it!"

I couldn't escape his painful grip on my shoulder. Drawing my hand inside my dress sleeve, I turned the lock with shaking hands. Even with the wool fabric for protection, I jerked away as the dial burned my fingertips. If this didn't work, I would die. Without telling Blackford my answer.

It suddenly became incredibly important to give Farkas his Bible. To help the man who killed my parents. That was the only way to get what I wanted. Out of here alive. Married to Gordon Ranleigh, Duke of Blackford.

The safe door swung open and I breathed a sigh of relief. I realized my mistake as I doubled over, coughing uncontrollably as I tried to rid my lungs of smoke. The heat on this upper level was singeing my face and the inside of my throat.

The count pushed me aside to reach inside the metal box. As he pulled out his Gutenberg Bible, other, smaller treasures fell on the weakened floor and began to shrivel. The ancient prayer book Lord Barnwood had just purchased was among the volumes.

These were Barnwood's prized possessions. The books he would mourn if they burned in this inferno. I had to rescue them; embers had already fallen into the safe. Nothing would survive the conflagration. Staying bent over, I snatched them all up, balanced them in my arms, and raced down the iron staircase. The heat burned my feet through my shoes.

The bobby was just beginning to regain consciousness. I grabbed him under one arm and tried to drag him toward the door. All I managed was to drop the books I was carrying. As I started to pick them up, a coughing fit stopped me in my tracks.

At least the heat wasn't as murderous on this lower level.

I felt a nudge at my shoulder and then Jacob began to help the bobby rise and escape. I glanced up to see Count Farkas, huge Bible hugged in his arms, reaching the bottom of the staircase. His face was fiery red and his eyes were nearly swollen shut from the smoke. His scalp was shiny with sweat.

He'd never let us live. He hadn't let my parents live. I grabbed up all the books I'd spilled, all of Lord Barnwood's priceless tomes, and backed away, never taking my eyes off the madman.

"Hurry!" Jacob managed to get the bobby out into the hall. Other hands reached around him and took the young man to safety.

As I stepped into the doorway, Lord Barnwood stumbled into me.

"My library!"

"You can't go in there." I would have said more, but I started to cough again.

Jacob put a hand on his arm to stop him, but Lord Barnwood shoved him aside.

"I must save my library."

"No." I tried to block his way and show him the volumes in my hands. "It's not safe. I have the important books."

"I bought that Gutenberg from Lupton. It's mine! I told Farkas he can't have it. I must save it. It's my library. I must save them all." Lord Barnwood pushed me away, struck Jacob in the face with the side of his hand, and rushed into the encircling fire. He headed straight to the middle of the room and collided with Count Farkas in an effort to pry the Bible out of the count's grip.

I stood in the doorway, transfixed. Lord Barnwood had bought the Bible that had led to the deaths of so many and Sir Broderick's terrible injuries. All these years he'd known the truth about what happened, yet acted as if he were our friend.

I watched as the two men struggled, each with their arms around the huge volume. The bindings began to give way under the assault. Then the heat began to make the pages blacken at the edges.

A section of the balcony collapsed with a roar, sending burning wood and fiery books everywhere. I think I screamed as sparks showered over me. The two men seemed to glow, standing in the center of the heat in a ball of flame. I stared, mesmerized, seeing not only the two book collectors through the flames, but also my parents.

Tears blurred my smoke-hazed vision. "Mama! Papa!"

Jacob grabbed me around the shoulders and rushed me

down the hall and out the front door.

I dragged my feet at every step. "Stop!" I gasped out to him. "We must save them. I can't fail my parents again."

CHAPTER TWENTY

OUTSIDE I could see two fire engines, hoses outstretched, pumping water from the front and side streets. Puddles of water and sheets of ice were everywhere. Constables held onlookers back while firemen aimed the streams of water and manned the bucket brigades in an effort to save what they could of the house.

"We can't go in there," Jacob told me, holding me in place with both hands.

"But I can't let Lord Barnwood die like my parents. I failed them. I can't fail him, too." I frantically tried to break free of his grasp, tears running from my stinging eyes down my hot cheeks.

"Stop it, Georgia," Jacob said, putting his arm around me and pulling me away from the house.

"There are still two men inside," I cried out to the nearest fireman and then began coughing.

"Where?" a bobby asked.

"In the library. The back of the house." I said among coughs and gasps.

"We can't get in there. The back of the house is about to collapse. Get back!" a fireman shouted.

"We must! Jacob, we must do something."

As soon as the words came out of my mouth, a rumble began. It grew louder and seemed to shake the earth. Then smoke and flames shot out the open front door and broke the windows over our heads.

I ran in terror toward the street. In front of me, the crowd tumbled back, staring over my head.

When the roar stopped, I turned and found Jacob still at my side. I looked at the house and saw the night sky where the roof should be. Every window was alight with flames as snow fell.

"Lord Barnwood," I called out.

"No one could survive that," a constable told me. "Are you all right, miss?"

"Yes." I pulled my singed coat closer around me as I shivered in the cold. "We'll wait, Jacob. Hopefully someone will come out alive."

The firemen packed up their equipment and put blankets on their horses. Constables began to return to their beats, snowflakes lingering on their helmets.

And still no one appeared.

We stood on the pavement, staring at the empty front doorway in the half of the wall still standing. Beyond that was the smoldering hallway. My feet were numb from the cold. I clung to the books I'd saved until Jacob took some of them from my tired arms.

"Dear heavens, what happened?" Grace took a few steps forward and then turned to gaze at us.

"Lord Barnwood had the copy of the Gutenberg Bible that my parents were killed for. He and Count Farkas fought over it and started a fire. Neither would leave without possession of that book and were trapped." I shook my head. "I'm sorry, Grace."

"I came over from Sir Broderick's. He knows nothing of this," she told me, staring at the ruins. "Lord Barnwood is gone? Truly?" She looked stunned, her mouth slightly open.

"Yes. Come back with us to Sir Broderick's. Get something warm inside you." I linked an arm with Grace.

"Georgia and I got him out once," Jacob said. "He went back in a second time. We tried to stop him."

"I'm sure you did. But those books were his life." Grace pulled out a handkerchief and wiped her eyes, then blew her nose.

"I saved the other books from the safe after Count Farkas took the Bible. I showed Lord Barnwood, but he went after Farkas and the Gutenberg. They both died for the sake of a single book." I'd known devoted antiquarian collectors, but none so single-minded.

Grace looked at me through teary eyes. "What Gutenberg?" Then she stared at the smoking pile and said, "I can't look at this anymore. Let's go to Sir Broderick's."

She led us back at a quick pace, ignoring every effort we made to console her on the loss of her employer and friend. From her silent sniffles, I knew she'd become close to him, growing oblivious to his eccentricities and enjoying the freedom he'd given her in her job.

When we arrived, Sir Broderick was wheeling himself out of the parlor. I saw on his face that he immediately read the situation correctly.

"Nothing could be done?" he asked.

"Jacob and I carried him out of the library, which was already on fire. He went back in to confront Count Farkas."

He sat up straighter. "Farkas was there?"

"There was a Gutenberg Bible in Lord Barnwood's book safe."

"He had a Gutenberg?" Sir Broderick asked, looking at Grace.

"I never saw inside the book safe. It wasn't on the list of

contents he gave me." Grace burst into tears. "I can't believe he's gone."

Mrs. Hardwick came toward us from the direction of the dining room. "Have you eaten yet, Grace? I think some of Dominique's soup and a cup of tea would help."

She looked at Jacob and me. "Wash some of that soot off you before you come to the table. And let me know if you have any burns you need ointment for." Then she put an arm around Grace's shoulders and led her away.

Jacob and I walked over to Sir Broderick and stacked the books I'd rescued next to him on a table. "This is all we saved. The entire house is in ruins. When we escaped the flames..." I pictured my parents looking at me through the fire and my heart was squeezed as if crushed under a terrible weight. "Neither Lord Barnwood nor Count Farkas could have survived."

"Are you sure?"

Jacob nodded. "We barely made it out the front door. No one was behind us, and no one could have escaped."

"Maybe they didn't want to. Not without the Gutenberg." Sir Broderick shook his head. He picked up the wilted-looking volumes and said, "These are all fabulously valuable in their own right. I wonder who they belong to now."

I handed Humphries my coat while still looking at Sir Broderick. "It seems a shame to have these wonders and then lose his life over one book."

"But what a book. I'd love to have seen it. Why did he never show it to me? We showed each other our antiquarian volumes all the time."

I hated telling him this, but he had a right to know. "Sir Broderick, I heard Lord Barnwood say that he bought the Gutenberg from Lupton. Those were his last words before he charged back into the fire to take the Bible away from Count Farkas. Lord Barnwood has had this book all these years while people died because of it. And he said nothing." My voice sounded anguished to my ears, but I couldn't hide the horror I felt.

"I never guessed." Sir Broderick looked down at his weakened legs and then scrubbed his face with his hands. I couldn't imagine the emotions that had to be running through him. He and Barnwood were friends.

"I failed Lord Barnwood. Like I failed my parents."

"No, Georgia, you didn't fail your parents. And Barnwood made his own choices." Sir Broderick looked away from the antiquarian volumes for a long moment of silence.

Then he slammed his hands on the arms of his wheeled chair and said, "Come on. You must be frozen. Get cleaned up and have some dinner. Jacob, thank you for looking out for Georgia. I take it you didn't see anything of Lady Carstaire?"

"No. It's strange, but I was so sure she'd killed Lady Hale and her husband. Could I be wrong?" I didn't believe I was.

"Perhaps she's just forcing your hand."

"Then I'll have to tell Inspector Grantham what I think, and let the police deal with her."

We went upstairs and cleaned up. Fortunately, I hadn't received any serious burns, but my shoes would have to be resoled because of charring and my dress was destined for the rag bag. By the time I repinned my hair and went downstairs, I found everyone had started on their soup.

It wasn't until Sir Broderick pushed away his fish course that he said, "Did you lose much in the fire?"

"Besides a friend and my job? No. I live a block away." Grace stopped shoving her fish around her plate and set down her fork.

Mrs. Hardwick asked, "Do you think there's any chance Lord Barnwood survived?"

I shook my head. "Jacob and I barely made it out of there. They were surrounded by flames and burning books."

"They?"

"Count Farkas was with him."

"Who?" Mrs. Hardwick looked from one of us to the other. Only then did I realize that while she was well aware of Sir Broderick's terrible injuries, she didn't know the name of the man who was responsible.

"A Hungarian nobleman who's been chasing after his stolen Gutenberg Bible for over a decade. He caused the fire that injured Sir Broderick. He killed my parents along with many others over the years in his search for his book. Thank goodness he won't get the chance to kill anyone else."

"I didn't know Lord Barnwood was meeting with anyone today. When I left to go to the Carstaires' neighborhood, he was here with Sir Broderick. I should have been there." Grace shoved her plate away.

"There was nothing you could have done," I said as the next course, of chicken and greens, came in and the fish course was removed.

"Maybe, but I'll never know that. I'm a member of the Archivist Society. I'm supposed to help people, and I wasn't there when one of my friends was in trouble." Grace looked like she might burst into tears.

Sir Broderick spoke in a sympathetic tone. "I'm sorry, Grace, because I do understand your feelings. I couldn't save my business partner and his wife. Instead, this same man who killed Lord Barnwood condemned me to a life in this wheeled chair. Georgia is still upset that she couldn't save her parents that day. He's injured or killed people over half the world looking for that Bible. Count Farkas has left none of us unscarred."

We were silent with our thoughts for a few minutes until Grace gave a sigh and said, "I need to give you a report about Lady Carstaire, don't I? I'd nearly forgotten.

"I went to the Carstaires' street and spoke to several people, including Lady Moffatt. She saw a hansom cab pull up in front of Carstaire's house after dark two days ago. She thinks it was almost six. Being across the street, she couldn't see who got out of the carriage. She assumed it was Sir Henry, but we know he was dead by then, or at least down at Cheyne Walk."

"So very possibly it was Lady Carstaire," Jacob said. His plate was already empty.

"Did anyone see her out of doors that day?" I asked.

Grace nodded. "A maid at a house two doors down from the Carstaire home was sent to the market in the late afternoon, her mistress having run out of something the cook needed for a special dinner. The girl hurried because she still had chores to do before her tea and she was hungry. She was almost to the corner of their street on her way back when she saw Lady Carstaire hurry down their road. The lady stopped at the corner and waved down a hansom cab."

"Did Lady Carstaire see her?" I asked.

"No. She said Lady Carstaire was in an obvious hurry. When the girl got home, it was just after four." Grace smiled at me. "It would have given the lady plenty of time to meet you and Sir Henry at five."

"I'll need that maid's name and address. I'm going to Inspector Grantham in the morning to tell him all we know."

"You don't think Lady Carstaire is going to try to silence you?" Sir Broderick said.

"No. She's very cold, very correct. She knows all she has to do is keep her wits about her and no one will be able to prove anything," I said.

"And she believes her position as a daughter of an earl protects her from all unpleasantness. That's a direct quote from Lady Moffatt," Grace told me.

Jacob was walking Grace home when the telephone rang in Sir Broderick's study. I ran upstairs and answered to hear Blackford's voice rumble out of the receiver. "Georgia, are you all right? I just heard about the fire."

"Yes, I'm fine, but Count Farkas was killed." I smiled to myself. Blackford had called me. "Where are you? How did you find out I was at the fire?"

"I'm dining with a business associate who has a telephone. One of the other guests is a neighbor of Lord Barnwood, saw the fire, and learned about your role before he came here tonight. Really, Georgia, you shouldn't take such risks."

How dare he lecture me. "Says the man who just traveled across a continent and an ocean in mid-winter."

I could hear his sigh over the telephone wires. "I didn't call to lecture you, Georgia. I called for the pleasure of hearing that you are safe."

I wondered if he could hear my answering sigh. "Thank you for caring."

"I do care. I've cancelled my plans for tomorrow night. I'll call on you, if I may."

"Please do, Blackford. We have so much to talk about. Will you come to dinner?"

"It may have to be later than that. I'll let you know. And now, I must return to my host. Please be careful, my love. I don't want anything to happen to you."

"Thank you. I—I don't want anything to happen to you, either. I care for you, Ranleigh."

"I love you, Georgia. Good night."

I stood with the receiver against my ear for many minutes after the call ended, still hearing his last words in my mind. When I finally set it in its cradle, I stroked the earpiece with one finger.

FIRST THING the next morning, I went to Scotland Yard and asked for Inspector Grantham. At Sir Broderick's insistence, Jacob went with me. I was shown to Grantham's office within a few minutes and found him behind his battered, cluttered desk. "What can I do for you, Miss Fenchurch?"

"I think Lady Carstaire killed both her husband and Lady Hale."

He stared at me, blinking, for a moment. "Why?"

"I hate telling you this. I've learned secrets and I hate having to share them with anyone. But if I don't, a murderer will go free."

He nodded. "Fogarty was here yesterday morning filling me in, but I suspect you know more about this business than he does. Why don't you start at the beginning? And should I invite Superintendent Marcum?"

"No. I'm not sure he'd listen to me. Once you investigate our information, you can tell him. He'll listen to you." I settled myself and began to tell him what I knew.

I started with all the details I was told about the love letters now in my possession. I told him we'd now matched the handwriting to that of Sir Henry Carstaire. When I reached the point where the feuding Lady Hale gave Sir Henry a furnished house, Inspector Grantham stopped me.

"Where was the house located?"

I told him.

He pulled out a notebook and pencil from the shambles on his desk and wrote down the address. "Not a wealthy neighborhood. Not even a very nice one. Go on."

"What your pathologist didn't discover on autopsy was Lady Hale was four months or more with child."

Grantham frowned and shook his head. "I'll have to find out who performed the autopsy. I wish all of our doctors were conscientious, but we don't get a lot of choice." He made another note. "And Fogarty said you're sure her husband wasn't the father."

"Yes, on the evidence of the servants. They couldn't stand each other, and they'd been fighting over how to raise their son. If adultery could be proven—"

"Sir Edward Hale could divorce Lady Hale and keep their son away from her. She'd have been ruined." Grantham kept writing.

"But she'd just inherited a fortune and could move to Canada. By the way, I learned recently that had been her plan when she was hiding at Lady Imogen Fielding's. She had others cleaning up her business matters for her before she went overseas."

"Was Sir Henry going to run away with her?"

"Supposedly not."

Grantham steepled his fingers and studied me. "Then why would Lady Carstaire kill her husband?"

"Anger, jealousy, embarrassment. She claims to be frail, but frankly, Inspector, I don't believe it. Sir Henry may have changed his mind at the last moment and planned to leave her. Or maybe she just didn't believe him when he said he was going to stay."

"Have you spoken to her?"

"I sent her a note. She replied that if I spread the story, she would talk to her solicitor."

"That doesn't sound like a guilty woman."

I watched Grantham, hoping he believed me. "It sounds like a very brave and determined one. Someone with the nerve to look someone in the eyes while stabbing them in the heart."

He readied his pencil. "You'd better tell me in detail everything you've learned and who you've spoken to."

After I finished my interview with Inspector Grantham, Jacob walked me to my bookshop. Frances had already opened for the day and several customers were studying our stock of books on the shelves. The sunshine and slightly warmer temperatures were bringing people out of doors again and I had high hopes for our coffers.

I hung up my cloak, my coat having too many burns to ever wear again, and began to help the next customer. The stream of readers was steady and it seemed like no time at all before Frances left for lunch with her family.

I wasn't concerned about being on my own. I'd been alone at this stage of plenty of investigations and nothing had ever happened. I admit I felt a little unsettled when the last customer walked out onto the pavement with their purchases and the bookshop was empty. Rather than dust or shelve new copies, I decided I was tired and deserved to rest sitting behind the counter. That I was facing the door and had my back to the antiquarian book cabinets was only a detail.

I was lying to myself, but it made me feel better. At the moment, I was feeling rather fragile.

This would be the perfect time to try to reach Blackford. But when I called Blackford House, I reached Stevens. "His

Grace said he'd return late this afternoon. May I take a message?"

I felt abandoned, and I didn't want to be reasonable about it. "No message," came out in a wounded sigh.

The bell over the shop door jingled and I jumped. Jerking my head up, I saw Grace in the doorway, looking at me with a wistful expression.

I ended the conversation and hung up the phone before Grace said, "I don't suppose there's a chance you're hiring?"

"Of course there is, if the employee is you."

She came toward me, still looking hesitant. "But what about Frances?"

"Frances has always been free to work whatever hours she wants. She didn't replace Emma. You can, if you'd like."

"What if Emma chooses to come back?"

"Emma will be starting a family. And Sumner's ego probably won't let her work more than occasionally to help out. I need a full-time employee to replace Emma. I know you're reliable and you know the shop." I gave her a smile. "Now, are there any more 'what if's?' or will you accept the position?"

Grace's answer was to come around the counter and hug me. Then she stepped back. "I can't start today, though. I have to meet with Lord Barnwood's solicitor and the fire insurance people. And his heirs. Now that he's gone, they're stepping up with their hands out."

"I didn't know he had any heirs." I wondered what surprises Sir Broderick might produce if I asked him about his living relatives.

"None that he had anything to do with while he was alive. And I don't think they wanted anything to do with him." Grace headed to the door. "I'll start tomorrow, if I may."

"Gladly. And Grace," I smiled at her, "welcome."

By the time Frances returned, I'd shaken off my silly disquiet as I helped customers. People came in and out of the shop all afternoon, leaving me no time to worry. Frances must have seen my nervous state, because she stayed with me while I waited for Jacob. When he didn't arrive, I finally closed the shop. Frances walked a few blocks with me until our paths diverged.

"Tomorrow we'll have Grace here, too. We'll keep you safe, Georgia," she told me as she said good night.

When Humphries opened the door for me, Sir Broderick looked out from the parlor and said, "Isn't Jacob with you?"

"No. Is he supposed to be?"

"We can't be sure Lady Carstaire isn't planning to stab you."

"Well, I'm home now and I doubt she'd break into a house full of people."

I was enjoying a cup of tea with Sir Broderick and Mrs. Hardwick when we heard the telephone ring. Thinking it was Jacob calling to explain his absence or Blackford phoning to say he was on his way here to finally have our conversation, I rose and hurried up the stairs to Sir Broderick's office. "Hello?"

"Miss Fenchurch?"

"Yes."

"This is Mrs. King from the jewelry shop next door. Someone is breaking into your bookshop. Do you have anything valuable in there?"

I thought of my antiquarian books and the fire in Lord Barnwood's library just the evening before. "Thank you. I'll be right down. Have you seen the constable on his beat?"

"Not yet. He should come by here soon."

I hung up and rushed down stairs. "Someone is breaking into my bookshop. I'll be back as soon as I get it sorted out."

"Shouldn't you wait for Jacob? Or the duke?" Mrs. Hardwick said.

"No." I finished pinning on my hat. "I don't know when either of them will arrive."

"Yes, you should wait," Sir Broderick said. "Where is that lad?"

"Tell him to come to the shop when he gets here." I yanked on my gloves and hurried out the door.

"Wait. I'll come with you," Mrs. Hardwick called from inside.

"There's no time," I shouted back and rushed off. Visions of how fast Lord Barnwood's library went up in smoke sped my feet. I refused to lose my business.

Normally, I thought of the walk from Sir Broderick's to my bookshop as short. Tonight it seemed to take hours. Traffic rushed by whenever I wanted to cross a street. Wind seemed to push me backwards. And all the time, I kept thinking *I hope the burglar hasn't set fire to my shop.*

I was out of breath when I finally reached the bookshop. The cold air blew newsprint and leaves down the gutters and jabbed my cheeks with its arctic blast. The lights were off next door at the jeweler's. Where was Mrs. King? I checked the front of my shop. The door was locked and the windows unbroken. There was no bobby around. No one was walking on our block.

Had the burglar tried to enter from the rear? Mrs. King and the constable might be there now.

I turned to head around the corner to the alley and my shop's back door when I heard "Miss Fenchurch." Lady Lydia Carstaire stood directly in front of me, close enough to plunge a dagger into my heart.

I gasped. She stood not three feet away, and there was no one else around. The way she'd met her first two victims. Light from a streetlamp glittered in her eyes, making them hard. Lethal. Mad.

"How dare you send the police to my door asking questions about Alice and my husband?" In the flickering light of the streetlamp over my shoulder, I could see her face clearly. There was nothing beautiful or frail about it.

I glanced around, looking and listening for help. I didn't have time to chastise myself over how really stupid I'd been to fall for this trick after I'd fallen for the fake note to meet her husband at night in the fog.

"Police! To my door! What must the neighbors think?" She clearly was scandalized.

I backed up one step and then another down the pavement.

She matched me move for move, never taking her eyes off me. Then I saw the flash of a blade in the streetlight as she pulled it out from her coat.

I shrieked and jumped to the side as the knife tangled in my cloak.

She pulled it free. I refused to give up. I had too much to say to Blackford. Too much to do with Blackford.

She struck again, this time a downward thrust from beside her ear. I jumped back and as the knife was almost through its arc, near her skirts, I stepped forward and punched her in the face.

After the shocked look left her face she screamed, "You hit me! How dare you lay a hand on me? I'm the daughter of an earl. You're a nobody."

If she was going to give me time while I hoped the bobby

on this beat came by, I was more than willing to stand in the street and exchange shouts with her. "How dare you try to stab me? How dare you stab Lady Hale and Sir Henry?"

"*Lady* Hale? Alice? She was a whore!"

"You knew she was expecting Sir Henry's child, didn't you?"

The knife came up again by her ear, and as she plunged it down with a shriek, I jumped to the side and back. She missed, but I tangled my heel in the hem of my cape.

I landed hard on the pavement, at her mercy.

CHAPTER TWENTY-ONE

I sprawled on the paving stones. Lady Carstaire came forward as a blur sped by me and under her skirts.

She shrieked and stumbled as her strike missed. "You horrid little beast!"

Dickens must have clawed her as he had me so many times. I silently promised to feed him liver for the rest of his life if he'd stop this madwoman.

As the cat shot out from beneath the fine fabric, the woman kicked at him but missed.

She raised the knife again. Dickens raced back for a second attack, causing her to spin around in an attempt to stop him. At that moment, the glorious sound of the bobby's whistle rang out, followed by footsteps running toward us.

With a quick glance over her shoulder, Lady Carstaire made one more swipe at me with her knife. Missing, she ran with surprising speed past me into the night and away from the constable.

He gave two more blasts on his whistle as he reached me. "Are you all right, miss?"

"I am now, thanks to you."

"You're bleeding."

I looked down to where he pointed. Lady Carstaire's first strike had cut my arm as well as my cloak. Only then did I notice my arm hurt like the devil and I felt weak.

Dickens had disappeared.

MRS HARDWICK had bandaged my arm and I was giving my statement to Inspector Grantham when I heard Blackford's voice in the hall. Sir Broderick quickly wheeled his chair into the hall and exchanged hushed words with him for a moment before Blackford entered and knelt next to my chair.

"Georgia. You've got to stop taking these chances."

"I'm fine, Blackford. Sit down and have some tea." My voice sounded faint and I didn't have any energy for an argument.

"Sir Broderick said Lady Hale's killer stabbed you."

"No, but she did slice my arm. Blackford, we need to talk, but not until after I finish giving my statement." My head fell forward for an instant before I pulled myself together. I felt so weak.

He made a growling noise before rising and shouting, "Get Georgia some tea with plenty of sugar. She's in shock."

It arrived within seconds and Blackford hovered like an avenging angel until I drank a cup, daring Grantham to ask me a question with just a stare. Only then did he decide I was well enough to continue.

Actually, I did feel a little stronger. When I finished giving Grantham every detail I could remember, he told me, "We spoke to Lady Moffatt and then Lady Carstaire late this morning. Lady Carstaire wouldn't admit to anything, not even going out the evening Sir Henry was murdered. She claimed her husband never had an affair with anyone and the baby must have been Sir Edward's. She was highly indignant that we should call at her front door."

"Did she mention she's the daughter of an earl?"

He smiled. "Once or twice, yes."

"Inspector, would you care to stay for dinner?" Mrs. Hardwick asked.

"Thank you, but no. We need to have everyone looking for Lady Carstaire. And Georgia? Don't go anywhere alone again until she's captured." Inspector Grantham walked over to speak to Sir Broderick.

"Now, Georgia, we need to talk," Blackford said, looming over me.

"After dinner, Your Grace. Will you join us?" Mrs. Hardwick said in a no-nonsense tone.

He bowed to her. "Thank you."

We could hear Jacob's voice in the front hall. "Inspector! What's happened? I was sent on a wild goose chase into the suburbs by a note from Mr. Wylie. It turns out he didn't send it."

"When did you get this note?" Inspector Grantham asked, hurrying into the hall to speak to Jacob.

"Mid-afternoon."

"This could well be the work of Lady Carstaire, too. She seems to be fond of sending false messages. Georgia was sent back to her shop because of a burglary that never happened."

"Is she all right?" Jacob exclaimed and suddenly appeared in the doorway, looking into the parlor over Sir Broderick's head.

"Yes, she's fine. And it's time we had dinner. Certain we can't tempt you with some of Dominique's cooking, Inspector?" Sir Broderick said. "I'm sure your sergeant will be well taken care of in the kitchen."

Grantham and his sergeant exchanged a quick glance. No doubt they hadn't had any tea, much less dinner. "Thank you. I think we will accept your hospitality. I'll just make a call to the Yard about Lady Carstaire." At a nod from Sir Broderick, the inspector hurried upstairs to the study to use the telephone.

We went into the dining room. Blackford sat next to me, pulling out my chair and offering to cut my meat so I wouldn't have to work my arm too much. The soup was warm and spicy and I felt each spoonful give me more energy.

The inspector soon joined us, and we found ourselves called on to tell Blackford and Jacob what had happened. I could feel tension rolling off Blackford as I told him about my near escape in the fire, the death of Farkas and Barnwood, and the fight in front of the bookshop.

"If the note I received was fake, what about the phone call from the jeweler's wife? Are you sure that was from her?" Jacob asked.

"It was a female voice, but I couldn't say for certain whether it was Mrs. King or Lady Carstaire. When I first arrived I checked, and it didn't seem that the shop had been disturbed. I didn't realize Dickens had left the shop this afternoon."

For the first time since he arrived, I saw a pleased smile on Blackford's face. "I always thought there was something special about that cat."

"He reminds me of you," I murmured, giving him a sideways glance.

His smile widened.

We were through the fowl dish before I asked, "Sir Broderick, what will happen to the prayer book I sold to Lord Barnwood now that he's...?"

"He paid for it. I have the money. It's part of his estate and ownership will be determined by the solicitors." He shrugged. "I know he was happy with it."

A gloom settled over the table.

"There is one thing that needs to be settled," Mrs. Hardwick said. "Where will Teddy go?"

"We can assure Lady Imogen and Mrs. Coghill that Sir Edward had nothing to do with the death of his wife and Teddy is in no danger. I'm sure they'll let us return him to his father without any difficulties." I turned to Blackford. "Will you go with me while we give them the news and then to take Teddy back to his father?"

"I'd be honored." He gave me a look that seemed to say, *Do you think I'll let you out of my sight?*

After my experience that night, I'd be glad for Blackford's close presence for quite a while.

Conversation veered onto normal topics such as Blackford's recent trip to America and Jacob's law studies. I finally found myself relaxing, only to discover my arm burned at the site of my wound.

We'd only begun our coffee when the sergeant appeared at the dining room door. "Sir, it's about time…"

Grantham rose. "Yes it is. Thank you for your hospitality, but we have a criminal to catch before we can call it a day. Georgia, take someone with you everywhere you go. Lady Carstaire only seems to strike where she isn't expected and her victim is alone."

We all rose and saw the policemen off. Then we went into the parlor for coffee. After a few minutes of polite chitchat, I said, "I'd like to take Blackford to the study for a conversation. Is that all right, Sir Broderick?"

"Why don't you two talk here? Jacob and I will be busy in the study and Mrs. Hardwick will be…" He shot her a look.

"I plan to retire early. If you will excuse me?"

Blackford and Jacob rose when Mrs. Hardwick did, and

then the other three left the parlor. Blackford began to pace. "You've made up your mind, haven't you, Georgia?"

"No. I have a question to ask you. How long will your egalitarian thoughts last on who can be a duchess? And do you love me enough to accept the fact I have neither the training nor the temperament to be a good duchess?"

"That's two questions." He grinned at me.

"Blackford."

The smile slid off his lips. "My thoughts on who can be my duchess will last the rest of my life. I've learned inborn nobility triumphs over aristocratic birth every time. Why do you think I didn't marry as soon as I came into the title? My beliefs said I needed to create an heir and perpetuate the line as soon as possible. But among the aristocracy, there was no one worth marrying just to extend my title. Then I met you."

"I'm liable to embarrass you on a regular basis with my middle-class manners and ideals."

"There will be times when you'll get flustered at our arcane habits, but you'll never embarrass me. You're too good-hearted."

I was thrilled with his kind words, and I did love him. Why not say yes? But something kept the word in my throat. "Believe me when I say I love you, Ranleigh, but I fear I won't make you happy. I'll make too many mistakes. You'll grow tired of me. Your peers will make fun of me."

"They won't. They won't dare." His tone told me he simply didn't allow his fellow aristocrats to express opinions about his friends in his hearing. At least, not twice.

"Oh, they'll dare. And my current friends will treat me differently. They'll keep their distance, not certain how to treat a duchess. I'll be left friendless." Finally, I'd admitted to myself and to Blackford what I feared.

"You're not giving your friends, or mine, a chance. There will be a few, I'm sure, but most people will see what I see and what your friends see. Georgia, a good and kind and fascinating woman."

"I've seen how Lady Phyllida has been treated. She's the kindest woman I know, and she's often snubbed in society. She doesn't have a home or family except for Emma and me, and Emma's married now. Caring for Lady Westover is purely temporary. Could we—?"

"Lady Monthalf will always have a home with us. You needn't worry on her behalf. Besides, doesn't she want you to marry me?" A sly smile crossed his face. He knew she had been pushing me to marry him.

"Yes. But is it what *you* want?" I gave him my best wide-eyed look.

"Give me a little credit, Georgia. I know my own mind. You're the only woman I will ever consider marrying."

"You can't know the future." I wished I could.

"But I know me. I've been hopelessly in love with you for a long time. Now I realize that my resistance to proposing marriage to you has been foolish in the extreme. I want you to be my wife." He stopped his pacing to sit next to me on the sofa. "Do you believe me?"

"Yes. I believe you."

A smile grew on his face like sunrise. "Then marry me, Georgia."

"What about the practical issues? What about the bookshop?" I managed to ask as I fought down a desire to agree to anything and everything he requested. "And Archivist Society investigations?"

"You can lease out the bookshop or set up a manager. It is yours absolutely. I'll have my solicitor write up an agreement to that if you'd prefer. And there is no way I could stop you from assisting the Archivist Society. I wouldn't want to try. But please, Georgia, be more careful than you were tonight. There will always be a footman around to escort you if I'm not available."

"I can choose any manager for the bookshop I want?"

"Of course." He scowled. "Who are you thinking of?"

"Grace. She knows books and she's out of a job."

A puzzled look crossed his face. "I thought you would say Frances Atterby. Or Emma."

"No. Frances likes to work at the shop on her own hours. And Emma will be too busy being Mrs. Sumner to manage the shop. We need to go together to the bookshop in the morning to tell Grace about her new job."

The look of pure joy that crossed Blackford's face mirrored my own. He pulled me into his arms.

"Say yes. Yes that you'll marry me. Yes that you'll love me forever."

"Even if you'd never asked me to marry you, I'd love you forever. I love you, Ranleigh. Yes."

And then neither of us spoke for a long time.

CHAPTER TWENTY-TWO

SIR Broderick, Mrs. Hardwick, and Jacob were all at the dining table when I came down to breakfast the next morning. They turned to stare at me, waiting in silence for me to speak. Even Humphries hovered over the breakfast dishes as if waiting to hear the good news.

I decided to draw out the suspense, despite the smile I couldn't quite keep off my face. I felt as if a great weight was lifted from me and my steps were feather light. "It appears to be a sunny morning. I wonder if it will be any warmer."

"It will quickly become a great deal warmer if you don't satisfy Mrs. Hardwick's curiosity," Sir Broderick said. And then he smiled. "Best wishes, my dear girl."

Mrs. Hardwick echoed him.

"How did you know I said yes?"

"Oh, for pity's sake. The duke wouldn't have left here whistling if you'd said no," Jacob said. "And you're grinning like a fool."

My cheeks suddenly heated to an alarming temperature. "He's coming over this morning. First we'll go to the bookshop and offer Grace the job as manager, and then we'll go collect Teddy Hale and take him home." I couldn't wait to see him.

"Oh, that's excellent." Sir Broderick sounded relieved. "I can work with Grace quite well. Of course, we'll both have to train her, but at least she knows books."

I was only halfway through breakfast when the front bell rang. Humphries went out to answer it. After an exchange of male voices, Inspector Grantham came in the room.

I set down my fork. His face was grave as he faced me.

"We found Lady Carstaire in the Thames this morning. She drowned."

"Perhaps that was a better end than hanging. She could never have withstood the public humiliation of a trial." All the joy from my evening with Blackford dissipated like morning mist.

"It's a shame her anger at her husband's betrayal led her to such violence," Mrs. Hardwick said. "I'm just glad she didn't succeed with you."

"So am I." The relief I felt was nothing less than overwhelming. "If she'd just not responded to my note accusing her, nothing could have been proven against her. Am I right, Inspector?" I found my breakfast no longer appealed to me and I pushed the plate away.

"Yes. As it is, she's faced her own punishment for her crimes," Grantham said.

"Breakfast, Inspector?" Sir Broderick asked.

He made a face. "I'm afraid I lack an appetite this morning."

"At least wish Georgia well. She and Blackford are to marry."

Inspector Grantham stared at Sir Broderick for a moment before turning to me. "Then on the evening I came here to take you to Scotland Yard, you two…"

"He'd asked. I hadn't accepted yet. Now I have, which should make your grandmother and Aunt Phyllida happy. They'll be able to turn their efforts toward you full time."

"Oh, dear." The man looked a little green. "I wish you

every happiness, Georgia."

"You'll be glad to know Georgia is riding with Blackford this morning to pick up little Teddy Hale and take him home," Sir Broderick said.

"I'm glad to hear it. I suppose I'm still not to discover where he's been," the inspector said.

"How much do you know about this?" I hadn't wanted to explain to Inspector Grantham why I was law-breaking.

"Sir Broderick has kept me informed about the child. At least as informed as you've kept him. Really, Georgia, that was a matter for the police."

"I agree, but there was a network in place to keep Teddy hidden for as long as it took to find his mother's killer. I didn't want to see policemen chasing all over London in a futile attempt to find the boy. Terrible waste of police resources." I hoped he bought my story.

"Very civic-minded of you, Georgia. But please, don't be so thoughtful next time." Fortunately, he didn't look angry.

"Of course, Inspector." I managed to hide my smile. That morning, I wanted to smile at everything.

As soon as he left, I rose to get ready.

"What will you wear outdoors today?" Mrs. Hardwick asked. "Your coat has burn holes in it from the fire and still smells of smoke. And your cloak has a slice and bloodstains."

"How noticeable are the slice and the stains?"

"Not too bad."

"Then that will do. I don't want to see Grace wearing something that will remind her of the fire at Lord Barnwood's."

Mrs. Hardwick gave me a dark look. "No, that will not do. You're a future duchess. Borrow my cloak for this morning, and then this afternoon we'll go to the dressmaker for a new cloak and a couple of new tea and dinner gowns."

"My life isn't going to change that much." Blast. Deep down I knew it would. Those women dressed up for tea and dinner, and I was soon to be one of those women.

Mrs. Hardwick raised her eyebrows.

For a morning that had begun in such happiness, it was quickly darkening with the sorrows of the last few days. I drew in as deep a breath as I dared. "You're right. Thank you. I'll borrow the cloak if you don't mind."

She smiled at me. "I'll go get it."

Jacob finished his breakfast and said, "Best wishes, Your Grace."

"Oh, for pity's…"

"Get used to it, Georgia. It'll be your title. Duchess of Blackford," Sir Broderick said.

"But not with you. Oh, please, not with you. You're my friends." I thought I'd weep.

"Only privately," Jacob said. "It would be wrong not to 'Your Grace' you in public. In private, you'll still be that Georgia who breaks down doors and pretends to be other people and does crazy, scandalous things. And you'll still be our friend."

Sir Broderick smiled his agreement.

I was truly fortunate in my friends. And I realized my deepest fears had been for naught.

Blackford arrived before Mrs. Hardwick returned with the cloak. "I've sent my man of affairs to obtain a special license."

"That shouldn't be necessary. I'd like to wait until Emma and Sumner return for our wedding."

"They're in Paris. They'll be back tomorrow."

"What? The last letter I received had them in Nice."

"Telegrams are quicker and I am impatient." He smiled and his dark eyes shone with laughter.

Mrs. Hardwick returned with her cloak and I slipped it on. "It appears I'll need one more gown when we go to the dressmaker's this afternoon. I'll need something for my wedding."

"Then we'll need to pick up Lady Phyllida on our way. She enjoyed Emma's wedding so much, she needs to be involved in yours, too," Mrs. Hardwick said.

Linking arms with Blackford, I said, "But first, let's go reunite Teddy with his father."

We went outside and I discovered he'd brought the Wellington coach. Some things were going to be more difficult to get used to than others and climbing up into the old carriage was one of them.

Then Blackford lifted me up and climbed in after me. For one of the few times since I'd known him, he sat next to me. He gripped my hand and then grazed my gloved knuckles along his lips.

Okay, maybe some changes wouldn't be difficult to accommodate.

After giving Grace the good news and receiving congratulations from her and Frances, we rode to Mrs. Coghill's. We walked together to her front door where we both presented our cards. We were shown into the parlor rather than the morning room. Already my position was being elevated.

Mrs. Coghill bustled in and dropped a curtsy. "Your Grace. Miss Fenchurch."

"We've come to tell you Sir Edward Hale has been absolved of any connection to his wife's murder. Teddy can go home now. Today."

"Really, Miss Fenchurch? Then who—?"

"Lady Lydia Carstaire murdered both Lady Hale and Sir Henry Carstaire. She was a very jealous woman."

"What's going to happen to her?"

"After failing to kill Miss Fenchurch, she drowned herself. Her efforts to keep her crimes secret had failed," the duke told her.

Mrs. Coghill scowled. "What is your interest in this, Your Grace?"

"Miss Fenchurch and I are to be married." He beamed when he said it. I smiled too. It was beginning to seem real.

"Congratulations," she said after a shocked silence. "Teddy is upstairs with Lady Imogen. I'll get them."

A minute later, the young boy raced down the stairs. "You've come to take me to my father?"

"Yes. Come along. I've brought my best coach to deliver you home in," Blackford said.

Lady Imogen looked slightly amazed. Apparently, Mrs. Coghill had told her all. "Congratulations seem to be in order. Both on finding the culprit and on your impending marriage."

"Thank you."

A maid brought down a small case of Teddy's things, which she handed to Blackford's footman.

I knew Lady Hale and Teddy hadn't left with anything but the clothes on their backs. "You've taken good care of him."

Mrs. Coghill lifted her chin. "It was what Alice would have wanted."

We said goodbye and took Teddy outside. He raced to the carriage as if he'd been freed from something fearful. When we rode off, I asked, "Are you excited about going home to your father?"

"Yes. I've missed him. I miss Mother, too, but she's not..." He looked down as his lower lip quivered.

"They told you?" Blackford said.

"They said she'd been murdered, and they thought my father killed her. Then they said it was possible someone might try to kill me. But nobody would, would they?"

"No. And we found the person who really killed your mother."

"Good." He nodded and then looked out the window in fascination at the busy streets.

"We're here," he cried out when we arrived in front of his house. It was all we could do to keep him from jumping from the carriage before the steps were pulled down and a footman could assist him to the ground.

The door to the house opened before he reached it and Sir Edward was out the doorway and onto the landing. The boy leaped into his outstretched arms. "Open all the curtains, Johnson. We're not a house in mourning any longer," Sir Edward called out. Then he looked at me, his voice bitter as he said, "So you discovered I didn't kill Alice."

"I learned who did kill her. It's much easier to be certain of a fact than the absence of something and to convince the police of facts. So now everyone knows it's safe for Teddy to come home. No one is trying to harm him."

"Thank goodness for that. Sir Broderick contacted me a little while ago to tell me you were on your way with my son." For the first time, I saw a smile on Sir Edward's face above the boy he still clung to. "Thank you for bringing Teddy home."

I smiled back at him. "The Archivist Society is glad any time we can bring families together."

"Or start new ones," Blackford murmured in my ear

while he helped me back into the carriage.

I was going to have a family again, a real family, for the first time since I was seventeen. Blackford was making all my dreams come true. "I love you so much, Ranleigh. I can't believe my good fortune."

His smile stretched across his normally serious face as he sat down next to me. "I love you, too, my dear Duchess Georgia."

I thought my heart would burst with happiness. I knew I'd found my future. Beside Blackford through all the decisions and investigations in our long and happy future.

Coming soon,
a new mystery series from Kate Parker.
Death, scandal, and fashion in pre-war London
as a newspaper society reporter struggles to separate
the secrets from the lies to catch a murderer.

Deadly Scandal
the first in the Deadly Series

London, September 1937

CHAPTER ONE

What I saw was all wrong.

I gasped as I looked down at Reggie's face and reached for him. My hand jerked to a stop as reality hit me.

Reggie wasn't sleeping on that cold metal table. He looked too sunken and gray. A large, round red spot marked the bullet's entrance above his right ear. The damage was to the other, the left side, of his head. Even at this angle, I could tell we'd need to keep the coffin closed. What I saw, despite everyone's attempts to keep me from seeing, would never go away.

My vision shattered like glass into shards. The room became disconnected visions and sounds. I took a deep breath and choked on the overwhelming smell of bleach. I felt Sir John grab my arm as if he feared I'd faint.

"The foreign office has already identified him," a man's voice said as he attempted to take my other arm. "You don't need to be here."

I shook him off. "Yes, I do." They were wrong. Reggie didn't commit suicide. He couldn't have shot himself on the right side of his head.

Reggie had been murdered.

I couldn't mourn him. Not yet.

The garishly lit room smelled of disinfectant, smoke, and

rotting meat, incompletely masked by a strong scent of perfume. I became aware of other people, living people, moving about the large basement space and murmuring. A lifetime of training at boarding school and living under my father's roof forced me to pull myself together.

One did not break down in public.

When and where had Reggie been discovered? I realized I hadn't asked even that basic a question. And I needed answers. "What was he killed with? And where?"

"A Webley British Bull Dog." Another man joined us. He was large, solid, rumpled. He introduced himself as a police inspector. He and Sir John shook hands.

"Who killed him?"

"He killed himself, Mrs. Denis," the inspector said. His tone said, *I'm tired. Let's get this over with.*

"How did he shoot himself in the right side of his head if he shot left-handed?" I stared at the inspector.

"Our records say your husband was right-handed."

"He was. But he didn't shoot right-handed. He couldn't. His right trigger and middle fingers didn't bend." I looked at the men's faces staring blankly back at me. "Don't you understand? He couldn't have killed himself. Not this way."

The doctor shared a glance with his assistant, who draped the sheet over Reggie's head. "Mrs. Denis, I realize this is a shock—"

I grabbed Sir John's arm. "He didn't do this. He was murdered. Where was he found?"

The inspector reviewed some notes. "In the service alley behind St. Asaph's Hotel. A couple of waiters leaving for the night found his body with the gun lying next to him. A suicide note was found in his pocket. He hadn't been dead long, maybe a couple of minutes."

"May I see the note?"

The inspector nodded and handed me a torn scrap of paper. "There were no fingerprints."

The note said, *This can't continue. I should have done something earlier. I accept responsibility*

"Do you recognize his handwriting?"

"Yes. But he accepts responsibility for what? And why had he gone to St. Asaph's after the theatre? He was never out past eleven or midnight on a weeknight. Ever." The more I learned, the less Reggie's death made sense.

"Apparently, your husband went to the theatre with some work colleagues. They split up after the performance. No one saw him after that. Didn't you wonder when he didn't come home last night, Mrs. Denis?" the policeman asked. His tone held implied criticism.

"I wasn't home. I was visiting friends in the country when the Foreign Office came to tell me of his death." There. I hadn't lied.

"Your husband owned a Webley British Bull Dog, didn't he?" the inspector said, taking back the note. "We'll have to go to your home and make sure it's still there."

I peered into the inspector's eyes. "Of course, but you don't think you'll find it, do you?"

"No."

"Reggie had no reason to take his life." This was turning into a nightmare. My temper pounded in my head. How could anyone do this to Reggie?

The inspector looked down, avoiding my gaze as he folded his arms across his chest. "The coroner will determine the reason."

"You're wrong, Inspector." He didn't know Reggie at all. The whole idea was preposterous.

I was about to continue arguing when Sir John pulled me aside. "Keep quiet. They'll find out you didn't come down to our place until..." His whisper ended in a throat clearing. "And usually, husbands are killed by their wives. They'll think you killed him."

"I couldn't kill him, Sir John," I whispered back.

"I know that."

"But somebody did."

"Now is not the time to discuss it. Do you want to see any more?"

I shook my head. All I wanted was to get the sight of Reggie, gray and broken, out of my memory.

Sir John told the doctor to release the body to the mortuary when they were done and hustled me out of the room.

When we reached the sidewalk and I could no longer smell disinfectant and the metallic tang of blood, I took a deep breath. We traveled with the inspector and a constable to the flat and found the short-barreled gun missing from the drawer where Reggie kept it. I couldn't think of anywhere else it could be. After a cursory search, the policemen thanked me and left.

I wandered from room to room. The flat felt achingly empty. Yesterday morning, Reggie had gone into work, promising to meet me the next night at Sir John's estate, Summersby Lodge, taking the 17:12 train into Sussex. He'd been his usual self, wishing me a safe journey, nearly forgetting his umbrella, kissing my cheek. I'd burnt the toast.

I gasped from the pain of the memory. The refrain of our mornings for the past three years would never happen again.

I needed the truth.

I faced Sir John and said, "I want to see where he died."

"Livvy—"

"Please. I really need to see the spot. He's dead, Sir John, and it makes no sense. Help me, please."

"It's not a good idea, Livvy. None of this is."

"Someone murdering Reggie wasn't a good idea, either," I snapped. Then I put up my hands in a conciliatory gesture. "I'm sorry. I won't get hysterical on you, I promise. Please. I want to retrace his steps."

Sir John glanced at me, sighed, and said, "Oh, all right."

We took a cab to Soho and, at my request, climbed out in front of the Windmill Theatre. I don't know what I was expecting, but it was a dreary brick building with triple entrance doors chained shut at this time of the day. Posters for the revue flanked the entrance.

"If we leave for the station now—"

There was more for me to discover. I was sure of it. "Where is St. Asaph's Hotel from here?"

He glanced around. "I think down Haymarket and then Pall Mall to cross St. James Park."

I began to walk in the direction he pointed.

"Livvy, we have a train to catch."

I glanced back at Sir John, who reminded me of a teddy bear as he trundled down the pavement in his brown suit. "There will be other trains."

I kept walking, checking the pavement and gutters for a clue. If Sir John had asked me what I was looking for, I wouldn't have known. I was only sure Reggie had gone to St. Asaph's Hotel for a reason.

A short distance down Pall Mall I came to an abrupt stop. "That's the German Embassy over there."

Sir John gave me a dry look. The huge swastika flag flying from the roof was a giveaway.

"Would he have had some reason to come down here?" I turned toward the embassy entrance on Carlton House Terrace.

"I hope you're not planning on dropping in at the embassy and asking them," Sir John said, looking horrified.

"Not today." I'd been told the reason for his suicide was that Reggie was suspected of giving secrets to the Nazis. To have the route to his murder site go past their building made me uneasy.

I kept walking until I passed the Foreign Office, where Reggie worked. "Did he see something here, Sir John? Something that meant he had to be killed?"

He didn't answer. There was no answer.

I'd reached the alley that ran next to St. Asaph's Hotel when I spotted a garishly colored booklet a few feet away. When I retrieved it, Sir John looked over my shoulder as I skimmed the pages. It was a theater program for the Windmill Revue, damp and wrinkled, with a few notations in Reggie's handwriting.

"It's his program. See? He always made notations about performances. He has every program for every show he's ever seen, going back to his school days." A moment later, I caught my mistake. Had, not has.

Sir John ignored my verbal slip. "So he dropped it and it blew over here."

"It's a clue."

"You're not Agatha Christie and it's not a clue. Keep the program by all means if it makes you feel better." Sir John's voice had an edge.

I walked to the spot where Reggie must have died and looked around, but I found no other sign that Reggie had ever been here. It felt as if he had vanished. Two men in white cook's aprons came out a back door and stared at me as they lit cigarettes.

I started back the way I came.

"Hold on, Livvy. We need to return…"

I slid the program into my purse and kept walking. It would have taken Reggie ten or fifteen minutes to reach the spot where I found the booklet from the time he left the theatre. The street was well lit. People would have been out on this street at that time of the evening, even in the rain we'd had last night. Plus, rooms of the hotel overlooked this spot.

"Why did no one hear the gunshot?"

Sir John shrugged his wide shoulders. "Perhaps they did. There was only one shot. People don't usually respond to one of something. It takes a few noises to make people sit up and take notice."

I nodded. He was probably right. "No witnesses have come forward?"

"Apparently not. Now, let's go." He took my arm and walked to the front of the hotel, where he hailed a cab. Once I was seated, I discovered how very tired I was. We rode to the train station in silence and didn't exchange a word until we settled into a first-class compartment by ourselves.

Sir John, who'd kept his mouth clamped shut, now blasted out his words at me. "Olivia, suspecting your husband was murdered is one thing. Setting yourself up to be hung is quite another."

"You went hunting with Reggie. You know he couldn't shoot right-handed." I stared at his face as he turned his gaze to the grimy floor. "You think he was murdered, too."

"Yes, all right, what you say makes sense. But it's dangerous for you to say so. Whoever killed him did so for a reason. He might come after you next. And the police might decide you're the murderer. You have no alibi."

"I had dinner with my father last night."

"Well, that's something. How is Sir Ronald?"

"Unchanging and unchangeable."

"Ah." He knew my father well.

We arrived back at Sir John's country house to find my father, like bad news, had arrived there ahead of us. When the footman opened the door for me, Father pivoted around in Abigail's best parlor and marched into the hall. "Olivia, are you all right? What is the meaning of this, Summersby?"

Sir John's eyebrows rose to his thinning dome. "She was determined to see him. I couldn't let her go on her own."

"Of course not. Good thinking. But Olivia. Why put yourself through something so distressing?"

"At least now I know he was murdered."

Abigail, Sir John's wife, gasped as she came over and took my hand. "Are you sure?"

"Very," Sir John said. I caught the look that passed between them. Sir John believed me, and now Abigail did, too.

"Preposterous," my father said.

"Have you ever known Reggie to shoot right-handed? Have you ever known him to stay out late on a work night? Has he ever taken his pistol to a theatre performance? None of this makes sense." I was very near tears and not doing a good job of hiding them.

Reggie and I were seldom apart for long. His job was one of minutiae, details of documents, ceremonies, diplomatic credentials. Sometimes he would work late at the office. I know he never came home smelling of brandy or sex. No lipstick smudges. Never a hair out of place.

He was my anchor, my rudder, while I dashed off in all

directions. Writing, sketching, going out with girlfriends, always busy while he sat observing.

I'd married him against the advice of my father, which was a major point in Reggie's favor. I'd never had an instant's thought that my father could be right.

My father's tone turned pedantic. "I always knew he was capable of deceiving you, Livvy, but I never thought he'd do anything like this. There's an investigation into papers stolen from the Foreign Office. Probably from his section. Reggie must have done it. His note is a confession."

"I don't believe it."

"He said he took responsibility. What else could he mean?"

"I plan to find out. Reggie wasn't a traitor."

"Well, someone in his department is working with the Nazis."

"It's not in Reggie's character," Abby told my father with her lips thinned in anger.

"Don't be too sure. You're his cousin. He could have hidden all sorts of secrets from you," my father told her.

"I've known him all my life. He might as well have been my brother." She took my hand. "Oh, Livvy, I don't believe any of this. He was too bookish for his own good, but he didn't have a criminal bone in his body. He'd never steal, he certainly wouldn't commit treason, and he didn't like the Nazis."

"I know. People don't suddenly change like this." Reggie certainly hadn't.

"He worked for the Foreign Office. You have no idea what those people are capable of," my father said.

"You work for the Foreign Office," I snapped at him. I'd spent my childhood furious over his deceits.

"And I'm a better judge of character than you."

That stung. "I'm going to find out what Reggie was capable of."

"There's more." My father stood there in his black three-piece suit, his back soldier straight, and stared at me with a grim face.

"I've been told my husband died by his own hand, he's suspected of being a traitor, and now you tell me there's more?" My voice rose in a wail.

"Reggie had been under investigation for the theft of those papers for some time. The Foreign Office won't admit it publicly, but they believe he was the one who committed treason. They were closing in on him. And he knew it. This would explain why he," he drew in his breath, "took this step."

I looked at their faces. Abby's concern was written on her features; Sir John looked shocked.

"Never." Why would my father think my calm, brilliant, sweet husband had killed himself? "Reggie would never divulge secrets from the Foreign Office. He was an honorable man, not a traitor. He followed all the rules. And now that he can no longer defend himself..."

Uneven breaths shook my body. I took the handkerchief Abby had been holding out to me and dried my eyes.

My father's expression softened a little. "I don't like telling my only child her husband was a traitor. Naturally, the Foreign Office will do what we can to avoid a scandal."

I looked him straight in the eye. "I'm going to investigate the circumstances of my husband's death."

"Livvy. No. It will only mean more pain for you. Leave the investigation to the professionals."

"He was my husband. I have to do this." I'd seen the

professional detective. He had no interest in digging in to find the truth. And that wasn't the only reason. Some compulsion was driving me on; anger, disbelief, a rejection of all I'd been told, but I couldn't admit this out loud. They'd have stopped me.

My father put on his best Victorian head-of-the-family tone. "You'll do nothing until after the funeral. Then we'll talk about it. Oh, why did I let you attend university?"

"Why did you *let* me...?" I allowed my anger to boil. It was the only thing that was holding me together after the shock. I knew I'd need all my nerve and every ounce of my wits if I was going to catch Reggie's killer.

Acknowledgments

This book would never have seen the light of day without the help of a great number of people. My family, in particular my very patient husband, have been unflaggingly supportive.

Technical and critical help has been freely and kindly shared by Hannah Meredith, Anna D. Allen, the Ruby Slippered Sisterhood, and the members of HCRW.

I thank all of you for bringing me through this process. All mistakes are my own.

About the Author

Kate Parker grew up reading her mother's collection of mystery books by Christie, Sayers, and others. Now she can't write a story without someone being murdered, and everyday items are studied for their lethal potential. It's taken her years to convince her husband she hasn't poisoned dinner; that funny taste is because she can't cook. Her children have grown up to be surprisingly normal, but two of them are developing their own love of literary mayhem, so the term "normal" may have to be revised.

In addition to the Victorian Bookshop Mysteries, next year will bring a new series featuring a young widow in late thirties London who lands a job as a society reporter for a major newspaper. With Europe on the brink of war, the newspaper publisher finds a secondary assignment for her, one that can't appear in the press. The first in the series will be *Deadly Scandal.*

As much as she loves stately architecture and vintage clothing, Kate has also developed an appreciation of central heating and air conditioning. She's discovered life in coastal Carolina requires her to wear shorts and T-shirts while drinking hot tea and it takes a great deal of imagination to picture cool, misty weather when it's 90 degrees out and sunny.

Follow Kate and her deadly examination of history at www.KateParkerbooks.com
and www.Facebook.com/Author.Kate.Parker/

Made in the USA
Lexington, KY
22 November 2018